D0389186

House Rivals

Also by Mike Lawson

The Inside Ring

The Second Perimeter

House Rules

House Secrets

House Justice

House Divided

House Blood

House Odds

House Reckoning

Rosarito Beach

Viking Bay

House Rivals

MIKE LAWSON

Atlantic Monthly Press
New York

Published simultaneously in Canada
Printed in the United States of America

FIRST EDITION

ISBN 978-0-8021-2360-2
eISBN 978-0-8021-9132-8

Atlantic Monthly Press
an imprint of Grove/Atlantic, Inc.
154 West 14th Street
New York, NY 10011

Distributed by Publishers Group West

www.groveatlantic.com

15 16 17 18   10 9 8 7 6 5 4 3 2 1

To my agent, David Gernert.
This is the tenth DeMarco novel and were it not for David,
the first one would never have been published. Words cannot
express how much I appreciate all he's done for me.

House Rivals

Prologue

———◆———

She was young and strong, but she didn't stand a chance against them.

There were three of them, all wearing black ski masks. One was skinny, shorter than her, and if it had just been him, she was sure she could have taken him. She would have beaten the shit out of him. But the other two were bigger than her; they were fat, but strong.

It was after midnight and she'd been forced to park to the side of the restaurant, and they took her just as she was about to get into her car. They rushed her as a group, and before she could scream, one of them clamped a hand over her mouth. Then they manhandled her to the back of the restaurant, out by the Dumpsters where she couldn't be seen by passing cars.

They groped her a bit. The big guy who had his hand over her mouth was squeezing her right breast with his other hand, and the other big one cupped her crotch. He laughed and said, "Oh, yeah. This is gonna be good." The little one didn't touch her; he just watched.

The next thing she knew, she was on the ground and one of them was sitting on her chest with his hand still clamped over her mouth and the other big guy had ahold of her wrists so she couldn't use her fists. She thought they'd try to pull her jeans off next, and she tried to get her hands free to fight and started kicking at the short one who was still standing, but he was able to evade her thrashing legs.

The short guy watched her struggle for a while, then knelt down and put his face close to hers. "You're going to stop," he said. "You're gonna knock off all the bullshit and quit telling lies." His voice sounded familiar but she didn't know who he was. "You're gonna quit before people lose their jobs. You saw how easy it was tonight. If you don't stop, the next time we're gonna take you someplace and take turns raping you, then we'll tie you naked to a tree and leave you for the wolves. You understand?"

She couldn't speak because the one man still had his hand over her mouth and she couldn't even nod because he was pushing her head into the gravel. But she stopped struggling. When he'd said *next time*, she knew she was going to be okay.

"Let's go," the short guy said to his pals and the one got off her chest, giving her left nipple a hard tweak before he did, then they all took off running.

It took her a while to get to her feet and when she did, she almost collapsed back onto the ground. Her legs felt like they were made of rubber. She started crying as she walked back to her car, and it pissed her off that she'd been so scared they made her cry. She opened the door and picked up her cell phone, which she'd left in the cup holder, and dialed 911.

As she was waiting for the cops to arrive, she thought: *Fuck you. I'm never going to stop.*

1

Marjorie Dawkins was the mother of two boys: Bobby was ten, Tommy was twelve. She was a busty five foot four, had a photogenic smile, and her hair was a lustrous chestnut brown. She used to wear her hair shoulder length but got tired of fussing with it. Now she had Carla over at Selene's—for sixty bucks every three weeks—keep it short and simple so all she had to do was blow dry it after she showered. Marjorie didn't have time to spend more than five minutes in the morning on her hair. Whenever anyone described her they didn't say she was pretty; they always said she was *cute*.

Her husband, Dick, was a good-looking, easygoing guy who could spend hours perfectly content doing nothing but punching a TV remote. When asked what he did for a living, he would say he was a day trader. The truth was that Dick was a stay-at-home dad, a nanny for their boys. As for the day trading, she'd give him five hundred a month to play with and figured that so far this year he'd made a profit of maybe nineteen bucks. Since Marjorie earned a quarter million a year, she figured any money Dick lost playing the market was a cheap price to pay to salvage his pride, plus it gave him something to talk about at parties. He was also, she had to admit, a good father—Bobby and Tommy adored him—and after fourteen years of marriage he could still jump-start her libido. Like with her hair, Marjorie didn't have a lot of time for sex so she was glad she had someone handy with the proper appendage when she was in the mood.

———◆◆◆———

Bill Logan was six foot one and weighed exactly the same as he had in college: one hundred and eighty pounds. He had thick dark hair, an attractive widow's peak, and when he smiled, a dimple appeared in his right cheek. Women loved that dimple.

Bill's first name was actually Leslie—he was Leslie William Logan—and he'd never forgiven his mother. After he started to catch shit for the name—which began when he was about six—he asked her why in the hell she'd named him that. She told him that Leslie had been her father's middle name and that there were a lot of famous people named Leslie. There was Leslie Howard, the British actor in *Gone with the Wind,* and Leslie Nielsen, the guy in all those funny movies, like *The Naked Gun.* You know, his mom said, the movie O.J. Simpson was in. And then there was the most famous Leslie of all: Bob Hope. His real name had been Leslie Townes Hope—which was why, Bill Logan said to his mom, Hope changed his name to Bob!

Like his partner, Marjorie Dawkins, Bill made a cool two hundred and fifty grand a year. Unlike Marjorie, he didn't have a useless spouse and two kids to gobble up what he earned. He'd been married for a year when he was in his twenties, cheated on his bride three months after they said their vows, and was divorced fourteen months after the wedding. There'd been nothing wrong with his wife; she had been, and still was, a sweet, attractive woman. The problem, Bill knew, was his nature: he just couldn't stay faithful. He could have been married to the actress Scarlett Johansson, who some magazine had just named the sexiest woman on the planet, and he would have cheated on her.

He'd always figured that it was a *good* thing that he'd learned this about himself when he was young and before he had kids. He never again subjected any poor woman to the agony of marrying him.

Bill Logan figured—all false modesty aside—that he'd probably slept with more women in North Dakota than any man his age. In Bismarck, he could hardly go into a bar or a restaurant and not run into some woman he'd bedded. The one woman he hadn't slept with and never would was Marjorie Dawkins. They just had too good a thing going, business-wise, to screw it up with sex.

Bill parked his fire-engine red Porsche Boxster next to Marjorie's black Jeep Cherokee. He drove the Porsche from May until September but after that switched to a practical four-wheel drive Chevy Tahoe with studded snow tires. Winters in North Dakota were a bitch. Their office was in a strip mall with four other businesses: a HairMasters staffed by a bunch of Vietnamese girls; a Subway operated by a cheerful, overweight Hispanic lady; and a FedEx-Kinko's place that was really convenient for him and Marjorie.

The fourth business had a sign next to the door so small you could barely read it that said LAPTOP REPAIRS. More than half the time, the door had a CLOSED sign in the window. The guy who owned the laptop repair shop was a long-haired doofus named Gordy Hewlett, and Bill and Marjorie hired him whenever they had any computer-related work they needed done—including a few jobs that some nitpickers might consider illegal. Gordy bathed infrequently, liked to wear jeans with holes in the knees, smoked a lot of pot, and quite often when Bill went into his shop, Gordy would be playing video games. And all those things were okay with Bill and Marjorie because when they needed Gordy, he performed okay.

When Bill walked into the office he and Marjorie shared, Marjorie waved a hand at him but kept talking to whomever she was talking to on the phone. She'd been there since six thirty. This was the way it had always been in the ten years they'd worked together: Marjorie arrived at six or six thirty and stayed until three thirty or four because she was always attending her boys' after-school functions: soccer, basketball, baseball, whichever sport was in season. She wouldn't let her sons play football.

Bill usually arrived at nine or ten and stayed as long as necessary. If there was something that needed to be done at night, like meeting a guy on a backwoods road, Bill handled that sort of thing. Business-related social events were different and they both attended a lot of those: fund-raisers, parties, rubber-chicken dinners. Sometimes they'd both go to the events and sometimes only one of them would go. Marjorie was just as good as Bill when it came to schmoozing folks.

So they worked whenever they needed to, splitting the time and the various jobs in a way that suited them both. No one paid any attention to how many hours they worked or if they were in the office or not. The only thing that mattered to old man Curtis was that they got results.

Their office was as bare-bones as you could get. They had serviceable desks they'd bought at a place called Office Furniture for Less, and both had comfortable, ergonomic, tilt-back leather chairs. There were also a couple of rarely used visitor chairs and four tall metal file cabinets. They were *really* careful about what they put in the file cabinets. If they were ever served a subpoena or if someone executed a search warrant, there couldn't be anything in those cabinets that could bite them on the ass. This meant that the only things in the file cabinets were phone directories and documents that were a matter of public record, like bills going through state legislatures, property records, and environmental studies. The stuff that could land them in jail was encrypted and stored in the Cloud, and Gordy—the pot-smoking laptop repairman—had the files rigged so they could be wiped out in three seconds from their smart phones if it ever came to that.

One reason the office was so poorly furnished was that they really didn't need anything better. If they wanted to impress someone, they rented a suite in a hotel. The other reason was that Curtis didn't mind paying their salaries, but he'd go crazy if he thought they were wasting his money on things they didn't need. Curtis may have been worth over a billion dollars but as the old saying goes, he'd squeeze a nickel 'til the buffalo shits.

Marjorie hung up on whomever she'd be gabbing with and said to Bill, "I went to a parent-teacher conference last night and one of the other moms said she saw you and Bobby's math teacher at the American Grill. I mean, for Christ's sake, Bill. Do you think you're invisible? And in case you didn't know it, my kid's math teacher used to be married to a cop and the cop still has a thing for her."

"Aw, she just happened to see me there at the bar and sat down for a minute to chat."

Marjorie knew he was lying through his teeth. "So what's going on?" he asked to change the subject.

"You know Buchanan, state senator, ninth district?"

"Yeah?"

"I just found out his septic system failed and it's going to cost about twenty-eight grand to make things right. So I had Gordy do a little research on him. It looks like Buchanan's barely able to make his mortgage and the main reason why is his daughter's going to Reed College over in Oregon, which is costing him a boatload."

"Sounds like what Senator Buchanan needs," Bill said, "is a good contractor who can give him a deal on fixing that septic system."

"That would help," Marjorie said. "Also a guy who can get him a permit to build the new system on the same spot where the old one is. Buchanan's septic system sits near a creek, which was okay at the time it was built, but today that won't fly. It's going to cost him double to relocate the drain field."

"Well, I know a guy who can take care of that."

"I know you do. So you wanna go talk to Buchanan?"

"Ah, jeez. He lives in Belcourt, doesn't he? I mean, that's two hundred miles from here."

"Hey, you're the guy with the Porsche. What's the point of having one if you don't drive it once in a while?"

"Yeah, okay. I'll do it."

"One other thing. Curtis is flying in on Tuesday. He's particularly anxious to hear how we're doing with Judge Morris. He's got a real hair up his ass over Morris."

"Which Morris? South Dakota Morris or Montana Morris?"

"Dakota, of course. What's wrong with you? Did that teacher screw your brains loose?"

"Aw, enough with the teacher. So what are we going to tell him about Morris?"

"I don't know. We'd better come up with something before Tuesday. But that's not the big thing. The big thing is that goddamn girl."

2

DeMarco was standing in the basement of his Georgetown home next to a professional killer. The killer's name was Ralph. It said so right on his shirt, the name in red thread over the pocket.

Yesterday, DeMarco had been doing about the most useless thing a man can do on a Sunday afternoon. He should have been outside mowing his lawn, but instead he was watching a professional golf tournament on television, wondering if Tiger was ever going to get his game back. He had a bowl of popcorn in his lap, a Budweiser clenched in his right hand, when he caught a motion out of the corner of his eye: something small and gray—and *very* fast. "Son of a bitch!" he yelled, and the popcorn went flying as he leapt up and he sloshed beer down the front of his pants.

He'd seen a mouse. A fucking mouse!

He tried to find the critter, but couldn't. It had vanished. He wandered through his house for the next two hours armed with a broom, looking for places where rodents might dwell. He searched in closets and under sinks; he pulled out cardboard boxes filled with crap he should have thrown away years ago. He removed boxes of cereal and pasta from his kitchen cabinets to see if they'd been nibbled on. He found some rice spilled on one of the shelves but didn't know if that was evidence of mice dining or his own sloppiness. By the time he finished, he'd found nothing and his home looked like a team of DEA agents had executed a search warrant.

Realizing he needed professional help, he called an exterminator with a twenty-four-hour answering service. He told them to send over a cold-blooded killer, but was told that one wouldn't be available until tomorrow morning. That night he couldn't sleep. He kept hearing things—or he imagined he was hearing things—scurrying about behind the walls in his bedroom. He could see, in his mind's eye, one of the little bastards gnawing on an electrical wire.

Ralph showed up at eight a.m. the next day. He was a swarthy, overweight, balding guy. DeMarco suspected that Ralph's forefathers had disembarked on Ellis Island from a ship originating from Sicily. DeMarco's ancestors could have been on the same ship.

"I've never had a rodent problem before," DeMarco said.

"Well, it happens," Ralph said. "And it's not about cleanliness, per se."

"Per se? What the hell does that mean?"

"It means there's rats in every city in America and just because you live in Georgetown and don't have garbage strewn all over your house, doesn't mean you won't get rats."

"It wasn't a rat. It was a mouse."

DeMarco didn't want to hear the word *rat*. Mice were cute little things. Some people even had 'em for pets. Rats were vicious-looking varmints with red eyes, bigger than squirrels, and they would bite your nose off while you slept.

"All they need," Ralph said, "is a hole big enough to get their head through. If they can get their head through, then they can squeeze their whole body through. I'm talking a hole not even as big as a nickel."

Ralph begin his search down in the basement because, in his professional opinion, and considering the construction of DeMarco's seventy-year-old home, that was the most likely point of entry. DeMarco's basement was unfinished, with concrete floors and walls, and contained his washer, dryer, and furnace. Five minutes after walking down the steps, Ralph pointed at a couple of small black particles that looked like peppercorns. "There you go," he said. "Rat turds."

"It was a mouse," DeMarco said.

Ralph focused next on the insulation. The floor joists for the first floor of DeMarco's house sat on the foundation and batts of fiberglass insulation were crammed between the joists to minimize heat loss. About a minute after Ralph found the mouse turds, he said, "Yep," and tugged on an insulation batt and *hundreds* of mouse turds came tumbling out.

"Aw, Jesus," DeMarco said.

"There's your nest," Ralph said, "or at least one of them."

"Aw, Jesus," DeMarco repeated.

"I'm going to have to rip out most of this insulation."

"But how did they get into the house?" DeMarco asked.

Ralph ran his flashlight along the top of the basement walls and near the electrical panel he stopped and said, "See that?"

"What?"

"That hole where that one cable is coming through. Looks like it might be an Internet cable. You see how much space there is around the cable? Whoever ran it should have filled the hole with caulk. I'm not saying that's the only entry point, but that's one of them."

DeMarco's cell phone rang. He was going to ignore it but then looked at the caller ID. It was Mahoney.

"Yeah, hello," he said.

"I need to see you," Mahoney said.

"Can it wait? I've got a big problem here at the house."

But Mahoney had already hung up.

"Look, that was my boss and I have to go," he said to Ralph, "but do whatever you gotta do. Wipe 'em out. Give me whatever I have to sign and I'll call you later and you can tell me what the plan is—but wipe 'em out."

DeMarco passed through security, entered the Capitol, fought his way through a cluster of camera-wielding tourists to reach the stairs, and walked up to the office of the House Minority Leader: John Fitzpatrick Mahoney.

Mavis, Mahoney's secretary, was on the phone, chewing somebody out. From what DeMarco could hear it sounded like some kind of conflict in Mahoney's schedule and Mavis was blaming the conflict on whomever she was talking to. She finally slammed down the phone and said, "Idiot."

Looking up at DeMarco, she said, "What are you doing here? He's already an hour behind schedule and it's not even ten, and right now he's supposed to be in two places at once."

DeMarco shrugged. "He told me to come see him. I don't know why."

"Well, he shouldn't have done that," Mavis snapped.

"What can I tell you? He called. Hey, have you ever had mice in your house?"

"What? Of course not. Now you just wait right here," she said and marched over to Mahoney's office, rapped on the door, and let herself in. She came out two minutes later and said, "You can walk with him over to the DNC." She took a breath and said, "I don't know why in the hell he wants to walk. That's going to put him even farther behind."

The Democratic National Committee's office was on South Capitol Street SE, about half a mile from the Capitol. If Mahoney had a car take him, he would get there in two minutes; if he walked it would take him at least twenty minutes because Mahoney walked slowly and stopped and bullshitted with everyone he met on the way. DeMarco felt sorry for Mavis. It was impossible to keep Mahoney on schedule and the main reason why was because Mahoney didn't care about his schedule. At his rank, people would usually wait for him if he was late—and he didn't care how long they had to wait.

Mahoney lumbered out of his office a couple of minutes later. He was dressed in a gray suit, a blue shirt, and a red-and-blue striped tie. On his feet were white Nike running shoes. He did this periodically: Made a half-assed effort to lose weight and get some exercise, the effort usually not lasting more than a week.

Mahoney was a handsome man with bright blue eyes and snow white hair. He was five foot eleven, the same height as DeMarco, but twice as broad across the back and butt. He drank too much, he ate too much, and he smoked cigars. A half-mile walk wasn't going to come anywhere close to offsetting all his vices.

He didn't say hello when he saw DeMarco; he just walked toward the door and DeMarco trailed along behind him. Nor did DeMarco try to speak to him as they were leaving the Capitol because about every two feet somebody would say: "Good morning, Mr. Speaker." If Mahoney didn't know the person, he'd say, "Hey, howze it going? How you doin' today?" If he knew the person, he'd stop, shake his or her hand, then chat about whatever popped into his head.

Mahoney was no longer the Speaker of the House; he'd lost the job when the Republicans took control a few years ago, but he'd held the job for so long that people still used the title. It was driving him crazy that the Democrats couldn't take back the House and he spent half his working hours scheming to make that happen—which was probably what he was going to do at the DNC this morning: more scheming.

When they finally got outside, DeMarco caught up to Mahoney and walked next to him. "There's a guy out in Montana named Doug Thorpe," Mahoney said. "If it wasn't for him, my name would be on that black wall down there on the Mall. He saved my life twice. He also saved the lives of a dozen other people, too. They gave him a Silver Star. He should have gotten the Medal of Honor."

Mahoney never talked about Vietnam. DeMarco had no idea what he did over there or how bad it had been. All DeMarco knew was that Mahoney had just been a kid, barely out of high school when he enlisted in the Marines. He ended up with shrapnel from a grenade in his right knee and he limped when it was cold. But that's about all DeMarco knew.

Mahoney was as corrupt as any congressman on Capitol Hill. He took money under the table; he did quasi-legal favors for people who helped him stay in office; he used campaign contributions to maintain his lifestyle. He would stab his enemies in the back—and sometimes he'd stab his friends in the back if it were politically expedient to do so. He loved politics more than he loved breathing. He loved the power, the intrigue, and being in the thick of things. But there was one area where Mahoney was above reproach: the proper treatment of veterans. It was the only area where he was above reproach.

"Anyway, I want you to go see him," Mahoney said.

"In Montana?" DeMarco said.

Mahoney ignored the whine in DeMarco's voice. "It's about his granddaughter. According to Doug, she's uncovered some conspiracy out there and somebody's threatening to kill her."

"What kind of conspiracy?"

"Hell, I don't know. Something political. I'd had a couple of drinks before he called last night."

. Had a *couple*? Knowing Mahoney, he'd probably had a lot more than two drinks. Mahoney was an alcoholic.

"All I know is that Doug's never asked for a damn thing from me in all the years I've known him. He's a fly-fishing guide and when I was younger I'd go see him and we'd go fishing and drink and tell lies about the war, but I haven't seen him in years. Anyway, he said he needed help and he didn't know who else to go to and his granddaughter won't listen to reason. So I told him you were going to help him."

Before DeMarco could say anything, Mahoney said, "Hang on a minute." He walked over to a street vendor and bought a Danish in a cellophane wrapper; the Danish was loaded with preservatives and had probably been baked a month ago. There was no point in DeMarco asking why he was walking if he was going to eat pastry as he walked.

"You don't need to go with me the rest of the way," Mahoney said as he ripped the wrapper off the Danish. "Get Doug's address from Mavis, and head on out there today. I told him you'd see him tomorrow morning."

"Tomorrow! But I got . . ."

"When you find out what's going on, let me know."

━━━━━◆━━━━━

DeMarco walked back to the Capitol, cursing John Mahoney every step of the way. He didn't want to leave today, not with his house infested with rodents. He could just see coming home from Montana and finding fifty mice in his kitchen, having a feast, dancing like cartoon characters in a Disney movie. He called Ralph. "Where are you?" he asked.

"I'm still here at your house, ripping out the insulation. I found another nest."

"Aw, Jesus. Don't leave. I'll be back in less than an hour and you can tell me what the game plan is."

DeMarco had worked for Mahoney for years. He had an office in the bowels of the Capitol, down in the subbasement. On the frosted glass door of his office, in flaking gold paint, were the words COUNSEL PRO TEM FOR LIAISON AFFAIRS. The words were absolutely meaningless; Mahoney had invented them. But DeMarco had an office, he had a title, and the U.S. government paid his salary. He was a GS-13, and had been a GS-13 for almost as long as he'd worked for Mahoney. His chances of getting a raise were between slim and none.

DeMarco was Mahoney's fixer—and sometimes his bagman, meaning Mahoney occasionally sent him to collect cash from people who wanted to contribute to Mahoney but didn't want to be known as contributors. More often, if Mahoney had some sticky issue with a constituent or another lawmaker or an old girlfriend—Mahoney had many of those: old girlfriends—DeMarco would be sent to deal with the issue. And usually, if DeMarco was sent to resolve a problem, it meant the problem couldn't be handled by Mahoney's legitimate staff in some legitimate fashion. The other thing Mahoney had done many times in the past was loan DeMarco to his friends when his friends had problems—as he was now doing with his buddy Doug Thorpe.

DeMarco got Thorpe's address and phone number from Mavis. When he asked if she'd mind booking him a flight and renting him a car, she basically told him to go fuck himself. She did this by simply sniffing. She worked for Mahoney and only Mahoney.

DeMarco descended to his hole-in-the wall office and used Google to learn that Doug Thorpe lived on the Yellowstone River about half-way between the towns of Forsyth and Miles City, Montana. He'd never heard of either town, and would have to fly into Billings. The best flight he could get left National at five thirty p.m. and arrived in Billings seven hours later, stopping along the way in Salt Lake City. Then it would be a two-hour drive to Thorpe's place. If DeMarco had had a little voodoo doll of John Mahoney it would have looked like a pincushion.

DeMarco made reservations—flight, hotel, and car—then went home to pack and talk to Ralph. He wanted to know Ralph's agenda for genocide.

"You got two or three choices here," Ralph said. "You got your traps. The good news with traps is the body stays in the trap and you just chuck out the body with the trap. The bad news is the traps aren't all that effective. Rats must have some sort of genetic memory transfer thing where they know the traps will kill 'em."

Genetic memory transfer? It sounded like the creatures had been created by a mad scientist in a laboratory, some superbreed capable of taking over the world.

"Then you got your sonic devices," Ralph said. "They send out this ultrasonic noise that's supposed to drive 'em out of the house, but most of the time it just drives them insane and they run back and forth inside the walls bumping into things but they don't leave. You just end up with deaf, insane rats."

"Great," DeMarco said.

"I recommend this stuff," Ralph said and showed DeMarco a small, flat box containing little blue-green pellets.

"What's that?"

"It's called d-CON. It's basically a super blood thinner and it makes them hemorrhage internally and turns their guts to mush. For some reason they love this shit more than I like clam linguini."

"Yeah, but where do they die? Inside the walls?"

"Well, sometimes. But what's supposed to happen—and what usually happens—is after they eat the stuff it makes 'em really thirsty, and they go outside to find water and they die outside. That's why I'm not going to plug up any entry holes for a week or so."

Now DeMarco had an unwanted image of a mouse, bleeding from every orifice, tongue hanging out, as it crawled, gasping, toward a pool of water.

"But what if they don't die outside? What if they rot inside the walls?"

"Well, that's a possibility—but I'd still recommend the d-CON."

DeMarco signed a form—like a death warrant for mice—giving Ralph permission to poison the little suckers and absolving Ralph's company of any liability for anything. He also gave Ralph a key and the security code to the house so he could do the work and remove the corpses. For some reason he trusted Ralph. Then he went to his bedroom and packed for the trip.

He normally wore suits when he was working but this didn't seem like a wear-a-suit trip, visiting some guy who was a fly-fishing guide. He packed one suit, one dress shirt, one tie, and a bunch of casual Montana-like clothes: jeans, sweaters, tennis shoes. Not sure how long he'd be out there, he packed enough underwear for a week. If he was stuck there longer than a week, he'd have to decide if he should wash the underwear or turn his boxers inside out.

3

The only good thing about flying to Billings as far as DeMarco was concerned, was that it was the first of May. This meant his chances of spending two days sleeping in an airport terminal due to weather-related delays were slightly less than normal.

The flight, in fact, turned out to be uneventful, meaning his luggage arrived the same time he did and the planes departed and arrived almost on time. These days, airlines consider *almost on time* to be outstanding performance. He checked into a Holiday Inn Express about midnight and slept without dreaming of rodents. He awoke at eight, feeling good, gorged himself on pancakes, and took off for Thorpe's place. He found it two hours later and thanked the Lord, as he always did, for the guy who'd invented the GPS. Whoever the guy was, he deserved the Nobel Prize and possibly sainthood.

Thorpe's home was an honest-to-God log cabin perched near the banks of the Yellowstone River and surrounded by ponderosa pines. In addition to the cabin there were two sheet-metal buildings the size of two-car garages. One of the buildings was open and DeMarco could see a snowmobile, a wood splitter, and a large rubber raft on a trailer. Next to the open garage was a shiny black Mercedes that looked out of place in the rural setting. A pile of firewood big enough to last through a cold Montana winter was stacked next to the house, and on the front porch were two rocking chairs. Some mixed-breed of black-and-white dog slept between the rocking chairs, and the dog barely raised its head when it saw DeMarco.

DeMarco knocked on the front door and nobody answered. He pulled out his phone and called the number Mavis had given him for Thorpe and heard a phone ringing inside the cabin. Having no better idea, he sat down in one of the rocking chairs, ruffled the dog's head, and looked out at the Yellowstone. Montana, he had to admit, was in a gorgeous part of these United States and he wouldn't mind spending a week at Doug Thorpe's cabin, sitting on the porch, reading mysteries, and enjoying the sound of the river going by.

An hour later, a pickup truck with a crew cab, towing an aluminum boat, pulled into the driveway. Three men got out of the pickup. The driver saw DeMarco on the porch, gave him a wave, then shook hands with the two men who'd been his passengers. DeMarco heard one of the men say, "Thanks again, Doug. We'll see you next year."

The two guys, both overweight and in their sixties, wore fancy fishing vests with multiple pockets and hats with fishing flies stuck into the crowns. They didn't look like fishermen; they looked like bankers. They got into the Mercedes and took off.

The dog got up and walked slowly down to greet the driver. The way it moved DeMarco figured the mutt was about a hundred in dog years. The man gave it a pat on the head and said, "Hey, Daisy." To DeMarco he said, "Can I help you?"

"My name's Joe DeMarco, Mr. Thorpe. John Mahoney sent me."

Doug Thorpe was in his seventies, tall, lanky, and tanned. His hair was gunmetal gray and his eyes were nested in a mass of wrinkles from squinting into the sun. DeMarco was willing to bet the man had better than twenty-twenty vision. He was wearing a green-and-red Pendleton shirt, faded blue jeans, and old hiking boots. He looked like the kind of guy who always wore boots. When he shook Thorpe's hand, DeMarco could feel nothing but calluses.

"I appreciate John sending you out here," Thorpe said. "I hope you can help. How's John doing?"

DeMarco wanted to say: He's doing fine considering the fact that he's a devious, self-centered, crooked, conniving, wife-cheating alcoholic—but he didn't say that. Instead he said: "He's doing fine, sir. He told me he owed you his life."

"Well, I don't know about that," Thorpe said. "You want a beer? I figured we could sit on the porch and talk about Sarah."

"Sure," DeMarco said.

Thorpe opened the front door, which DeMarco noticed wasn't locked, and Daisy followed him inside. He came back a moment later with two cans of Coors. He handed one to DeMarco, popped the top on his beer, and said, "About Sarah. She's my granddaughter. In fact, she's the only family I have left. My wife's been dead for twenty years and my daughter died four years ago. Jenny married a handsome idiot named Johnson and he liked to fly small planes—you know, Cessnas, Piper Cubs, and such—and he killed them both. So Sarah's the only one I have left and I love her to death. Anyway, she's got it into her head that there's some kind of big conspiracy going on."

"Conspiracy about what?"

"You need to talk to her. The story's too complicated for me to follow, but she claims state legislators and judges in Montana and the Dakotas are being bribed. Some of it has to do with natural gas, but to hear her talk it's about more than gas. Anyway, she's been working on this story—I guess you'd call it a story—for almost two years."

"Is she a journalist?"

"No, not really. She doesn't have a job. She dropped out of college her sophomore year because she couldn't figure out what she wanted to do, hooked up with some environmental group, and then started doing her own thing. I guess you'd call her an activist. But the thing about Sarah is she's rich. Really rich.

"My daughter was as smart as a whip and she bought stock in Microsoft and Apple and Starbucks and any other company you can think of that's hit it big in the last thirty or forty years. Jenny just knew how to make money. She always managed to buy the stock when it was worth pennies and always sold it before it tanked. And real estate. She'd buy a plot of useless land and next thing you know somebody's offering her ten times what she paid for it. Jenny was just an incredible woman; I don't know why she married that idiot flyboy.

"Well, Sarah's smart, too. Not as smart as her mom, but smart. But the main thing about Sarah is she's stubborn. And because she's rich, she can afford to be as stubborn as she wants. My daughter was the smartest person I've ever known; Sarah's the most hardheaded person I've ever known."

"You told Mahoney that someone was threatening to kill her?" DeMarco said.

"Yeah. About a year ago, she must have hit a nerve with somebody and she started getting these harassing phone calls. This guy would call her two, three times a day and usually about two or three in the morning. He'd say she was telling lies that could cost people their jobs, and if he lost his job, he was going to kill her. The guy called her so much she changed her phone number, but somehow he was able to get her new number."

"How did he know she was telling anybody anything?" DeMarco said.

"She's got one of those blogs on the Internet and she writes about all the stuff she says is going on. I can't imagine many people read it because . . . Well, please don't tell Sarah I said this, but she's a horrible writer. Anyway, she's been harassed with phone calls, they've tried to buy her off, and they've filed lawsuits." Thorpe laughed. "These guys must not know how rich Sarah is, because she was actually delighted when they filed the lawsuits. She said, bring 'em on. She was just looking for the opportunity to have her lawyers depose these guys or make them testify in court. The lawsuits are moving forward, but you know how the courts are. It'll be months or even years before the suits are settled."

"Who's they? Who filed the suits?" DeMarco asked.

Thorpe waved the question away. "Talk to Sarah. She can give you the details, and I don't really care about the lawsuits. If that's all that was going on, I never would have called John. But a week ago it got serious.

"She was leaving this diner late at night, and these three guys come up to her in the parking lot wearing ski masks. They drug her back behind the diner, knocked her down, touched her in places they shouldn't have, and told her to quit telling all the lies she's been telling. They said the next time they'd take her into the woods, have some fun with her, and leave her there for the animals to eat. They didn't hurt her but they scared the hell out of her."

"Did she call the cops?"

"Sure, but the cops couldn't find 'em. If I ever find 'em, I'll kill 'em."

He said this in a soft voice but DeMarco had no doubt the man meant what he'd just said. *I'll kill 'em* wasn't hyperbole, not when it came from Doug Thorpe.

Thorpe crushed the beer can he was holding like it was made of paper. "I just want her to stop, DeMarco. I think she's tilting at windmills and isn't going to accomplish a damn thing. She's been at this for almost two years, and as near as I can tell, nobody believes her. At least nobody with any authority, like a state attorney general or a federal prosecutor. But she's not going to stop. I know her. She'll keep pushing until somebody does kill her. What I'm hoping you can do is figure out what's going on and then get John involved. John's got the clout to force somebody with a badge to help her."

"I'll go see her, Mr. Thorpe. Where does she live?"

"She has a house in Billings. In fact, thanks to her mom, she's got property all over the place. But she's in Bismarck right now. She spends so much time there she leased an apartment."

"Oh," DeMarco said. "How far is Bismarck from here?"

"Four, four and a half hours."

"Four and a half *hours*?"

"Yeah. If you leave now you can be there by supper time. I'll send her an email and tell her you're coming." Thorpe shook his head. "I'd call her but she's become so paranoid she thinks her calls are being monitored. And, hell, maybe she's right."

4

Bill and Marjorie met Curtis at a restaurant called the Pirogue Grille near the Radisson where Curtis was staying. The Pirogue Grille was an elegant place with old redbrick walls, dark furnishings, intricate brass chandeliers, and eye-catching artwork on the walls. It had an excellent wine list and a menu that included venison and buffalo as well as more traditional fare. But the menu and the elegance were wasted on Curtis, a man who usually had a bowl of soup for dinner. If a restaurant had a children's menu, Curtis would often order from it not only because the portions were small but because the kiddie meals cost less.

Curtis was a complete mystery to Bill and Marjorie. The man was seventy-four years old, worth over a billion dollars, and if the insurance actuaries were right, he was most likely entering his last decade. A man with that much money and that little time left on earth ought to be enjoying all the money he'd made, but it seemed as if Curtis had only one interest in life: making more money.

He stayed in modestly priced hotels like the Radisson. He didn't drive a luxury car. He didn't own a yacht. He did own a jet, but only because he needed one to get around the country and didn't like to be tied to the airlines' schedules. His clothes looked like the sort you'd buy at Macy's—nice enough but nothing fancy; Bill spent more on his clothes every year than Curtis did. In the time they'd worked for him, as far as they knew, he'd never taken a vacation. He didn't go on cruises. He didn't play golf. He didn't have any hobbies. He spent most of his life on his plane or in conference rooms and law offices. What in the hell was the point of living that way?

When they first met him, Marjorie tried to get him to talk about himself and his family. They knew he was married and had been married to the same poor woman for almost fifty years. He had two children. His son was still a bachelor and a doctor in Austin. His daughter was the mother of two, like Marjorie, and owned an art gallery in Dallas. But even as good as Marjorie was at getting people to talk about themselves, she couldn't draw Curtis out. When he was with them the only thing he wanted to talk about was whatever problem he was having at the time that was preventing him from making more money. Marjorie eventually stopped asking how his wife, kids, and grandkids were doing. She came to the conclusion that Curtis honestly didn't care how they were doing.

Curtis was a small, thin man, about five foot six. His body was almost bird-like and his head seemed disproportionately large in comparison to his slight frame. The little hair he had left was white and wispy, his eyes were watery and pale blue. He had hearing aids in both ears. He almost always wore suits but instead of a dress shirt he usually wore polo shirts or golf shirts under the suit jacket. He'd been born and raised in Texas—his home and headquarters were in Houston—but he didn't have a Texas accent and didn't wear a Stetson or cowboy boots. His shoes were soft, black Dr. Scholl's.

His first name was Leonard and they imagined his wife must call him Leonard or Len or Lenny or something, but the only thing they ever called him was Mr. Curtis. Most often when they met him he was alone but sometimes he was accompanied by a couple of lawyers—and the lawyers always called him Mr. Curtis, too. He was a miserable, miserly, sour old son of a bitch but he paid Bill and Marjorie so damn much that he could have beaten them with a hickory stick and they wouldn't have cared.

Curtis sipped his coffee, made a face as if it didn't taste right, and got down to business. "So what's happening with Morris?"

Walter Morris was a circuit court judge representing the second judicial district in South Dakota. Circuit court judges in South Dakota ran for election every eight years but Morris was planning to retire when his term was up. This meant that Marjorie and Bill couldn't use campaign contributions to sway him. Morris also made a decent salary—he wasn't rich but he was comfortable—and didn't have any debt.

Nor did Morris have any vices that they had been able to find, such as cross-dressing or philandering. Marjorie even had Gordy look at his Internet history; if Morris had been looking at child pornography, they would have owned the judge for life—but no such luck.

The problem with Morris was a pending case having to do with sales tax. One of the many businesses Curtis owned was a company involved in the transportation of refined petroleum products—a pipeline, in other words—that covered thirteen states, including South Dakota. It was a complicated case and the laws governing pipeline taxes were poorly written, but the bottom line was that the company hadn't been charging sales tax for some of its services and the state treasurer said they should have—meaning the company now owed back taxes. Curtis, naturally, didn't want to pay the back taxes—Curtis didn't want to pay taxes on *anything*—and he and two other pipeline companies filed a lawsuit. The next stop for the lawsuit was Judge Morris's bench. Win or lose, the case would go to the South Dakota Supreme Court, but Curtis wanted a win in Morris's court because he was confident the state Supreme Court wouldn't reverse Morris.

"He's been taken care of," Marjorie said.

"How?" Curtis asked.

"The judge," Marjorie said, "has been looking online at condos in Palm Springs." Gordy had discovered this while examining the judge's

Internet history. "Apparently he and the missus have a hankering to go south in the winter."

"How much will it cost me?" Curtis said.

"Fifty-two," Marjorie said.

"Shit, is that all?" Curtis said.

It had actually been pretty easy to deal with Morris, a lot easier than Marjorie had expected. She simply sent him an email. In the email, she said she'd heard that he was looking for a California condo, she included a link showing a condo that was much nicer than the ones he'd been looking at on the Internet, and said the owner might be willing to sell for fifteen percent less than the listed price. Curtis would pay the fifteen percent—which was about fifty-two thousand on a three-hundred-and-fifty-thousand-dollar condo—but she didn't say that in the email. Marjorie said that if Morris was interested, she'd be happy to meet him for a drink and fill him in on the details.

When Marjorie met with Morris she went straight at him. The fact that he'd shown up for the meeting was enough for her to know that she didn't have to pussyfoot around with the guy. She told him that she was hoping for a favorable outcome on the pipeline sales tax case as the man she represented—who she never named—thought that being required to pay back taxes because of a confusing law was not only unfair, but in order to scrape up the money to pay the state, her employer might have to let a few people go.

"Are you trying to bribe me?" the judge said, trying to act all stern and righteous and shocked—but he couldn't have been *that* shocked. He had to know before he met with Marjorie that she was going to want something in return for the great price on the condo.

"Of course not, Your Honor," Marjorie had said. "No one is offering you any money. I'm just telling you that you can get a good deal on a Palm Springs condo, a deal you could probably get for yourself if you negotiated hard enough."

"And if I don't rule the way you want?" the judge said.

"The real estate market in California is pretty volatile, Your Honor. You can never tell what will happen. Why don't we wait until after you rule on the case and if you're still interested, give me a call. I can promise you that the buyer won't sell until after your ruling."

The judge didn't say yes or no. He just sat there scowling as if he smelled something foul in the room, then said he was late for a meeting and left the bar—a bar he'd picked that was about as far from his normal watering hole as it could get. But Marjorie knew what was going to happen next. She had no doubt. Morris would find a way to convince himself that the right thing to do was rule against the tax-grabbing state of South Dakota.

Ninety percent of the time, Bill and Marjorie behaved the same as most people representing a special interest group or a particular business: They paid attention to legislation that could cost Curtis money or make him money; they supported, through legitimate campaign contributions, politicians likely to favor Curtis; they pooled their resources with like-minded folks to pay for television ads to pass or defeat various bills and get the right people elected; they hired lawyers to throw monkey wrenches into the machinery when a monkey wrench was needed. In other words, just politics as usual. But every once in a while a little extra effort was needed to solve a problem, as was the case with Judge Morris—and this was why Curtis paid them so well.

You can't teach people to do what Marjorie and Bill did. They had a God-given instinct, guided by experience, to know who was corruptible and who wasn't—and then the ability to persuade those people to take a bribe in such a manner that the person wouldn't feel that he or she had really been bribed at all. Like with Morris.

Morris could, legitimately, rule either way with regard to the sales tax issue. He just needed to come up with a basis for his ruling that would morally satisfy himself that his decision had nothing to do with the condo but was instead in accordance with the constitution of the great state of South Dakota. In his own mind, Morris wouldn't even connect his good fortune to the ruling he made. He was a righteous and honorable man—and just lucky when it came to real estate.

"Now what about the goddamn kid?" Curtis said. "I've had enough of that little bitch."

5

——◆——

Two hours after leaving Doug Thorpe's cabin, driving eastward on I-94, DeMarco crossed the Montana–North Dakota border and stopped at a scenic vista near Medora, North Dakota (population 112). A sign informed him that he was looking out at the badlands of the Theodore Roosevelt National Park. He'd always thought that *badlands* was just a name for the places where outlaws like Butch Cassidy and Sundance went to hide, but learned that it was a geological term for rocky terrain extensively eroded by wind and water. The sign also said he might see—although he didn't—bison, feral horses, elk, and prairie dogs. He wanted to see a prairie dog, having never seen one before.

An hour or so later he stopped again to get the kinks out of his back and to be treated to the sight of Salem Sue: the world's largest black-and white Holstein cow. It was made of fiberglass, stood thirty-eight feet high, and was fifty feet long. Not a sight he would have seen had he not traveled fifteen hundred miles from Washington, D.C.

He crossed the Missouri River and drove into Bismarck, almost five hours after leaving Thorpe's place. The white, nineteen-story state capital building, the tallest structure in the city, dominated the view. He checked into another Holiday Inn Express and his room seemed identical to the one he'd had in Billings. Even the abstract art over the bed was the same.

He called the number Thorpe had given him for Sarah Johnson and she answered on the second ring. "Hi. This is Joe DeMarco. Would you like to get together to talk?"

"Yeah, you bet. There's a Starbucks—"

"How 'bout picking a place that serves a decent martini. It's been a long day. I need alcohol, not caffeine."

"Oh, well, let's see." After a long pause she said, "We could go to Minervas, I guess. It's near the Capitol. I don't drink much, but I've heard it's okay."

"I'll find it," DeMarco said. "I'll see you in an hour." DeMarco figured in a city the size of Bismarck he could get anywhere in an hour. "How will I recognize you?"

───── ❖ ─────

With a name like Minervas, DeMarco had been expecting a traditional tavern: neon Budweiser signs in the windows, photos of the softball team Minveras sponsored behind the bar. Or even better, maybe Minerva was the name of a famous madam back when they were building the railroads across the Great Plains, and the bar would be located in a historical brothel with embossed red wallpaper and portraits of plump naked ladies on the walls. It turned out, however, that Minervas was in a low brick building with a green roof and was a family-friendly restaurant with a well-lit bar, tables set with white cloth napkins, large comfortable booths, and a wholesome girl-next-door-type bartender.

DeMarco ordered a martini, and about five minutes after his drink arrived, Sarah Johnson walked through the door dressed as she'd told him she would be: blue jeans, a white turtleneck, and a woolly green vest. When he saw her eyes scanning the patrons looking for him, he raised a hand.

Sarah was six feet tall and according to her grandfather, twenty-two years old. She had alabaster-white skin, blue eyes, a flawless complexion, and butterscotch-blond hair reaching halfway to her shoulders. She wasn't beautiful, but she was striking because she was young and tall and had a nice figure and just glowed with good health.

She took a seat across from DeMarco and started off by saying, "Grandpa's email said you work for John Mahoney and might be able to help me, but he didn't tell me exactly what you do."

"You want a drink?" DeMarco asked.

"Uh, not really. I've got a lot to do tonight, and would just as soon get to the point."

"Okay. Well, as for what I do, I don't actually work for Mahoney. I mean, I'm not on his staff."

"Oh," she said, looking disappointed.

"I'm a guy Mahoney calls from time to time when he's got a problem or when one of his friends is having one. Like your grandfather. He sent me out here to see if I can help."

"Does Mahoney listen to you?"

DeMarco shrugged. "As much as he listens to anyone. Mahoney's a politician, and like most politicians, he acts primarily out of his own self-interest. But he's loyal to his friends and he told me your granddad saved his life in Vietnam. So he'll probably help you if he can, and if he doesn't have to stick his neck out, but that's the best I can tell you."

He could see Sarah wasn't enamored with his answer but said, "Well, since nobody else is willing to do anything, I guess talking to you can't hurt."

"Tell me what you're doing that's making people want to kill you. All your grandfather said is that you think there's some kind of big conspiracy going on."

"I don't *think*. I *know*. I just can't prove it and I can't get anybody in law enforcement or the big-time media to listen to me."

"I'm listening," DeMarco said.

"You know anything about state government in Montana or the Dakotas?"

"No."

"Yeah, well, the chances are if you lived in one of those states, you still wouldn't know anything. People pay attention to national politics because that's mostly what's on the news. They know if the president's thinking about bombing Iran or screwing with Social Security, but they don't have a clue what's happening in their own state legislatures. To find out what's going on in a state legislature you have to really *want* to know. You have to watch some little local channel that nobody watches and that's drier than dirt. You have to read bills that are written in some language other than English. So nobody pays a lot of attention to what's going on in Helena, Pierre, or Bismarck, but that's where the action really is. If a state can pass a law that's not covered by federal law, they can make anything happen. Hell, the states can even pass laws that go *against* federal law and sometimes the federal government can't do anything to stop them. To use a simple example, it's like in Washington and Colorado where they passed laws legalizing pot even though the feds say pot's illegal."

Sarah Johnson's intensity was palpable. After two minutes with her, DeMarco could tell that she was completely committed to whatever she was doing. He could sense her seriousness, her resolve. No, maybe *resolve* wasn't the right word. Maybe *obsession* was more accurate. Whatever the case, he could see the passion blazing in her eyes and he thought: Joan of Arc. That's who this young woman was. She was so zealous about what she believed in that she was willing to be burned at the stake. She wasn't an *activist*; she was a crusader and a would-be martyr.

"The other thing you need to understand," Sarah said, "is that the people elected to state legislatures are paid hardly anything. They barely make minimum wage. In South Dakota, a legislator is paid twelve thousand dollars a year and gets a hundred and ten dollars a day in per diem when the legislature is in session. If you do the math, that's less than eighteen grand if you don't take special sessions into account. And it's about the same in Montana and North Dakota.

"What this means is that these legislators, unless they're rich or retired with pensions, all have other jobs. They're ranchers and farmers and salesmen and teachers. Hell, half of them take the job because they *need* the lousy salary it pays. The other thing is, a lot of times they'll run unopposed because who else wants a job that pays so little?

"So what I'm trying to tell you is if you want to control what happens in a state, you don't waste your money bribing Montana's only congressman in the U.S. House of Representatives. What you do is introduce a bill in the Montana statehouse that does what you want, and if you need the votes, you pay off these part-time politicians who need the money."

"And that's what you're saying is happening? That somebody is bribing state legislators?"

"Yeah, but that's not all. They're bribing judges, too. If a law gets passed they don't like, they'll file a lawsuit and then if they need to, they'll bribe judges to overturn the law."

"Who's this *they* you're talking about?"

"There are a lot of theys," Sarah said. "I mean there are a lot of individuals and political organizations and corporations who are manipulating state legislators and judges, but the guy I'm after is Leonard Curtis."

"I've never heard of him," DeMarco said—and Sarah's expression said: *And why am I not surprised by this?*

"Curtis is an independent natural gas driller," she said.

"But what makes you think—"

"The biggest thing happening in this country, energy-wise, is natural gas and North Dakota has been called Kuwait on the Prairie. South Dakota and Montana also have gas and oil reserves, and huge corporations like Exxon and Conoco, and big independents like Devon and

Anadarko, are all going after the gas. It's like the California gold rush out here. Workers are living in shantytowns in trailers and RVs, and so many people are coming here that housing prices have skyrocketed and it's hard to get a motel room. They just can't develop the infrastructure fast enough to support all the drilling. At the same time, there are all kinds of issues—environmental issues, property issues, tax issues—related to natural gas. I mean, you've heard of fracking, haven't you?"

"Sure," DeMarco said. "That's when they pump in water to get the gas out."

"Not just water but chemicals, and fracking can contaminate ground water and cause earthquakes."

"Earthquakes? Is there any scientific evidence that fracking—"

"My point," Sarah said impatiently, "is that there are all sorts of legal issues related to natural gas, which means laws are getting passed to regulate the industry, and sometimes the laws are good for the gas companies and sometimes they're not. And what Leonard Curtis is doing, in every way he can, is making sure the laws are favorable to him."

"Aren't other companies doing the same thing?"

"Yeah, probably. Almost certainly. But I *know* Curtis is doing things that are illegal and I can't take on an entire industry. I figured if I focused on one guy I'd have a better chance of making a case. And Curtis is into everything: drilling, land leases, pipelines, drilling equipment. Anything to do with natural gas."

"And you think he's bribing people?"

"Quit saying that! Quit saying *I think!* I *know* he is."

"How many people are in these state legislatures?" DeMarco asked.

"In Montana there are a hundred in the House and fifty in the Senate. North Dakota is about the same as Montana. In South Dakota there are seventy in the House and thirty-five in the Senate."

"And Curtis is bribing all of them?"

"Of course not. Don't be stupid. First of all, the statehouses in all three states are currently controlled by the Republicans, and a lot of

Republicans support drilling because they want the United States to be energy independent and because the industry creates jobs. Right now, North Dakota has the lowest unemployment rate in the nation thanks to natural gas. So the statehouses are tilted in Curtis's favor and he doesn't have to do much to get a lot of these folks to vote the way he wants. He contributes to their campaigns, and these are little local campaigns where a few thousand bucks goes a long way.

"But these Republicans aren't a bunch of sheep, and a lot of them are farmers and ranchers and they care about the environment and anything that affects their property and mineral rights. And Curtis doesn't always need to get a law passed. Sometimes all he needs to do is slow things down, so legislation gets delayed. Or if there's a politician who's ranting against something Curtis wants, he just needs to quiet the politician down."

"Sarah, have you actually got any evidence that Curtis has bribed anyone? I mean, have you witnessed him bribing somebody or has anyone been willing to go on record that Curtis bought them off?"

"No."

"Then how do you know . . ."

"Let me give you an example. You know what a blowout preventer is? The device that failed in the Deepwater Horizon and dumped five million barrels of oil into the Gulf of Mexico?"

"Yeah, I know what you're talking about," DeMarco said.

"There was bill going through the North Dakota statehouse to increase inspection requirements for blowout preventers, and naturally Curtis was against the bill because more inspections would delay production and increase his costs. This one Republican named Stevens sided with the Democrats on the bill and he was pushing his party to approve it. Stevens is actually a pretty good guy when it comes to balancing energy production against environmental concerns.

"Well, Stevens is a farmer and to get to his farm he uses a road that passes through another farm. Stevens has an easement from the other farmer allowing him to use the road, and his dad had it before him. But one day, the other farmer says he's not going to allow Stevens to use the road anymore, and this meant that Stevens would have to drive an extra twenty miles to get to his place. To make matters worse, the road he'd be required to use has a bridge that goes over a little creek, and it's not rated for heavy loads. Stevens filed a lawsuit, of course, but the lawsuit was going to drag on for a year and in the meantime, Stevens would go broke. The next thing that happens, don't you know, Stevens stops supporting the bill, it fails in the Senate, and he gets the easement back. You see?"

DeMarco shook his head. "And that's it? A guy won't let him use a road and then the guy changes his mind and Stevens changes his vote?"

"Yes. Nobody gave Stevens a bag full of cash. Curtis just created a situation where Stevens would go bankrupt if he didn't play ball."

"How did you find all this stuff out, about Stevens and the easement and the other farmer?"

"When Stevens changed his position I wanted to know why, and I started digging. I talked to people, like the Democrats he'd been working with, and his lawsuit, of course, was a matter of public record."

"But you don't know for sure that Curtis made the other farmer cancel the easement, or why he did it, or if that's the reason Stevens changed his vote."

"I do know! I just can't prove it. Stevens denies it, of course, and when I asked the other farmer—who his neighbors all said is a shitty farmer and up to his neck in debt—he refused to talk to me. But I know!"

Before DeMarco could object again, she held up a hand to silence him. "There was another case. A Democrat, who lives in Williston, which is right about in the middle of the Bakken oil field. She was making a big stink about flaring and saying that Curtis was one of the biggest polluters."

"Flaring?" DeMarco said.

"Jesus," Sarah muttered, appalled by DeMarco's ignorance. "Flaring is where they vent off and burn waste gases that supposedly can't be efficiently captured and processed. If you were to go up in space it would look like there are ten thousand bonfires burning on the Great Plains. They actually have satellite pictures showing this. Flaring is bad in that it not only contributes to greenhouse gases but it actually wastes a lot of gas. They're burning off *millions* of cubic feet of gas a day."

DeMarco wondered if she was exaggerating—but he doubted she was. "So why do the gas companies do it?" he said.

"Because it's cheaper to flare the gas than it is to install the equipment to capture it. Or they'll say it's for safety reasons. Anyway, this legislator from Williston runs a bakery and she was pushing for legislation to reduce flaring. Then out of the blue comes an old lady, who looks like everybody's grandma, and she files a lawsuit saying she was poisoned by a cupcake."

"A cupcake?"

"Yeah. She said she found rat feces in the cupcake and it made her sick, and she got a lawyer to file a suit. This baker couldn't afford to fight a lawsuit, and if a rumor got out that she had rat shit in her flour, it would kill her business. Then the same thing happened, just like with Stevens. The lawsuit was dropped and the baker quit being a squeaky wheel. When I asked her about it, she started crying and wouldn't talk to me. Shouldn't you be taking notes or something?"

"No," DeMarco said. "I don't need to take notes, not at this point. I get the gist of what you're saying but the thing is, I'm not sure what to do next. I have to give it some thought."

"Well, I know what you need to do," Sarah said, her eyes blazing like they might set DeMarco's martini on fire. "First you need to go read my blog and then get Mr. Mahoney to read it."

DeMarco almost laughed out loud. Mahoney never read anything. The people who worked for him read the documents that Mahoney was supposed to read, then told him what the documents said.

"Then what Mahoney needs to do is convince the attorney general to investigate Curtis. What Curtis is doing isn't happening in a single state, so it would be appropriate to get the FBI and the Justice Department involved. They need to form up a federal task force."

"A federal task force?" DeMarco said. "Based on a cupcake lawsuit?"

"Shit, I'm just wasting my time with you," Sarah said. She started to get up but DeMarco placed a hand on her forearm. "Hold on, Sarah. I just need to think about all this, then maybe I'll talk to Mahoney." He had no intention of talking to Mahoney.

"Okay," Sarah said, then tears welled up in her eyes. "I just can't get anybody to take me seriously and this is serious stuff. Curtis is making a mockery out of democracy and nobody cares."

"I care, Sarah." Actually the only thing DeMarco really cared about was this girl not getting hurt. Although he admired her courage and her commitment, he thought she was being naïve if she believed she could change a political system that had become blatantly corrupt. She also didn't seem to understand that without solid evidence—which she didn't appear to have—she would never be able to prove to the satisfaction of any court in the land that Curtis was doing anything illegal. But his job wasn't to help her advance her cause; his job, as far as he was concerned, was to keep her from getting killed.

"Now tell me," DeMarco said, "about these death threats and the other things people have done to try to get you to stop."

6

"Do you hear me?" Curtis said. "I want that bitch to quit writing about me."

Marjorie and Bill were still sitting in the Pirogue Grille with Leonard Curtis, less than two miles from where DeMarco was meeting with Sarah Johnson. By now their coffee was cold and the waitress didn't bring them fresh cups because Curtis had rudely instructed the waitress to leave them alone.

Sarah Johnson's blog was the bane of Curtis's existence. It was a disorganized, unstructured mess that if printed out would run two thousand pages, and it served three purposes. First, Johnson used it as a journal or a diary in which she recounted what she'd done that day in her relentless pursuit of Leonard Curtis. It discussed, in mind-numbing detail, legislation or legal cases she'd researched. She also named people she'd talked to, usually castigating those people for incompetence or stupidity. Marjorie and Bill, therefore, pretty much always knew what Johnson was doing because she told the whole world.

The second part of the blog was an ongoing rant against the American political system, and Johnson raved about how Curtis manipulated politicians with campaign contributions, took them on junkets, and paid for misleading television ads. She admitted that what Curtis was doing was arguably legal, but she wanted everyone to know how he was using his vast wealth solely to benefit Leonard Curtis as opposed to the common people.

It was the third part of the blog that was the real problem, however, and the reason for Curtis's angst. What Johnson would do was look for any legal or legislative issue in the tristate area that affected Curtis. Next, she would identify people who appeared to be pivotal to the legislation passing or failing, or to a lawsuit being decided in Curtis's favor. Marjorie couldn't even imagine the hundreds of hours Johnson spent researching and investigating. Johnson's final step would then be to find some evidence, no matter how circumstantial or far-fetched, that a key person had been bribed, coerced, or otherwise unduly influenced. However, the evidence—if you could even call it evidence—could never be tied directly to anything Curtis had done personally. Nor had Johnson been able to find a single person willing to admit that he'd been bribed or coerced.

But the problem was that Johnson was right! In the past two years, she had uncovered eleven instances where Curtis had in fact bribed or coerced politicians.

Marjorie had tried dozens of times to convince Curtis that Sarah Johnson wasn't worth going after and that he should simply ignore her. She told Curtis that less than fifty people a week read Johnson's rambling blog. For that matter, they weren't sure that anybody actually *read* it; they could just see that less than fifty people a week visited her website—and eight of those people were Bill, Marjorie, Leonard Curtis, and five lawyers.

One reason so few people read her blog was that Johnson didn't have the ability to make the complex legal issues she wrote about simpler and more understandable, and the way she wrote wasn't engaging and put people to sleep. Furthermore, in person, Johnson was rude and antagonistic, and she alienated the people whose help she needed. The bottom line was that no law enforcement organization had been persuaded by her and her incomprehensible blog.

But Curtis didn't care. Curtis wanted her stopped.

So Bill and Marjorie had tried to stop her. They started off with a low-key approach. They had a lawyer send a cease-and-desist letter to Johnson warning that she would be sued for libel if she continued to make blatantly false accusations against certain people named in her blog. Letters from lawyers terrify most normal people. Normal people can envision spending massive amounts of money and time battling a lawsuit, and then, ultimately, losing the lawsuit and everything they own to pay off the lawyers and penalties imposed by the court. But Sarah Johnson wasn't normal, and the letter from the lawyer didn't deter her one tiny bit. She posted the letter verbatim in her blog, citing it as an example of the kind of thing Curtis would do to stop any investigation into his criminal activities.

Next, Leonard Curtis *did* sue her for libel—and Johnson's lawyers responded with a motion for discovery, asking for virtually every document Curtis's businesses had generated in the last two years. Curtis's lawyers were now fighting Johnson's lawyers to keep her from getting the documents. Curtis also had courts in three states issue restraining orders against Johnson, specifying she couldn't call him or come within a hundred yards of him. These orders were granted—and frankly, reasonable—because for a while Johnson was essentially stalking Curtis.

When Curtis's lawsuit didn't stop her, they tried to scare her by having a crude, rough-sounding guy make harassing phone calls, saying he was going to kill her if he lost his job because of the things she was doing. They figured Johnson *had* to know there were violent yokels all over Montana and the Dakotas and they all owned guns. In other words, they thought she'd take the threats seriously—and maybe she did—but she didn't stop going after Curtis.

Then Marjorie had an idea she was sure would work. Using Curtis's money, she convinced an editor at a major East Coast newspaper to offer Johnson a job investigating coal mining in West Virginia and Kentucky—places where they literally blew the tops off mountains to get at seams of coal. Marjorie figured that working for a legitimate newspaper on a big-time environmental issue would appeal to Johnson's ego as well as her crusading nature. But that didn't work either because by this point, Johnson's primary focus wasn't the environment—her mission was to nail Leonard Curtis.

Marjorie and Bill's next move was to have Gordy completely fuck up Johnson's website, figuring she wouldn't have the resources to fight off a cyberattack. They also had three more people file lawsuits against her, thinking that she wouldn't have the money to fight four lawsuits simultaneously. And that's when they found out that the twenty-two-year-old college dropout was extraordinarily rich thanks to her dead mother. Sarah's lawyers were now doing everything they could to turn the lawsuits into jury trials where Leonard Curtis would be subpoenaed to testify.

The last thing they did was send three guys to rough her up. This had been Bill's idea. Marjorie said at the time she thought it was a mistake but Bill said that a young woman, all on her own, might be brave when it came to lawsuits and harassing phone calls but real, physical violence was a whole different story. So Bill told the guy he hired not to hurt her, but to do his best to scare the living shit out of her. But, as Marjorie had predicted, all the assault did was piss Johnson off and the cops were now looking for the people who had assaulted her.

"So what are you going to do next?" Curtis asked, as they sat there drinking ice-cold coffee.

"Mr. Curtis," Marjorie said, "I know you don't want to hear this but I really think we ought to just leave that crazy girl alone. Nobody's listening to her. Nobody takes her seriously. Nobody reads her stupid blog."

"*I* read her damn blog!" Curtis said, smacking one of his small fists on the table. "I want her stopped."

"Okay," Bill said, seeing that Marjorie was getting nowhere and just making Curtis angry. "We'll regroup. We'll come up with something."

"Yeah, well, if you don't, I'll find somebody who can," Curtis said.

That was the very last thing Bill and Marjorie wanted to hear. They knew Curtis was happy with their work, but they also knew he wouldn't hesitate to fire them. Curtis fired people the way cats shed fur, and they knew they'd never find jobs that paid anywhere near what Curtis was paying them.

7

---◆---

Curtis left the Pirogue Grille at nine thirty to go back to the Radisson. Curtis was a man who went to bed every night at ten p.m. and he allowed nothing to keep him up any later. As soon as he left, Marjorie and Bill ordered drinks—a Glenlivet neat for Bill, a glass of good Merlot for Marjorie. They never drank when they were with Curtis because Curtis didn't drink.

"What are we going to do?" Bill said.

"I don't know," Marjorie said. They sat there for a couple of minutes, sipping their drinks, saying nothing, as they tried to come up with an idea to stop Johnson that might actually work. Finally Marjorie said, "There's always Murdock."

"Aw, Jesus, Marjorie. Murdock? Are you serious?"

"Yeah, I guess I am. I don't want to do that but . . . Johnson's irrational. She's insane! She's been butting her head against a brick wall for two years, yet she refuses to stop. She's too rich to buy off and she's too crazy to scare off. I mean, she's like those fucking Muslim suicide bombers: she's willing to blow herself up to blow *you* up. How can you deal with a person like that?"

"But Murdock?" Bill said.

"Hey! If you got a better idea, spit it out."

When three men in ski masks terrorized Sarah Johnson in a dark parking lot, the short ringleader had been Bill's ex-brother-in-law. His name was Tim Sloan, and Bill could understand why his sister had divorced him. Tim was a lazy, shiftless, useless slug whose primary source of income—after Bill's sister divorced him—was a Social Security disability check for a nonexistent back problem. But Tim wasn't totally stupid and he was always desperate for money as long as he didn't have to work too hard for it, so Bill used him occasionally.

Bill and Marjorie's territory covered three large states, and Tim would be sent to pick up documents that they didn't want emailed as emails left a traceable record. A couple of times, Bill had Tim volunteer to help out on the campaigns of candidates Curtis opposed hoping Tim might overhear something that would give Curtis's guy an advantage. One time they had Tim deliver photos to a certain judge when they wanted to impress upon him the inadvisability of a ruling he'd been about to make. And Tim was the gravelly voiced man who had harassed Johnson with nasty phone calls, threatening to kill her if he lost a job that he didn't have.

But Murdock was in a completely different league than Tim Sloan.

The first and only time Bill and Marjorie had used Murdock was six years ago. It was so long ago they could almost convince themselves they'd never used him at all. A lawsuit Curtis couldn't afford to lose had made it all the way to the South Dakota Supreme Court and if the court ruled against him, it was going to cost him millions. To make matters worse, this occurred during the great recession of 2008 and even Curtis was having financial problems.

The problem was that there were five justices on the South Dakota Supreme Court and Bill and Marjorie knew that two were going to rule against Curtis, two were going to rule in his favor, but they had no idea what the fifth justice was going to do. The swing judge was an unpredictable screwball named James Wainwright III who had no consistent record on anything. It was as if he flipped a coin every time he made a decision. To make matters worse, Bill and Marjorie hadn't been able to find anything they could use to persuade Wainwright. He was rich and, as best as they'd been able to tell after having a private detective watch him for two months, had no vices they could use to control him.

If Wainwright was gone, however, the governor would appoint his replacement. Curtis had no strong hold over the South Dakota governor but the governor was "gas-friendly" and Bill and Marjorie were about ninety percent sure he would pick a guy who would rule in Curtis's favor. So they just had to get Wainwright off the bench—they *had* to—and after everything else they'd tried had failed, Curtis told them to call Murdock. They had no idea how Curtis knew Murdock and Curtis, being Curtis, wouldn't tell them. It was apparent, however, that he'd used the man before.

Bill met with Murdock in a steam room at a small gym in Denver clad in nothing but a white towel, a practical precaution to ensure Bill wasn't wearing a wire. Murdock turned out to be an average-looking guy of indeterminate age; he could have been forty-five or a decade older. He had receding dark hair, brown eyes, a bony nose, and thin lips. He was in good shape but he wasn't physically impressive; he wasn't any more muscular than Bill. Nor did he look the way Bill imagined a contract killer would look: evil, steely-eyed, cold as ice. If Murdock had said that he sold vacuum cleaners at Sears, Bill would have believed him.

Bill told Murdock that Judge Wainwright of South Dakota needed to have a fatal accident within the next three months, but the judge couldn't be obviously murdered. Murder could lead to all sorts of problems, and the last thing Curtis wanted was some hotshot law enforcement team investigating Wainwright's death.

Six weeks later, Wainwright drowned. He owned a cabin in the Black Hills and liked to fish for trout in the small streams near his place. His body was found lying in less than a foot of water in Spearfish Creek. It appeared as if he'd slipped, hit his head on a rock, fell into the water unconscious, and drowned. He was still holding his fishing rod in his hand when he was found. The rock that he'd smacked his head on was lying near him, his blood was on it, and there was no evidence that anyone else had been with the judge—such as fingerprints on the rock or footprints that didn't belong to the judge or tire tracks from a second vehicle parked near the scene—at least no evidence that a local county sheriff could find.

But Bill didn't want to bring in Murdock to deal with Sarah Johnson. He'd lost ten pounds and didn't sleep soundly for three months after Wainwright's *accident*. "Goddamnit, there has to be another way," he said to Marjorie.

"Bill," Marjorie said, "I don't want to do this either, but I've got two boys to send to college one day, and my house isn't going to be paid off for another fifteen years. I am *not* going to let that girl destroy my life."

Before Bill could respond, Marjorie's phone beeped the signal for a text message. "It's Heckler," she told Bill. "Let me see what he wants." Marjorie left the bar to call Heckler, and the reason she did was because she needed a cigarette. She never smoked around her kids but she'd sneak one every once in a while when she was under stress.

Heckler was a local private detective who they were paying to watch Sarah Johnson. He'd been following her for the last three months, although he couldn't stick with her twenty-four hours a day as he needed to sleep sometime. Heckler also recorded her cell phone calls and used the GPS feature in Johnson's phone to keep tabs on her location. When it came to technology, Heckler was a dinosaur but Gordy—Bill and Marjorie's grass-smoking associate—had downloaded the necessary spyware onto Johnson's phone.

Marjorie had actually been amazed to learn that there were companies that legally sold software that could be used to monitor cell phone calls and track people's movements. According to these companies' websites, you had to have physical access to the phone you wanted to monitor and, of course, the owner's permission, but Gordy was smart enough to load the spyware onto Johnson's phone by embedding the software in an email he sent to her. Marjorie had told Bill she was think-ing about having Gordy put the software on her kids' phones so she'd always know where they were and what sort of mischief they might be planning.

Thinking about getting Murdock involved, Bill decided to have an-other scotch. He looked around for the waitress and didn't see her, so he walked up to the bar. He ordered a drink from the bartender, then glanced down the bar. Aw, shit. There was a woman sitting there—glar-ing at him. He'd slept with her once, couldn't remember her name, and he hadn't ever called her back after the one time. He was trying to make up his mind if he should go say hello or just ignore her when Marjorie came back into the bar. She walked over to him and said, "Come on. We don't have time for you to get laid."

They sat back down at the table and Marjorie said, "Johnson met with a guy tonight."

"You mean she had a date?"

"No. Heckler said the guy was older than her. Heckler said he was a hard-looking SOB. Those were his words. He said Johnson and the guy had a drink together and she left an hour later. Heckler said it didn't look like a social thing."

"So who is he?"

"His name's Joe DeMarco. Heckler got his name when he called Johnson. Then Heckler followed him back to his motel and paid a clerk to get a peek at the registration form." Marjorie paused before she said, "DeMarco's from Washington, Bill. I mean, D.C. not the state."

"D.C.?"

"Yeah. We better find out who he is before you talk to Murdock."

Bill didn't bother to say that he hadn't yet agreed to talk to Murdock. All he said was, "I think you're right. I just hope he isn't carrying a badge. Curtis will go through the roof if he is."

8

DeMarco stopped at a liquor store after his meeting with Sarah, bought a bottle of Grey Goose, and went back to his room at the Holiday Inn Express. The ice machine on his floor wasn't working and he had to go up two floors before he found one that was. He dropped ice into a plastic glass, added two ounces of vodka, and plopped onto the bed with his laptop.

For the next hour he read Sarah Johnson's blog. He stopped when it felt like his brain cells were turning to mush and starting to dissolve. The girl may have been smart but she couldn't tell a story. She wrote in convoluted sentences that went on forever and sometimes a single paragraph would fill an entire page. She was repetitive—making the same argument over and over again in case the reader didn't understand it the first time—and her stories were filled with trivial details that she apparently thought were necessary to prove she'd done her research or to validate whatever she was saying. She used capital letters to emphasize her points, and every other sentence had some phrase or word capitalized and, as if that wasn't enough, sometimes double exclamation points served for periods.

But the gist of the blog was basically what she'd told him in Minervas: Leonard Curtis, and the many companies he owned, had incredible luck when it came to state laws and rulings handed down in various courtrooms. However, there was nothing even close to proof that Curtis had done anything illegal. In one case, Sarah concluded a state legislator in Montana—who was also a wheat farmer—had changed his vote based solely on the fact that the man got a good deal on a farm implement called a seed drill.

DeMarco had no idea what a seed drill was, but the story about the legislator and the seed drill illustrated the depths Sarah went to in order to get information and, at the same time, how tentative her conclusions could be. In this case, Sarah learned a Democrat named Reynolds had strayed from the party line and changed his vote on a bill proposing to increase taxes on natural gas to aid school funding. She went to see Reynolds and asked him why—and he refused to talk to her.

So Sarah started talking to other Democrats who had a stake in the bill to see if they could explain Reynolds's treachery. One of the legislators, a man named Franklin, who was also a farmer, was quoted in Sarah's blog saying: "I actually wonder if it had anything to do with that seed drill he got at Colson's for ten grand. I mean, I've never heard of a guy getting a deal like that, and he was bragging about it, so it wasn't like he was trying to keep it secret, but it was right after that he started arguing against the bill."

When Sarah asked Franklin if he was saying that he thought Reynolds had been bribed, Franklin started backpedaling, saying he wasn't about to accuse a fellow Democrat of doing anything illegal.

It took Sarah a week to learn that Colson's was a farm that had gone into foreclosure, and that Curtis had bought the land and then hired a broker to sell off the farm equipment. One of the items being sold was a practically new White 8186 seed drill that would normally sell for about twenty-five thousand. Based solely on this information—the fact that Reynolds changed his vote on a bill Curtis didn't want passed and was given an extraordinary deal on a piece of equipment that Curtis owned—she concluded the seed drill was a bribe.

The problem, DeMarco immediately realized, as would any other lawyer, was that no one could prove that Reynolds had done anything illegal. Reynolds would argue that he was just a shrewd negotiator and Curtis's broker didn't understand the value of the item he was selling but, whatever the case, the price he got for the used seed drill had nothing to do with his vote.

In another section of her rambling blog, Sarah listed by name every politician and law enforcement person she'd contacted in an attempt to get these individuals to investigate Curtis. She called them obtuse, lazy, and blatantly corrupt. The girl did not know how to make friends and influence people, and DeMarco had another image of Sarah as Joan of Arc on a big white stallion, dressed in chain mail, wielding a broadsword, whacking the heads off English horsemen. And a few French horsemen, too, if they got in her way.

Which reminded him: he needed to tell Sarah not to mention him or Mahoney in her blog. He'd tell her if she did, that he'd walk and she'd be on her own again. The last thing DeMarco needed was to have his presence in Bismarck advertised, and Mahoney would go ballistic if his name appeared in her blog without his permission. The problem was, DeMarco wasn't sure he could control Sarah; he wasn't sure anyone could.

Tall, pretty, blond Sarah reminded him in some ways of dark, dour Ralph Nader. Nader was old now, around eighty, but he came to national prominence at the young age of thirty-one when he wrote *Unsafe at Any Speed*. Like Sarah, Nader was passionate, fearless, insensitive, and didn't care whose feet he stepped on. But in spite of a tendency toward bluntness that bordered on rudeness, DeMarco liked the girl. When he was her age, he was still in college and spent more time chasing coeds and drinking than he did studying, while here was Sarah, trying to make the world a better place. However, he had no idea how to help her. Nor did he have any idea how to keep her from getting killed if somebody really wanted to kill her. And after spending only one hour with Sarah

Johnson, he knew she wasn't going to give up until either she was dead or Curtis was in jail.

Then one thought finally occurred to him. He grabbed his cell phone and called Sarah.

———◆◆◆———

Marjorie got up the next morning at five thirty as she usually did, took a quick shower, and blow-dried her hair. She stepped on the scale in the bathroom, made a face, then went and got dressed. As the coffee was brewing, she looked at the calendar on the refrigerator door. Bobby had a baseball game tonight. She'd try to make that. Tommy was going over to Henry Grove's house to play video games after school. Hmm.

Marjorie didn't trust Henry Grove—he was a sneaky little shit—and she was convinced that he was a bad influence on Tommy. The last time Tommy had been to Henry's house, Marjorie thought she got a whiff of pot off Tommy's hair but it was hard to be sure, the odor mixed in with sweat and all the other pungent teenage boy smells. She mentioned this to Henry's mom, suggesting she might want to poke around in her son's room and see if she could find a bag of dope. Naturally, Henry's mother had been offended and things were still a bit cool between her and Marjorie.

Marjorie left a note for Dick, giving him his marching orders for the day: drop off the dry cleaning; take the three boxes of crap that have been sitting in the garage for a month to Goodwill; call a plumber, like she'd told him two days ago, to come fix the leaky faucet in the master bath; pick up the boys after school, drop off Tommy at Henry's house, then take Bobby to the baseball field where she'd meet him. She'd pick up Tommy from Henry's place after the game so she could sniff his hair again. She signed the note *Love and kisses, M*, grabbed her purse, her keys, and headed out the door.

She didn't look at her cell phone until she got to work. Her plan that morning was to get on the phone and start calling people in Washington to figure out who this guy DeMarco was. When she pulled out her phone, she saw a text message from Heckler. He'd sent it at eleven last night. It said: Call me first thing in the morning. It's a big deal.

She called Heckler.

"Jesus, what time is it?" he said.

"Six thirty," Marjorie said. "Your message said to call you first thing in the morning."

"I didn't mean six thirty."

"Wake up, Heckler, and tell me what's going on."

"Hang on. I want to play you a call Johnson got last night from that guy DeMarco."

She heard Heckler getting out of bed, coughing, a cigarette lighter clicking, and then he said, "Okay. I'm going to play it back."

"Sarah, it's Joe DeMarco. I've been reading your blog and I wanted to ask you something."

"So now do you see what I mean about the shit that Curtis has been pulling?"

"Uh, yeah. Anyway, what I wanted to ask is this. Who paid these people you think were bribed?"

"What do you mean? Curtis paid them."

"I kind of doubt that Curtis paid them directly. I mean, I can't imagine him personally arranging for some legislator to get a good deal on a seed drill, whatever the hell that is."

"Well, of course he didn't do it personally. Curtis probably has twenty thousand people who work for him, with all the companies he owns. He retains a law firm that employs over eighty lawyers. Those are the people who are making the payoffs."

"I don't think so, Sarah. I think . . . I think Curtis has a guy like me."

"A guy like you? What do you mean?"

"I mean he's probably got a guy he uses for this sort of thing. A guy who fixes things for him. He wouldn't have two dozen people buying off politicians and judges. He'd want somebody he could trust, somebody he knew was competent, probably somebody who's worked for him for a long time."

And Marjorie thought: Oh, shit.

"So, Sarah, I wanted to know if you've ever come across somebody like that? A single person, an operator, who might have met with all these people you say have been bribed or blackmailed or whatever?"

"No."

"What I'm saying is, if you can find that person and if pressure can be brought to bear on him, maybe he can be forced to testify against Curtis because he's the guy who's really committed a crime."

"How would you pressure him?"

"I don't know. But the first thing we need to do is find him."

"If he exists."

"Yeah, if he exists. I'll talk to you tomorrow, Sarah."

And Marjorie again thought: Oh, shit.

"That's it," Heckler said. "But I thought you ought to hear that."

"You thought right. Now get out of bed and get back on her."

Marjorie sat for a minute, then reached into her purse for the pack of Marlboros and went outside. Bill would give her a ration of shit if she smoked in the office.

This was bad. Sarah Johnson had never mentioned Bill or Marjorie in her stupid blog. They had no documented connection to Curtis—at least none that Johnson would be able to find. Their consulting firm wasn't owned by Curtis—it wasn't one of Curtis's many companies— and Curtis was not identified in any public forum as being their client.

But if Johnson talked to the right people, it was possible—although highly unlikely—that some of those people might say that she and Bill had approached them on Curtis's behalf. Ninety-nine percent of them wouldn't talk, of course, because then they'd be admitting that they'd been bribed or influenced in some way. But maybe one of them would. Maybe one of them was no longer in politics and had grown a conscience. Maybe one of them felt that he or she had been screwed by Curtis in some way. All Marjorie knew for sure was that DeMarco had pointed Johnson in their direction—and that wasn't good.

She needed to find out who this damn guy was.

———————————◆◆◆———————————

Bill rolled into the office about ten. He wasn't his normal, cheerful self. He looked grim. He'd probably been thinking about the fact that he might have to go to Denver to see Murdock again.

"We have a problem," Marjorie said as soon as he walked through the door.

"I thought we might have. I saw the cigarette butts out by the door."

Marjorie told Bill about the conversation Heckler had recorded between DeMarco and Sarah Johnson. Bill's reaction was: *Oh, shit.*

"Who is this fuckin' guy?" Bill said.

"I've been on the phone for the last three hours trying to figure that out. He's a lawyer and he works for the House of Representatives but it's not clear what he does. He's not listed as being on anyone's staff. And get this. His father was an honest-to-God mafia hit man up in New York."

"Mafia? You think DeMarco's mafia?"

"No. Shut up. I said his *father* was mafia. He's not mafia, at least it doesn't sound like it. Anyway, I finally got to Peach."

Jeremiah Peach was an aide to Congressman Sam Erhart, Montana's sole representative in the House. It seemed as if Peach had been in D.C. since the British burned down the White House and whenever Montana elected a new representative—Democrat or Republican—the new congressman kept Peach on his staff because the new guys the new congressman brought with him didn't really know how things worked on the Hill.

"Peach told me that DeMarco is a shady character who works down in the subbasement of the Capitol. He's a lawyer, but as far as Peach knows, he doesn't practice law. When I Googled DeMarco, I found out he made the news about a year ago. You remember Bob Fairchild, that congressman from Arizona who paid an ex-cop to kill a woman in Tucson?"

"Yeah?"

"Well, DeMarco was the one who caught the killer but none of the articles made it clear as to why he was involved at all. But the main thing Peach told me is that DeMarco might work for John Mahoney."

"Mahoney? You mean the guy who used to be the Speaker?"

"Yeah. Peach said DeMarco's not on Mahoney's staff but it seems like whenever Mahoney has some sticky problem to solve, DeMarco shows up. Peach said it's like DeMarco's this dog Mahoney keeps in a cage, and he only lets him out when he wants someone bit. Peach also said that since John Mahoney is as corrupt as any African dictator, this means that DeMarco isn't some Boy Scout lawyer who plays by the rules."

"Why the hell would John Mahoney care about Sarah Johnson?" Bill said.

"I have no idea. But this is bad, Bill. The last thing we need is someone with a connection to Mahoney. Johnson can't get anybody in law enforcement to give her the time of day, but Mahoney can probably get the FBI involved with one phone call."

"What do you want to do?"

"I'm still thinking Murdock may be our best option. In fact, I think he's our only option."

"You want Murdock to . . ." Bill wasn't even going to say the word *kill* out loud. "You want him to take care of both Johnson and DeMarco?"

"Hell, no. If Johnson has an accident that's one thing. If something happens to *both* her and DeMarco . . . I don't even want to go down that path."

"But if something happens to her, even if it's ruled an accident, then DeMarco might keep digging anyway."

"Yeah, I know."

"Should we tell Curtis about DeMarco?"

"Not yet. He'd go ape shit if he knew a guy working for Mahoney was out here talking to Johnson. We need to come up with an answer before we talk to Curtis."

9

DeMarco called Sarah and suggested they meet for breakfast.

"I don't usually eat breakfast," she said.

"Well, I do. And pick a place that makes a real breakfast, not some coffee shop or a McDonald's."

He met her at a Denny's on Seventh Street and ordered French toast, sausage links, and eggs over easy. She had a coffee.

"Like I told you last night," DeMarco said, "Curtis probably has somebody working for him that's his go-to guy for payoffs. I mean, if you're right about Curtis."

"What do you mean, *if* I'm right?" she said, her eyes bugging out of her head. "I thought you read my blog."

"I read enough to know that you don't have any evidence that Curtis did anything illegal. On top of that, your blog's so damn convoluted and wordy, nobody can read it without going into a coma. Your grand-dad said you have money. Maybe you should hire a writer to turn your research into a book or a magazine article."

Then he immediately wished he hadn't said that. He could tell he'd hurt her feelings.

"I mean you have a lot of data and a lot of good arguments," DeMarco said, trying to sound soothing. "I'm just saying a pro could make it more . . . more accessible. But that's not what I wanted to talk to you about. Can you think of anyone who's taken a bribe that might be feeling some remorse, some guilt. Or maybe somebody who's now pissed at Curtis for whatever reason."

"I've been thinking about that ever since you called last night. I need to go back through parts of my blog again and look at my raw notes."

"Okay, do that. In the meantime, I think you should hire some security. A couple big guys licensed to carry."

"Yeah, maybe."

"Sarah, people have threatened to kill you twice. You've been assaulted. You need to take the threats seriously."

"Yeah, I know," she said—but DeMarco could tell she wasn't going to do anything. Like most twenty-two-year-olds, she thought she was immortal and invincible.

"How did you get into all this stuff with Curtis in the first place?" he asked.

"It started out when I got interested in fracking and all the damage that it was doing to the environment. I went to a couple of rallies, met some activists, and joined up with a group in Billings for a while. Then one night, my group went to a public hearing in Bismarck and . . . You remember what I told you last night about Stevens?"

"The farmer with the easement?"

"Yeah. We figured that Stevens was going to speak out in favor of the bill to increase inspections on blowout preventers, but instead he talked about how the existing requirements were good enough. But you could tell he didn't really believe what he was saying—I mean, the guy just *looked* ashamed—and one of the people I was with said it was obvious that Curtis had gotten to Stevens—bribed him or blackmailed him or something—but that we'd never be able to prove it. But I decided to see if I could.

"I knew if Curtis had given Stevens cash or transferred money to an offshore account I wouldn't be able to find out, but in Stevens's case it was easy because everything was a matter of public record. What I mean is, Stevens filed a lawsuit against the farmer who withdrew the easement and later, Stevens dropped the lawsuit, so it was easy to connect the dots."

DeMarco almost said: Well, you found some dots, but I'm not sure you really connected anything—but decided to keep his mouth shut.

"The next thing that happened," Sarah said, "was a circuit court judge named Hardy ruled in favor of something that benefited Curtis in a big way. You don't need to know all the details, and since you don't know anything about how they process natural gas you wouldn't understand anyway, but this judge's ruling didn't make sense. It was just absurd. Well, I found out that Hardy was running for reelection that year and about eighty percent of his campaign contributions were coming from Curtis and guys who worked for Curtis and companies Curtis owns."

DeMarco shrugged. "Yeah, well. You know."

"What the hell does that mean? That *yeah, well, you know*?"

DeMarco always told people that the United States of America has the best government that money can buy—and he was serious. And that's what he told Sarah. "Sarah, that's politics in this country. People and companies contribute to guys who see things their way. It's not a conspiracy. It's not illegal. It's just the way things are."

"That doesn't make it right."

"I'm not saying it's right. I'm just saying that Curtis didn't do anything illegal by supporting this judge for reelection."

It looked for a minute like Sarah was going to erupt like Vesuvius, then she took a breath. "Anyway, you asked how I got started. That was the beginning. After that, I just started digging into anything that favored Curtis. Bills in the legislature, court cases, lawsuits. I filed FOIA requests. I looked at key people to see if they benefited in some way. I looked at property records to see if they bought a second home and at building permits to see if they were remodeling their houses. I talked to their neighbors and their political opponents." She took a breath and said, "I'm a hell of a researcher, Mr. DeMarco. I may not be a writer but I work hard and I know how to dig to find things out."

And DeMarco believed that: that Sarah Johnson was a hell of a researcher. But she didn't seem to be able to grasp the fact that just because a politician benefited at the same time Curtis benefited that that wasn't prima facie evidence of bribery. Rather than argue with her, he said, "Okay. So go back over your blog and your notes and think about who might give us a lead on the person Curtis is using to fix things around here."

"I will," she said and stood up. "But then what? What do I do when I've got some names?"

"Then we go lean on these people and try to convince them to talk to you. I'm not much of a researcher but I'm pretty good at leaning on folks."

"You'll go with me? Seriously?"

"Yeah. For a while. I mean, I have a job in D.C. I need to get back to, but I'll give this a few more days."

Sarah marched out of the restaurant like a woman on a mission from God.

Actually, the only job DeMarco had back in Washington was doing whatever Mahoney told him to do and, for the present, Mahoney wanted him right where he was. DeMarco just wanted to get back home to see if Ralph had annihilated the rodents.

DeMarco finished his breakfast, then decided to call Ralph and ask how things were progressing.

"Things are going good," Ralph said cheerfully. He was a cheerful killer. "They already ate two boxes of the d-CON, so when I drop by your place tomorrow, I should find some bodies inside the house."

"You mean *outside* the house," DeMarco said.

"Uh, yeah, that's what I mean," Ralph said.

As he walked to his car, DeMarco thought about calling Mahoney to let him know what was going on, but then he couldn't help but notice that it was a lovely spring morning. There had to be a public golf course somewhere in Bismarck. He'd go rent some clubs and play a round—then call Mahoney. Nothing was going to change in four or five hours—except maybe the weather, which might preclude playing golf. He wished he'd brought his golf shoes with him.

"Maybe we're overthinking this thing," Marjorie said to Bill. She'd just come back into the office after another cigarette. Bill couldn't recall her ever smoking this much before; she must have gone through a pack since she'd arrived at the office.

"If something happens to Johnson," Marjorie said, "it'll end with her. Like we've tried to tell Curtis a million times, she doesn't have any proof that we or Curtis or anybody else has done anything illegal. She's just got a lot of conjecture and coincidence."

"Conjecture that's dead spot-on," Bill said.

"But it's *conjecture,* Bill. It isn't proof. If she's gone, this DeMarco character will go home. He doesn't have contacts here. He doesn't know how things work out here. But the main thing is, he can't be as screwy as Sarah Johnson. He won't spend the rest of his life investigating all the crap she's written about."

"I'm still not sure we should use Murdock. There has to be some other—"

"You know, I think it would be best if it looked like a home invasion or robbery or a rape."

"What?"

"I mean if she's just shot or something," Marjorie said, "the cops might think she was killed for some reason connected to all her political bullshit, and they might think that Curtis was involved. So you see what I mean? We shouldn't make it look like she was, you know, *assassinated*."

Bill was speechless. You look at Marjorie—cute, bubbly, bouncy little Marjorie—and you think: Soccer Mom of the Year. You'd never imagine that a woman who looked like her could be so cold-blooded. But there'd been plenty of times in the years they'd worked together when Bill had seen how she reacted to anyone trying to stop her from doing what she wanted—and although she didn't resort to murder—she could be downright brutal. Sometimes, she just scared the shit out of him.

"You know if DeMarco comes up with our names," Bill said, "we could end up being suspects."

"Which means we need to move fast, before he gets our names. You need to contact Murdock today."

"Why don't you contact him? I contacted him last time."

"And then what, Bill? I'm supposed to sit in a steam room naked with Murdock?"

"Maybe he has some other procedure for when he meets with female clients."

"Quit being childish. You're the one he knows. And what about my kids? I can't just go taking off for Denver."

"Yeah, well . . ."

"Hey, we're in this together, no matter who talks to him."

"Not exactly. I'm the guy who Murdock will give up if he's caught."

"And then you'd give me up," Marjorie said. "And don't tell me you wouldn't. We're in this together."

Bill didn't normally drink at eleven in the morning, but today was different. After Marjorie nagged him for half an hour—God, the woman could nag; he felt sorry for her husband—he finally agreed to call Murdock and that's what he was going to do. But he needed a drink first.

He didn't want to call Murdock. At the same time, he didn't want to lose everything he had. He liked his life the way it was, and he knew Curtis would fire him and Marjorie if they didn't solve the Johnson problem. Or maybe, knowing Marjorie, she'd blame their failure all on him and only he'd get fired—and no one was going to pay him what Curtis paid him. He didn't want to lose his job.

When Murdock had taken care of Wainwright, the swing judge in South Dakota six years ago, that hadn't really weighed on Bill's conscience all that much. He'd been scared, of course—he'd been scared for three months—that he might be arrested as an accomplice to murder and end up in prison for the rest of his life, but he hadn't really felt all that guilty. For one thing, the judge had been a disagreeable old fart. But Johnson . . . She was different. She was a young woman, practically a girl.

He knocked back a shot of Wild Turkey, then ordered another. Finally, he called Murdock from a pay phone in the bar. Murdock didn't answer the call and no way in hell was Bill going to leave a message.

He called again one hour—and two more shots—later. Murdock still didn't answer. Bill finally decided he needed to leave a message and stopped at a Best Buy and bought a prepaid phone using cash and giving a phony name. He called Murdock a third time and when Murdock still didn't answer, he left a message: "We met before, six years ago. You did some work for me. Please call me at 701-220-1048. It's urgent and I'll, uh, compensate you accordingly."

While he was eating some lunch to soak up the booze, Murdock called him. "This is the guy you called," Murdock said.

"Thanks for calling back. I need you to—"

"Stop. I don't do business over the phone. You remember where we met last time?"

"Yeah."

"Meet me there again."

Bill tried to figure out how long it would take him to get to Denver. "I'll be there some time late tonight," he said.

"Make it tomorrow morning. Ten a.m.," Murdock said. "And bring the down payment with you." Before Bill could tell him again that the matter was urgent, Murdock hung up.

DeMarco was on the eighth hole at a golf course called Hawktree, five miles north of Bismarck. Hawktree was an unexpected jewel, like an oasis in the desert: lush, emerald-green fairways and black sand bunkers surrounded by rugged, rolling hills covered with rust-colored, long-stemmed native grasses. He'd never played on a course in the middle of a prairie and he could imagine a million buffalo traveling over the fairways before they became fairways.

He'd just landed about fifty yards from the pin after making one of the best six iron shots he'd ever made. It was a shame there'd been no one with him to see it. He was just coming forward with his pitching iron when his cell phone went off like a burglar alarm and the ball went skittering off the end of his club and landed smack-dab in the middle of a sand trap.

"Fuck!" he cried. He took the phone out of his pocket. As he might have guessed, it was Sarah Johnson—a woman perfectly suited to screwing up what he was sure would have been a perfect shot.

"Yeah, Sarah, what can I do for you?"

"I've got four names. They're located in—"

"Just tell me when I get there. I can be at your place in a couple hours. Your grandfather gave me the address."

"Two hours!" she shrieked. "Where are you? What are you doing?"

"I'm just busy. I'll see you in two hours." He hung up before she could tell him to make it sooner.

It seemed only reasonable that he should take the shot over from where he was standing. It wasn't fair he should have to hack his way out of a sand trap because of a badly timed phone call.

10

"She just called DeMarco," Heckler said.

"Yeah?" Marjorie said.

"She said, I got four names."

"So what were the names?"

"No, you don't understand. All she said was *I got four names* and before she could say who they were, DeMarco said he'd meet her at her place and hung up. So I don't know who she was talking about. I'm just telling you she sounded excited and said . . . Well, I already told you what she said."

"You stay glued to that girl like, like . . . you stay glued to her."

"I will."

She called Bill to tell him that taking care of Johnson was even more urgent than she'd originally thought, but the call went to voice mail. She'd wondered if Bill was already on the plane to Denver. He'd better be on the plane; he'd better not be ignoring her phone calls.

But four names. What four names? Who was that crazy bitch talking about? What did these people know?

DeMarco pulled up in front of Sarah's place. He saw that she lived in a duplex—an old two-story white clapboard house with a big front porch and two brick chimneys—and not an apartment complex as he'd expected. He knocked on the left-hand door—the one with the letter B following the address—and she answered a moment later. Instead of inviting him in, she came through the door pulling a roll-on bag.

"Uh, what's with the suitcase?" DeMarco asked.

"I told you, I got four names. We're going to go see them."

"And you need a suitcase?"

"Yeah. We'll go to your motel first and you can check out."

"Wait a minute. Where are these people located?"

"The first one's in Minot. The next one—"

"Where's Minot?"

"In North Dakota," she said, looking at him like he'd asked where Paris was. "It's about a hundred miles from Bismarck. The next one's in Great Falls." Then she added, "That's in Montana. It's about eight hours from Minot."

"Eight hours!" DeMarco said. Then, because he couldn't help it, he said it again. "Eight hours!"

"Yeah. I figured we'd go in a loop. Minot to Great Falls, then Great Falls to Billings, then Billings to Rapid City."

"Jesus Christ," he muttered. "Can't we fly?"

"We could but it will be faster to drive. You can't get direct flights to most of these places."

He tried to think of a way to get out of this. Maybe he should tell her that he'd wait for her in Bismarck, and when she learned something, to give him a call. But he didn't. Instead he followed her down the sidewalk like a man walking to the gallows and opened the trunk of his rental car so she could toss her suitcase in. Thirty minutes later, he'd checked out of the Holiday Inn and gassed up his car. He wondered where they'd be staying that night.

She directed him turn by turn out of Bismarck until they reached US 83. Minot was due north of Bismarck.

"So who are we seeing in Minot?" DeMarco asked.

"A retired judge."

"And what did he do wrong?"

"He didn't do anything wrong."

"Then why—"

"This guy, his name is Parker, had a case before him involving forced pooling."

"Forced pooling? What's—"

"Curtis was suing landowners in Ward County for blocking surveys on their land to determine where to drill for gas. The lawsuit said Curtis's company had been negotiating in good faith with the landowners but the landowners weren't playing ball as required to do by the law."

"I still don't understand. What's forced pooling?"

Sarah gave an exasperated sigh to indicate what she thought of DeMarco's abysmal ignorance. "I'll keep this simple. Gas companies don't drill straight down to get the gas. What they do is get a lease to drill on one parcel of land that has gas under it, then they basically drill sideways or horizontally to get at the gas in adjacent parcels. The gas under all these parcels combined is called a *pool*. And you can look this up if you don't believe me, but thirty-nine states in this country have laws that essentially mandate that the owners of these adjacent parcels have to allow the companies to drill under their property if the company can get leases from a certain percentage of the landowners over the pool. That's what they mean by *forced* pooling."

This was just like Sarah's blog—totally confusing—but he imagined she was right about the law.

Sarah continued. "Both Republicans and Democrats in the areas affected are against these forced-pooling laws. Some people object for safety and environmental reasons, like they're afraid their well water will become contaminated. Others object on principal, feeling that they're being forced to give up their property rights, which they are. But somehow the gas and oil companies always prevail, no matter how many people object. Anyway, to get back to Judge Parker.

"Like I said, Curtis filed a suit in this one county against a bunch of landowners because they were doing everything they could to block him from drilling. Curtis's suit said they weren't acting in the spirit of the law. Well, Parker stands up in court one day and makes a raving speech about how he can't be bought but then recuses himself from the case to avoid the appearance of impropriety. It was obvious that Curtis had tried to buy Parker off, but . . ."

Once again, what was obvious to Sarah wasn't a matter of what could be proven; it was just her opinion.

". . . but when I asked Parker what happened he refused to tell me. He was a prick. He said that if he wouldn't discuss his reason for recusing himself with the legitimate media he sure as hell wasn't going to talk to some wet-behind-the ears blogger."

"What makes you think he'll talk to you now?"

"Because he's retired, so maybe he'll feel differently. The other thing is, Parker isn't really a bad guy. I researched him a little more after I started to think about who might help me, and he works at a homeless shelter on weekends, volunteers at polling booths, that sort of thing. I called him a prick, but he's more of a curmudgeon. I'm hoping now that he's no longer on the bench he'll change his mind about talking to me."

They arrived at Parker's home in Minot about four in the afternoon. The house was a nice-looking place with a well-tended front yard but not ostentatious. In other words, the kind of house an honest judge might own.

"You want me with you while you talk to him?" DeMarco asked.

"I don't think so. You look kind of intimidating."

"I thought that was the reason for me coming with you. To be intimidating."

"Intimidation isn't going to work on this guy."

DeMarco watched her walk up the sidewalk to Parker's house, sulking about the intimidating comment. He could *act* intimidating but he didn't think he *looked* intimidating, like he had a face that would scare little kids or something. He had dark hair he combed straight back, a prominent nose, blue eyes, and a cleft in his chin. He'd been told he looked just like his father, and he had to admit that his dad could look intimidating, particularly if he was angry, but he didn't think *he* looked that way, at least not when he smiled.

DeMarco saw Sarah ring the judge's doorbell and a moment later a balding guy in his seventies wearing an apron answered the door. Sarah talked to him for no more than a minute before he shut the door. She came back to the car and said, "What a prick."

"Where are we going next?" DeMarco asked.

"I told you. Great Falls. We can drive at least halfway there today, maybe stay in Glasgow tonight, and get up early tomorrow. We can be in Great Falls by midmorning tomorrow."

"Glasgow, Montana?"

"Yeah. Did you think I meant Scotland?"

———◆———

Marjorie's cell phone rang just as she was getting ready to leave the office to go to Bobby's baseball game. It was Heckler.

"What's going on?" she said.

"She went to see a guy named Raymond Parker in Minot. He used to be a—"

"Yeah, I know who Parker is. So what happened?"

73

"As near as I can tell, he slammed the door in her face. She talked to him for about two seconds and that was it."

"Good. Was DeMarco with her?"

"Yeah, but he just sat in the car when she talked to Parker. He's driving her."

"So where is she now?"

There was a long pause.

"Heckler," Marjorie repeated, "where is she now?"

"I, uh, I ran out of gas."

"You ran out of gas?"

"Yeah, they left Minot and started driving west. I didn't think they'd drive too far and . . . I mean, they just kept going and going and going and gas stations aren't all that close together on US 2 and—"

Marjorie just lost it. "Goddamn, son of a—"

"Jesus, I'm sorry, Marjorie."

"So what in the hell are you going to do?"

"I guess I'll head back to Bismarck and wait for her. By the time I get somebody way out here to gas me up, she'll have a three-hour lead on me."

"But can't you track her with the GPS in her phone?"

"She's out of range already," Heckler said.

Marjorie wondered if he was lying about the tracking software having some sort of limited range. She suspected that Heckler, the lazy shit, didn't want to drive any farther and try to catch up with Johnson. But she didn't know for sure and she didn't see any point in continuing to swear at him—but she felt like killing him. She wanted to know who that crazy girl was going to see next. The good news was that if Murdock did his job right they wouldn't need Heckler anymore because in the future Marjorie would always know where Sarah Johnson was. She'd be in a grave.

The problem with taking a long road trip with Sarah was that she only cared about one thing in life: crucifying Leonard Curtis. When she spoke about what Curtis was doing—undermining Mom, apple pie, and the American way—she became animated, waving her arms, talking so fast she sometimes sputtered. But there didn't seem to be much else that interested her.

At one point DeMarco asked, "Have you got a boyfriend?" Then he added, "Or a girlfriend."

She'd been looking at something on her smart phone when he asked the question and she sighed—as if she didn't appreciate the interruption—and said, "Not anymore. I was going with a guy in Billings for about six months. I met him at a Sierra Club rally. Then I found out he wasn't really passionate about anything. I mean he cared, but he wasn't really committed. When I told him this, he said I was too intense for him . . ."

No shit, DeMarco thought.

". . . and we broke up. I don't really have time for a boyfriend right now, anyway."

She sounded regretful, however, and DeMarco imagined she must get lonely. He almost said that Joan of Arc didn't have a boyfriend either—but decided it wasn't the time to be a smart-ass.

"Sarah, I admire what you're trying to do. Honest. I really do. But you're a young woman and there's more to life than chasing after Leonard Curtis. I mean at your age and with your money, you ought to be traveling through Europe, snorkeling in Tahiti. It's not healthy to be so obsessed with Curtis."

"Yeah, people are always telling me that. One of my friends said I should see a psychiatrist."

"Well, maybe . . ."

"The thing is, nobody else cares about what people like Curtis are doing. If somebody doesn't try to stop him . . ."

"That's not true, Sarah. Lots of people care. There are all kinds of folks out there trying to reform campaign financing and reduce the influence of lobbyists. But these people also have lives. They have families. They have hobbies. They have fun."

"Don't you understand?" Sarah said. "There's a crisis in this country! People like Curtis are buying politicians to get their way. Things have to change."

"Yeah, I know but—"

"Like judges. Why the hell do we elect state judges? Judges shouldn't be elected. If they're elected then it's easier for guys like Curtis to corrupt the legal system by contributing to their campaigns and running negative ads against them on television. State judges ought to be like the judges on the U.S. Supreme Court. You know, appointed for life."

DeMarco almost said: U.S. Supreme Court Justices are sort of elected, too. When you put a president in office, you're basically electing the kind of guy that the president will appoint to the Supreme Court if he gets the chance. But he knew that would just start her on another rant.

"Sarah, all I'm saying is that life is short. Enjoy it while you have the chance."

She just turned away from him and looked out at a field, a green sea of barley.

They stopped at about eight p.m. in Glasgow—the one in Montana —and checked into a place called the Star Lodge. Sarah offered to pay for his room but DeMarco said he'd pay for it, not bothering to tell her that if she paid taxes, she was paying for it anyway.

"I'm going to find out where to get a martini in Glasgow," DeMarco said. "You want to come along?"

"No, I've got things to do, people to call."

"Jesus, Sarah. Have you ever heard that expression about stopping to smell the roses?"

"And vodka smells like roses?" she said.

11

Bill Logan arrived at the steam bath in Denver an hour early, hoping the steam would lessen the hangover he had. When he'd arrived in Denver the night before, he had dinner, then just sat in the hotel bar and started pouring scotch down his throat. This thing with Murdock and Sarah Johnson was turning him into a drunk.

It was even affecting his sex life. He was a guy who usually got laid four or five nights a week. He knew so many women he could always get laid. But last night, sitting in the bar of the Hilton, there was a woman who looked like she might be a stewardess. She was close to forty, not a beauty queen, but not bad-looking, either. And she'd glanced his way a couple of times. Normally with a woman like her, Bill figured he'd have to buy her two drinks and then it would be off to her room to do the hokeypokey. But last night, he hadn't been able to work up the energy for romancing her, and he just sat there drinking scotch, imagining what it would be like to be in prison. With his luck, his roommates would be two psychopaths who would take turns beating and raping him.

Murdock walked into the steam room at ten, wearing a white towel around his waist. He made a motion for Bill to stand up and Bill did, knowing what he was supposed to do. He dropped his towel on the bench where he'd been sitting, and made a slow turn so Murdock could see he didn't have anything taped to his back. Then Murdock did the same thing, after which he looked under the bench to make sure Bill hadn't hidden a recorder there.

Murdock looked exactly as he had the last time Bill saw him six years ago. It didn't appear as if he'd aged a bit. Apparently killing people was good for his constitution. And like the first time Bill met with him, he couldn't help but think the guy just didn't look like a professional killer. He should've had barbed-wire tattoos circling his arms or those teardrop tattoos the gang guys had to show how many people they'd killed.

Bill told him what they needed him to do: take care of Sarah Johnson. He said, "It doesn't have to be an accident this time because we're in a hurry. Make it look like a robbery gone bad or maybe a rape."

"I don't rape people," Murdock said—and he said this like he was *offended*. Apparently killing people didn't bother him but he considered rape to be repulsive.

"Sorry," Bill said, not sure what else to say. "All I'm saying is, we don't need something fancy. Just make it look like it's part of some other crime, but not like she was singled out. You know what I mean?"

"Yeah," Murdock said.

Jesus, he couldn't believe what he was doing and saying. His hangover was almost gone thanks to the steam, but when he left the gym he was going straight to the airport and start tossing back drinks until the plane landed in Bismarck. They were going to have to carry him off that plane.

DeMarco was in a deep, dreamless sleep in his room at the Star Lodge in Glasgow, Montana, when someone began to pound on the door.

He looked at the bedside clock: six a.m. He got out of bed dressed in boxer shorts and his favorite Nationals T-shirt and opened the door. Not surprised, he found Sarah standing there, looking impatient.

"What are you doing, still sleeping?" she said. "We need to get going."

"Sarah, it's six in the fu . . . It's six. Are you insane?" Before she could say anything, he added, "Go away. I'll see you at eight, then we'll go have breakfast—or I'll have breakfast—then we'll take off." He shut the door, trudged over to the bed, and fell on to it. What a nut!

She spent the first hour of the drive to Great Falls sulking and he was in no mood to cajole her. Finally he asked, "Who are we going to see in Great Falls? Another judge?"

"Do you really care?" she said.

As he was trying to decide how he should answer that question, Sarah said, "I'm going to talk to a lawyer. She represented a group of ranchers suing Curtis for well water contamination caused by fracking. If she'd won, it would have been a huge blow to Curtis. Like this year, forty plaintiffs sued a natural gas company in New York and the gas company, after fighting the case for years, finally settled with them for millions and that's what could have happened to Curtis. Anyway, the lawyer involved was a woman named Janet Tyler. She's really good and it looked like she might have been able to beat Curtis. Then she backed out of the case and after she did, the whole case fell apart.

"I went to see her because it was obvious that Curtis had done something to get to her. I didn't think he'd bribed her because Tyler has money, and when I saw her speak on some local news program, I could tell she had a fire in her belly about the issue. I called her office and when she wouldn't speak to me, I hung around outside her office until she went out to lunch and—"

"Ah. So you stalked her."

"You're not funny, DeMarco. Anyway, when I asked her why she dropped the lawsuit I could tell she felt bad about what she'd done, but she wouldn't tell me what happened. I finally gave up but as I was leaving she said, "I didn't have a choice." When I asked her what she meant, she got into her car and drove away.

"After I met with her, I did some more research on her, the kind of research I should have done before I met with her. I found out that she had a son, but she was divorced and her son used her ex-husband's last name and she uses her maiden name. Well, her son had been busted by the cops. He was an oxycodone addict and he broke into an old lady's home to steal shit. He thought the old lady was gone but she wasn't and she tried to stop him, and he pushed her down and she smacked her head. But she was a tough old bird. She followed him out of the house after he ran, got his license plate, and called the cops. The cops went to his house to arrest him, and he punched one of the cops. So her kid was charged for breaking and entering, robbery, assaulting an old lady, assaulting the cops, and resisting arrest. They had like a dozen charges against him and he was going to do time, maybe four years. Well, voilà. After Tyler drops out of the well water contamination lawsuit, her son's case is pled down to two years' probation, drug counseling, anger management classes, mandatory community service, blah, blah, blah. Everything but jail time."

"Did you find anything resembling evidence that Curtis had anything to do with her son's case?"

"No. And fuck you for that *resembling evidence* crack. But the answer is no. I couldn't find any evidence that the judge or the prosecutor in her son's case had suddenly come into money or had some work done for free on their houses. But if you think it's a coincidence that her son got off scot-free at the same time she dropped the suit, then you're a complete idiot."

DeMarco was thinking maybe they should send *her* to anger management classes. Or charm school. "What makes you think Tyler will talk to you now?" he asked.

"I don't know that she will, but her son's dead. He got high, ran his car into a ditch, and broke his neck. I know she felt guilty about what she did, and since her son's gone, maybe she'll talk."

Sarah again decided to meet with Janet Tyler by herself.

DeMarco said, "I thought the whole point of me coming with you was for me to lean on these people. You know, I say I'm from Washington and I'm here to crush you with the entire weight of the federal government if you don't tell the truth."

"Yeah, but I've been thinking that's not the right approach, not with these people. The four I picked are all people who I think have a conscience and might feel bad about what they did, so I don't really want to scare them. I just want to convince them to do the right thing. And, frankly, you don't exactly look like you're from the government."

"What does that mean? What do I look like?"

"Well, you look like a guy a loan shark might send to break the legs of somebody who owes him money."

"You gotta be kidding," DeMarco said.

Sarah spent twenty minutes with Tyler and when she came back to the car she said, "I can't believe how bad that woman looks compared to the last time I saw her. She's lost about thirty pounds and looks like she's seventy years old. I know she's in her fifties."

"Yeah, but did she tell you anything?"

"No. She started crying and saying she was sorry about what she'd done and how I didn't understand that she had to do it for her son, but she wouldn't give me a name or tell me how they got to her."

"You sure you don't want me to talk to her?" DeMarco said.

"Yes. It won't do any good."

They spent the night at a Holiday Inn Express in Great Falls. DeMarco was thinking about buying stock in the outfit.

———◆———

The next morning—the day after seeing Janet Tyler in Great Falls—Sarah and DeMarco were on the road again, off to see the next two people on Sarah's list: a man in Billings, Montana, and a woman in Rapid City, South Dakota. Both people had served in their state legislatures but were no longer in office.

Only one memorable thing happened on this leg of their journey—or at least it was something DeMarco would remember for a long time to come. They were traveling southeast on Highway 87, along the eastern perimeter of the Lewis and Clark National Forest. DeMarco was driving and enjoying the scenery while Sarah was looking at her iPad. DeMarco figured she was investigating something online related to natural gas or Leonard Curtis, when she suddenly let out what he could only describe as a peal of joyful, girlish laughter.

"What's so funny?" he asked.

She laughed again and said, "One of my girlfriends sent me this YouTube clip of this kitten swatting this big dog on the snout. The dog, it's a huge St. Bernard, comes close to this little kitten and the kitten smacks it on the nose and the dog blinks a couple of times and backs up, then he comes close to the kitten again, and the kitten smacks him on the nose again. It's hilarious!"

DeMarco didn't say anything for a moment, then said, "You need to do that more often."

"What?" Sarah said.

"Laugh like that," DeMarco said.

But that was the only memorable thing that happened. The man who Sarah had planned to see in Billings wasn't home; they learned from a neighbor that he'd left unexpectedly the night before to go see a brother who'd had a heart attack. The woman in Rapid City refused to talk with Sarah, slamming the door in her face the way Judge Parker in Minot had. By the time they reached the duplex where Sarah lived, she looked like someone had killed her puppy and ate it while she watched.

"I gotta regroup," she told DeMarco as they pulled up in front of her duplex. "I think you had a good idea about running down whoever's acting as Curtis's middleman and I have to think more about how to find him. And you need to call John Mahoney and convince him to get the FBI involved."

She'd said this—about getting the FBI involved—maybe sixty times as they'd been making a trip that covered three states and almost fifteen hundred miles. He liked the kid, but she was starting to drive him bonkers and he was relieved when she got out of the car.

⸻

Marjorie was sitting in the family room, watching a stupid zombie movie with Dick and the boys. Dick was sulking as she'd just about ripped his head off when she got home because the kitchen was a disaster: unwashed dishes, food all over the counter, mustard spilled onto the floor, the milk just sitting there spoiling. So she had a right to get angry, but she probably shouldn't have called him names. Maybe she'd make it up to him by giving him a blow job tonight, something she considered the ultimate sacrifice for marital harmony.

She wasn't really watching the movie, either. She was stewing about her partner. Bill Logan was turning into a drunk. The day after he returned from Denver, he went out to lunch and came back to the office two hours later, completely shit-faced. Maybe after Murdock dealt with Johnson he'd get back on track. She sure as hell hoped so because things couldn't go on the way they were.

As for Johnson, she still hadn't gotten back from wherever she'd been. And because Heckler lost her when he ran out of gas, Marjorie still had no idea who'd she'd gone to see. All Gordy could tell from the spyware planted in her cell phone was that she made what appeared to be overnight stops in Glasgow and Great Falls, Montana. Marjorie needed to . . ."

Her phone rang; it was Heckler. Into the phone, she said, "Hang on a minute." To Dick and the boys she said, "Excuse me, I have to take this." Then she patted Dick on the thigh and said, "I'm sorry I got so mad earlier." But he ignored her and sat there pouting.

She walked into the kitchen. "Yeah, what is it?"

"She's back," Heckler said. "DeMarco just dropped her off at her place."

"Good. Now I want you to forget about her and get on DeMarco. I want to know what he's up to."

Heckler said, "Shit, then I gotta go. I gotta catch up with him before he's out of sight."

"Go," she said and disconnected the call.

She couldn't tell Heckler that the real reason she wanted him following DeMarco was because she couldn't afford to have him hanging around Sarah Johnson when Murdock made his move. Wouldn't that be the icing on the cake: Heckler stopping Murdock from killing the brat. Plus, she really did want to know what DeMarco was doing. She figured that after Johnson was gone, he'd most likely go home, but since she didn't really know why he was here in the first place, she couldn't be sure.

She called Bill next. "She's back home. Text the guy. You know who I mean."

Bill said, "Yeah, geez, okay." He sounded like he was drunk. Again.

"You better get your act together, Bill," she snapped. "This boozing shit can't go on."

"Yeah, I know," he said and hung up.

Men! If it wasn't her husband, it was Bill Logan.

She went back to the family room. The good guys were mowing down the zombies with machine guns. When she'd left the room to talk to Heckler, they'd been doing the same thing. That seemed to be the entire plot of the movie, but her sons didn't seem to care. "Anybody want popcorn?" she said, trying to sound perky and cheerful. The boys said, "Yeah!" Dick, he just pouted. Okay, no blow job for you tonight, asshole.

As she waited for the popcorn in the microwave to stop popping, her mind flipped back again to Johnson and DeMarco. What the hell had they been doing the last three days? Whatever it was, she sure as hell hoped it didn't come back and bite her on the butt.

⸻

DeMarco called Mahoney's cell phone to tell him what was going on and was shocked when Mahoney answered. DeMarco was in a bar in Bismarck when he made the call—not expecting Mahoney to answer—and it sounded like Mahoney was in a bar in D.C. when he took the call.

DeMarco summarized what was happening as quickly as possible. He had to be quick because Mahoney wasn't known for either patience or a long attention span. He told him that Sarah Johnson was obsessed with nailing a rich guy named Curtis who was bribing politicians and judges but she had no proof. On the other hand, she'd clearly pissed Curtis off because he was doing whatever he could to stop her.

"Is he behind the death threats?" Mahoney asked.

"I don't know. She names a lot of people in her blog, so Curtis isn't the only suspect."

"But is he really bribing folks?"

"Probably. But Sarah can't prove it. I just spent the last three days driving all over the American West with her. I was hoping to get a lead on Curtis's fixer, but I struck out. So I don't know what to do next, but I can't spend the rest of my life out here in the sticks following her around."

"You think she's in danger?"

DeMarco hesitated. "She could be. She's not going to stop investigating Curtis. She's the type who won't ever stop. And I don't know what to do about that either unless you want me to become her full-time bodyguard."

"What am I supposed to tell Doug?" Mahoney asked.

"Doug?"

"Her grandfather, my buddy. Have you gone soft in the head?"

"I guess you tell him you tried, but there really isn't anything you can do. You can't call up the attorney general and tell him to investigate Curtis just because Sarah *thinks* Curtis is doing something illegal. Then you tell him his crazy granddaughter needs to hire a bodyguard."

Now it was Mahoney's turn to hesitate. "You go tell him."

"Aw, come on," DeMarco said.

DeMarco had called Mahoney from a restaurant called the Peacock Alley American Bar and Grill. It was located in a historic building that began as a hotel in 1911, served as a speakeasy during Prohibition, and back in those days hosted illegal gambling and a few women of ill repute. The bar of the restaurant was located in what had once been the lobby of the old hotel. It was a place where the patrons dressed casually, which suited DeMarco, and it had large windows, a redbrick-like floor, a long, dark bar with comfortable high-backed stools, and an impressive number of beers on tap. There was a brass rail separating the drinkers from the diners and the walls were covered with black-and-white photos of Bismarck in the early twentieth century.

DeMarco was tired from driving all day and from listening to Sarah nag at him. He was thinking he should go to a laundromat because he was wearing his last pair of clean underwear, but who wanted to spend the evening in a laundromat? If he could get a flight out tomorrow evening, he'd go see Sarah in the morning and tell her he was sorry but he had to get back to D.C. If she ever found any real evidence—something more than a guy getting a bargain price on a seed drill—to give him a call and he'd try to convince Mahoney to lean on the FBI. He knew if he made that offer he'd regret it because she'd probably call him twice a day.

Anyway, that was the plan. See Sarah in the morning, then go see Doug Thorpe and tell him basically the same thing: that if Sarah ever found any actual evidence that Curtis had done something illegal, Mahoney would help. Until then, his granddaughter needed to hire a bodyguard, some strapping Montana lad with a license to carry a weapon. Insofar as the dirty underwear situation, after he had dinner, he'd go back to the motel and wash out the pair of boxers he was wearing in the motel sink. Or better yet, maybe he'd swing by Walmart and just buy a pair.

He ordered a second martini and took out his phone to look at flight schedules. Using one finger—he'd never been a thumb texter—he started to tap in the Travelocity website when a voice said, "You one of those tweeters?"

He looked over at the speaker: a blond in her late thirties. She was pretty, a little plump, but not too plump, and with a pleasant amount of cleavage showing.

"Uh, no, never tweeted in my life. I was just—"

"So what are you doing here in Bismarck. Are you a roughneck?"

"A roughneck?"

"You know, a driller, one of the guys who works on the gas wells. You got the build for it."

DeMarco figured that was a compliment. "I'm a lawyer from D.C." He added that his boss had sent him out here to help an old friend with a problem and before she could ask what the problem was, he asked what she did.

He found out that she was a math teacher, taught fifth grade, divorced, no kids. Deep into his second martini, he asked, "By the way, what the hell is a seed drill?"

"A seed drill?"

"Yeah, I heard the term a couple of days ago and was just curious."

"Well, city boy, a seed drill is a farm implement used to plant seeds. I mean, scientifically. These days, farmers don't plant by poking a hole in the ground with a stick and dropping a seed in. They use these fancy machines called seed drills that have computers and GPS systems and are calibrated so every possible inch of farmable space is planted."

"I'll be damned," DeMarco said. "You want another drink?"

And at that moment, his phone rang. It was Sarah. She was like a demon who had escaped from hell and couldn't be forced back down to the underworld where she belonged. "Just a sec," he said to the teacher. "Yeah, Sarah, what is it?"

"I think I found something. Come over to my place."

"Sarah, you need to get a life. We just spent the last three days together and, no offense, but I need a break from you. I'll stop by and see you first thing in the morning." Then he disconnected the call before she could argue with him. Then he turned the phone off—the only way to escape a modern demon.

"Who's this Sarah person you spent the last three days with?" the teacher asked.

Heckler could see DeMarco there at the bar chatting up some blonde. It didn't look like he was planning to leave any time soon—which wasn't good as far as Heckler was concerned. He was tired and needed to get some sleep. He walked up to the bar and made a motion for the bartender to come talk to him. Heckler and the bartender had gone to high school together and the bartender knew what Heckler did. He asked the bartender who the blonde was, and the bartender told him. He said the woman was practically a fixture at the American Grill.

An hour later, DeMarco and the blonde left together. DeMarco followed the blonde to her place and Heckler followed DeMarco. When DeMarco was still inside the blonde's house an hour later, Heckler called it a night, thinking he was getting way too old for this shit.

On the other side of Bismarck, Murdock sat in a car. He could see the lights were on in both sides of the duplex, meaning Sarah Johnson's landlady was home and awake. He'd wait until they both went to bed.

12

———◆———

DeMarco woke up feeling groggy, disoriented, and hungover. It took him a minute to figure out where he was: the teacher's bedroom. He turned his head. All he could see was the top of her head, a mass of blond curls, and one bare, freckled shoulder.

He eased out of bed trying not to wake her and got dressed. This was the one part of a one-night stand he hated: trying to figure out what to do in the morning before he left. He'd made it clear to the teacher—her name was Amelia—that he'd be leaving to go back to D.C. today. So he hadn't lied to her and he hadn't pretended that he'd be coming back to Bismarck for a second date. But still, it gave him that greasy lounge lizard feeling to sneak out of her house without even saying good-bye.

He went into her bathroom and used her toothpaste and his finger to brush his teeth. Then he hunted around the kitchen until he found paper and a pen. He scratched out a note saying he'd enjoyed last night and if he ever passed through Bismarck again, he'd give her a call. He had no intention of ever passing through Bismarck again.

He glanced at his watch as he started the car. Seven a.m. Knowing Sarah, she'd probably been up since dawn, ranting on her blog, but it still seemed a bit early to be knocking on her door. He stopped for coffee and an Egg McMuffin at the first McDonald's he saw, then proceeded on to his motel where he packed his clothes. He tossed his suitcase full of smelly clothes into the trunk of his rental car—he'd put a lot of miles on that car—and headed toward Sarah's place. She'd told him last night that she'd found something, but he'd interrupted her before she had a chance to say exactly what she'd found. Maybe she'd identified whoever was helping Curtis corrupt local politicians, but knowing the way Sarah tended to draw conclusions not necessarily supported by facts, he wasn't hopeful.

Marjorie had been in the office for more than an hour when Heckler called.

"DeMarco spent the night with a woman name Amelia Moore. He picked her up at the American Grill. Moore's a teacher . . ."

"I know who she is," Marjorie said. Moore was Bobby's math teacher, the same gal that Bill had been screwing. Jesus! What a slut!

"DeMarco went back to his motel about seven thirty this morning. Ten minutes later, he came out and tossed a suitcase into the trunk of his rental car. It's looks like he may be leaving town."

"Well, follow him to be sure," Marjorie said. It would be a relief to have DeMarco gone, although she still wished she knew what he'd been doing with Sarah Johnson after he left Minot the other day.

It was after eight by the time DeMarco arrived at the duplex where Sarah lived. He knocked, but no one answered. Then he noticed the door, the area where the lock goes into the frame. The wood had been splintered like someone had taken a crowbar or a big screwdriver and ripped open the door.

He thought to himself *Oh, shit,* and pushed on the door with the tip of one finger and it swung open without a sound. "Sarah?" he called out. There was no answer. "Sarah?" The silence was ominous and he had this awful feeling in the pit of his stomach.

He took a step into the apartment and there she was, on the floor, on her back, wearing boxer shorts and an extra-large T-shirt; probably the clothes she slept in. Her eyes were wide open, staring up at the ceiling. She wasn't moving. He noticed her long legs were white as milk as the girl never took time to just sit in the sun. DeMarco took two more steps and he could see that her T-shirt, which was a burgundy color, was soaked with another color that was almost burgundy. He knew it was a waste of time, but he went down on one knee and felt for a pulse in her throat. There was no pulse.

Sarah Johnson was dead.

DeMarco walked outside and dropped down onto the porch steps. He felt completely numb. He sat there for a minute, unable to think, his mind like a whiteout in a blizzard, then reached for his phone and called 911. Five minutes later a squad car arrived, lights flashing, no siren. Two cops, one male, one female, both young, walked up the sidewalk toward him, hands on their holstered sidearms. "Are you the one who called 911?" the female cop asked.

"Yeah," DeMarco said.

"Sir, we need you to stand up and keep your hands where we can see them."

Heckler called again while Marjorie was on the phone with one of Curtis's lawyers, and she let the call go to voice mail. She checked the voice mail five minutes later and heard Heckler say, "You need to call me. The cops just arrived at Johnson's house."

She called Heckler and said, "What's happening? And why are you at Johnson's house? You're supposed to be following DeMarco."

"I *was* following him. He went to Johnson's place and then he went inside and five minutes later a squad car shows up. Now there're two more squad cars here and a couple of guys I think are detectives. Shit. The medical examiner just pulled up."

"Hang on a second," Marjorie said. "I gotta think."

She knew what had happened: Murdock had killed Johnson and DeMarco had discovered the body. Should she tell Heckler to split or not? The last thing she needed was a cop spotting Heckler hanging around the crime scene. On the other hand, she wanted to know what DeMarco was going to do next.

"You stick with DeMarco," she told Heckler. Then she lied. "I don't know what the cops are doing at Johnson's house, but you make sure they don't see you. I don't want them questioning you. But stick with DeMarco and keep me posted."

———— ◆ ————

Two hours after discovering Sarah's body, DeMarco left the police station. He told a detective how he knew Sarah and why he'd come to her house that morning. He told him about Sarah's crusade against Leonard Curtis and how she thought Curtis was bribing judges and politicians. He said the police should read Sarah's blog, that everything she'd learned or suspected had been dumped into it. He also said that Sarah had contacted various law enforcement agencies regarding Curtis, and the people she'd contacted were listed in her blog.

The detective—a heavyset guy with kind eyes—told DeMarco that he'd investigate those things, but it looked to him like Sarah had woken up and interrupted a burglary in progress, and that's why she was killed. "All the small electronics were missing from Ms. Johnson's apartment. We couldn't find a laptop or cell phone. All the drawers in her bedroom had been opened and pawed through. If she had any expensive jewelry, it's gone, and there was no cash in her purse." The detective paused and added, almost apologetically, "Like lots of places around the country, we have a meth problem here in Bismarck. And thanks to all the gas and oil workers, there's a lot of cash floating around which tends to attract a bunch of bad actors."

"I don't think this was a robbery," DeMarco said.

"You think this guy, Curtis, had her killed?"

"I don't know, but the timing bothers me and it should bother you, too. She'd received two death threats and was assaulted once because she was writing about Curtis. And she'd just spent three days running around Montana and the Dakotas trying to find evidence she could use against him." DeMarco realized as he was speaking that he sounded like Sarah: No hard evidence, just conjecture based on coincidence.

"Did the person who lives next door to her hear the gunshots?" DeMarco asked.

"No. She didn't hear the door being ripped open, either. But the next door neighbor is seventy-six years old. She doesn't wear a hearing aid but she needs one."

"Or it could mean the killer used a silencer," DeMarco said.

The detective made an expression that DeMarco interpreted as: *Not likely—and please leave the detecting to us.*

The detective asked DeMarco if he knew who Sarah's next of kin was and DeMarco said, "Yeah. A man named Doug Thorpe who lives near Miles City, Montana. He's her grandfather. I have his address and phone number. Do you want me to notify him about Sarah's death?"

"No. You're a suspect and . . ."

When DeMarco opened his mouth to protest, the detective said, "I mean technically, since you found the body and admitted to spending the last several days with her. But do I really think you killed her? No, I don't. I'm just saying it wouldn't be appropriate for you to notify her next of kin. I'll call the right sheriff in Montana and have him go talk to Mr. Thorpe."

DeMarco was relieved that he didn't have to break the news to Thorpe—and felt like a coward because he was relieved. He could imagine what Thorpe's reaction was going to be; he remembered how Thorpe had said that Sarah was the only family he had left and how he "loved her to death." He could also imagine that Thorpe might blame him for what happened to his granddaughter—and Thorpe might be right to blame him. It was possible that someone had found out that a guy from D.C. who might have some political clout was working with Sarah, and that may have been the catalyst for her being killed. He also wondered if he'd gone to see her last night as she'd asked, if he could have prevented her death.

He remembered telling Sarah how life was short and how she ought to spend some time enjoying it; he'd just never imagined how short her life would turn out to be. He could see her the first night he met her, her unlined face, her eyes blazing as she spoke about her obsession with Curtis. He remembered the way she laughed at the YouTube video. She'd been so terribly young and naïve and earnest—and good.

DeMarco had heard the word *heartsick* before but had never been sure what the word really meant. Now he knew: he was heartsick.

13

DeMarco called Mavis—he didn't even bother to try calling Mahoney directly—and told Mahoney's secretary to tell Mahoney to call him right away. "Tell him Sarah Johnson was murdered."

Ten minutes later Mahoney called him back. "What the fuck happened?" Mahoney screamed. Then, being Mahoney, he had to add, "What the fuck did you do?"

DeMarco didn't answer Mahoney's question. He just told him that whoever killed Sarah had tried to make the crime look like a robbery, but he doubted it was.

"But I don't know for sure that Curtis was responsible," DeMarco said.

He also didn't tell Mahoney that Sarah had discovered something last night and wanted to talk to him about it, but that he'd been too preoccupied with getting laid to go see her. DeMarco didn't believe—maybe because he didn't *want* to believe—that whatever Sarah had uncovered had anything to do with her death. In two years of investigating she'd never found any hard evidence, so why would last night have been any different? And how would anyone have known *what* she'd found last night? But since the killer had taken her laptop and her cell phone and the police had locked up her house because it was a crime scene, DeMarco doubted there was any way to find out what she'd been working on the night she died.

So he didn't believe—and again maybe because he didn't want to believe—that Sarah had found something last night that was the cause of her death. What he suspected was that Curtis had simply taken the next logical step: Since Sarah couldn't be bought off, discouraged by lawsuits, or scared away by death threats and assaults, he decided to have her killed.

"So what are you going to do?" Mahoney asked.

"First, I'm going to go see Doug Thorpe and tell him how sorry I am."

"Ah, God, Doug," Mahoney said. "Does he know his granddaughter's dead?"

"By now, he probably does. The cops wouldn't let me tell him. They said they'd have the sheriffs where he lived notify him. I could call him and talk to him on the phone, but that doesn't seem right. I need to talk to him face-to-face, to explain what happened and to tell him how badly I feel, so I'm going to drive to Montana to see him."

"Yeah, okay. Call me after you've talked to him and I'll call him, too." Mahoney sighed. "I imagine that will be the last time in my life I talk to him. Jesus. He calls me to help his granddaughter and the next thing you know she's dead, and he'll probably think it was your fault, which means he'll think it was my fault."

DeMarco couldn't think of anything to say to that, so he didn't say anything. The worst part was that he knew it could indeed be his fault that she was killed.

"What are you going to do after you see Doug?" Mahoney asked.

DeMarco had been thinking about that question since the moment he saw Sarah's body. His first reaction to her death had been shock followed by an overwhelming sense of sadness and a good deal of guilt—but now the main thing he was feeling was anger.

"I don't know," he said to Mahoney, "but I do know that I'm not leaving this place until somebody pays for killing her. And I can tell you right now that the local cops aren't going to be much help. So one thing you can do is lean on somebody at the Bureau, and get an FBI agent to meet with me."

It occurred to DeMarco, after he talked to Mahoney, that it could be a mistake to drive five hours to Miles City to talk to Doug Thorpe only to discover that Thorpe wasn't home and on his way to Bismarck to talk to the cops and to make arrangements for shipping Sarah's body back to Montana. He went back to the police station and asked the detective if anybody had talked to Thorpe yet. The detective was nice enough to call somebody and a moment later told DeMarco that yes, Thorpe had been notified.

DeMarco hated to do this over the phone but he called Thorpe.

"Mr. Thorpe, it's Joe DeMarco. I'm sorry—"

"What the hell did you do?" Thorpe said. He didn't scream like Mahoney had. He spoke quietly but DeMarco could hear the cold fury in the man's voice. He also remembered the way Thorpe had sounded when he'd said that he would kill the people who had mauled Sarah and threatened her. His voice was the same when he asked what DeMarco had done.

"Mr. Thorpe," DeMarco said, "I don't know if I did anything that got her killed, but the truth is, I don't know for sure. The cops here think she was killed by a drug addict who broke into her house to rob her. I don't believe that but . . . Look, the reason I called, is that if you're coming here for . . . for her body, I'm going to wait for you and we'll talk when you get here. If you're not coming, I'll—"

"Of course, I'm coming. I have to bring her home, then make funeral arrangements. I'll bury her next to my wife and daugh—"

Then Thorpe started sobbing and hung up on DeMarco—and DeMarco had a vivid image of Doug Thorpe standing in front of three headstones in a small Montana cemetery.

Heartsick.

DeMarco returned to the Holiday Inn and got his room back. He unpacked his clothes and threw them into a couple of plastic bags he found in the closet and headed out to find a laundromat. He had no idea how long he was going to be in Bismarck. While his clothes were washing, he went to a nearby coffee shop and tried to figure out what to do next. Only one idea occurred to him.

Using his phone, he found out that he couldn't get a direct flight from Bismarck to Great Falls, Montana. The best flight he could find stopped in Denver and would take five hours. And he sure as hell wasn't going to drive from Bismarck to Great Falls, which would take nine hours. When it came to air travel this part of the country was like Siberia.

He called the Bismarck airport and after getting bounced around a bit found himself talking to a woman who had a voice deeper than his. He told her what he wanted: a pilot to fly him to Great Falls tomorrow morning.

He returned to the laundromat and tossed his clothes into a dryer. He was feeding quarters into the dryer when his phone rang. It was Mahoney.

"The FBI has a satellite office in Bismarck," Mahoney said, "but there are only a few guys there, and they're all busy. The main field office for North Dakota is in Minneapolis but—"

"Goddamnit," DeMarco said. "I have to go to fucking Minneapolis to talk to an FBI agent?"

"Shut up. An agent named Westerberg will be in Bismarck this evening. He'll call you when he gets there. He's got your number."

"Thanks," DeMarco said but Mahoney had already hung up.

Mahoney must have pounded on someone over at the Hoover Building and Mahoney was a hammer too big to ignore. At the same time,

DeMarco couldn't help but think: too little, too late. This is what he should have done in the first place: gotten the FBI involved *before* somebody killed Sarah Johnson.

DeMarco returned to his motel with his freshly laundered clothes. There wasn't anything for him to do until he talked to Doug Thorpe and the FBI. He pulled out his laptop and looked at Sarah's blog, hoping that she'd updated it since he spoke to her the night before. She hadn't. The last entry she'd made was when they were traveling from Rapid City back to Bismarck, and then she'd just rambled on about the depressing state of American politics.

DeMarco had fallen asleep reading Sarah's blog and was awakened by his ringing phone.

"This is Doug Thorpe," the caller said. "Where are you?"

"I'm at my motel," DeMarco said. "I was just waiting for you to call. Tell me where you are and I'll meet you."

"I'm down at the morgue," Thorpe said.

"Oh," DeMarco said.

"I need a drink. I gotta get the smell of this place out of my nose. I'll meet you at . . ."

DeMarco was on his way to meet Thorpe at a restaurant near the Bismarck morgue when his phone rang again. The caller ID showed a 763 area code.

"Hello," he said.

"This is Special Agent Westerberg."

Westerberg turned out to be a she and not a he as Mahoney had said.

"I've been ordered to meet with you." She said this like she wasn't happy that some politician had squeezed her boss's nuts. "I'll be in Bismarck by seven this evening. I'm staying at the Radisson. I've stayed there before and there's a place called the Pirogue Grille on Fourth Street. Meet me there at eight."

Westerberg said this like she was issuing an order, not making a request.

"Okay," DeMarco said. "How will I recognize you?"

"I'll probably be the only woman in the bar packing a gun in a shoulder holster."

With that, she hung up.

DeMarco saw Thorpe sitting at a table by himself, staring out the window. The sky was overcast and it looked as if a lightning storm might start any moment. Thorpe's face looked like the sky: like a storm cloud. DeMarco sat down across from him. Thorpe was drinking whiskey out of a shot glass, taking small sips.

Before DeMarco had a chance to say how bad he felt about Sarah's death, Thorpe said, "So what happened?"

DeMarco told him what he and Sarah had been doing before she died, how they had attempted to talk to four people, trying to find whoever Curtis was using to make payoffs to judges and politicians. DeMarco admitted that it had been his idea.

"I thought that if we could identify Curtis's fixer, we might be able to force him to testify against Curtis," DeMarco said. "But I don't know if that's why she was killed."

DeMarco watched as the blood rushed to Thorpe's face, turning his normally tanned complexion an angry shade of purple. "Are you telling me you think some robber—"

"No, Mr. Thorpe, I don't think she was killed by a robber. I'm saying that while I was with Sarah, she didn't find anything new. Nobody would talk to her. She didn't get any new evidence against Curtis or anybody else. The other thing is, as far as I know, nobody knew I was working with her or that she was talking to these people. So maybe Curtis ordered her death, but if he did, it was something he set in motion before I got here or maybe as soon as I got here. But the other thing is, Curtis would have to be crazy to have her killed. Sarah never found a thing in the two years she was going after him that could cause him a significant legal problem."

"So if Curtis didn't have her killed, who did?"

"I don't know. Sarah accused a lot of people in her blog about being in collusion with Curtis. Maybe one of them killed her. Or maybe Curtis's fixer somehow found out that we were looking for him. I don't know. But the main thing I wanted to tell you is that Mahoney talked to the FBI today and I'm meeting with an agent this evening."

"Why didn't you and John get the FBI involved in the first place?"

"Because we didn't have anything to *get* the FBI involved. Sarah had no evidence any crimes had been committed, but now—"

"Yeah, now you got a crime. Somebody killed her."

"I'm sorry, Doug. I'm sorry about everything."

Thorpe finished the whiskey remaining in the shot glass. He winced when he swallowed, as if he wasn't used to the taste. As he rose from the table he said, "I'm going to take care of Curtis."

DeMarco knew Thorpe wasn't talking about pursuing a legal case against Leonard Curtis. He was talking about killing the man.

"Leave Curtis alone," DeMarco said. "You do something to him, you're just going to end up in jail."

"With Sarah and my daughter both gone, DeMarco, I don't care about jail."

"Doug, I don't know for sure that Curtis had anything to do with your granddaughter's death. So I'm asking you to give me a chance to find out who killed her before you do anything. Please? I know I screwed this up but give me a chance. And let me get the FBI engaged before you do something you'll regret. I'm also flying to Great Falls tomorrow morning."

"Why?"

DeMarco told him why he was going to Great Falls—but Thorpe didn't seem impressed. At this point Thorpe had no confidence in DeMarco, and DeMarco couldn't blame him.

"Just give me a few days," DeMarco said. "Okay? You take care of Sarah. Let me know when the funeral is. And I'll keep you informed of what I'm doing."

"Well, you better do something, son, because if you don't, I will."

DeMarco watched Thorpe walk away. The first time he met Thorpe at his cabin near the Yellowstone River, DeMarco had been struck by how he looked: over seventy years old but strong, fit, and vigorous. Now he just looked like an old man that time had run over. He was a person who'd served his country in an extraordinary way and—unlike John Mahoney and Joe DeMarco—had probably lived a blameless life. But here he was in the waning days of his existence, stripped of everyone he'd ever loved: wife, daughter, and granddaughter. If there was a God, DeMarco had to wonder about His grand plan.

14

There were five women in the bar of the Pirogue Grille. Three of the women were with men. The fourth was a young lady with a blue streak in her hair, a ring through her left nostril, jabbering in a high-pitched voice on a cell phone. DeMarco doubted that blue hair and nose rings were allowed by the Bureau's dress code. The last woman was sitting alone at a table with her back to the wall.

The woman looked like she was about forty and had dark red hair, the color of mahogany. She was wearing a navy blue suit with a skirt—she had good legs—a white blouse, and a blue-and-white scarf tied to resemble a man's tie. Her face was narrow with high cheekbones and a wide, sensual mouth. She was attractive, but DeMarco's first impression was: *tough cookie.*

She appeared to be drinking a martini, and DeMarco decided to have one, too. He waved at her to let her know that he'd seen her, then walked up to the bar and ordered a drink. After it arrived, he walked over to her table.

"Agent Westerberg, I presume."

"Yeah," she said. Instead of pulling out her ID, she pulled back her suit jacket and showed him the Glock in the shoulder holster.

"I'm Joe DeMarco. Thanks for meeting with me."

"I wasn't given a choice. And all I was told was that a young woman named Sarah Johnson was murdered last night and the former Speaker of the House isn't happy that no one's solved the crime yet. So what's going on?"

DeMarco told her about Sarah's blog and how she'd been on a crusade the last two years to nail a rich gas guy named Leonard Curtis who was buying off lawmakers and judges to get his way.

"But she never found any hard evidence that Curtis had done anything illegal because he makes these tricky under-the-table deals with politicians that you would never be able to prove are bribes. Let me tell you about the seed drill."

"Seed drill? What the hell's a seed drill?"

He told her what a seed drill was, and how one state legislator miraculously changed his vote after he got a bargain on one.

"You gotta be shittin' me," Westerberg said.

"No. And everything Sarah found was like that, a circumstantial case for bribery based on the coincidence of a politician benefiting at the same time Curtis had some luck with a law or a lawsuit. But the harassment campaign against her was real. The hacker who fucked up her blog for a month was real, and the three guys who threatened to rape and kill her were real. And now she's dead and I'm ninety-nine percent sure it wasn't some meth head who broke into her house and used a silenced weapon to put two bullets into her heart."

"But Curtis may not have been the one responsible," Westerberg said. "You said she named a lot of people in her blog. Maybe one of them was the person who killed her."

"Yeah, maybe," DeMarco said.

"What have the Bismarck cops got on her murder?"

"I have no idea," DeMarco said. "They consider me a suspect because I admitted I was probably the last person who saw her alive, other than her killer, and I'm the one who found the body. They don't seriously think I killed her but they're not talking to me about their investigation."

"Do you understand that Ms. Johnson's murder is a local police matter and that the FBI has no jurisdiction?"

"Yeah, and I don't care. And neither does John Mahoney."

Westerberg shook her head. "So what do you expect me to do, DeMarco?"

"Start by reading Sarah's blog. That's going to give you a migraine but it will tell you everything she suspected about Curtis. Lean on the Bismarck cops to make sure they're doing everything they can. Take a look at Curtis's phone calls and emails and . . ."

"That would require a warrant."

"That's your problem," DeMarco said. "I'm just saying do whatever you have to do to find who killed her."

"Okay," Westerberg said—but DeMarco got the impression that her definition of *do whatever you have to do* wasn't the same as his. "Anything else?" she asked.

"No." DeMarco thought about telling her about the trip he was making to Great Falls tomorrow, but he didn't want to give Westerberg the chance to tell him he shouldn't go.

"All right," she said. "I'll give you a call in a few days and let you know what I've found." She handed him a card and said, "If anything else occurs to you, call me at that number. But don't call and ask for progress reports. When I know something, I'll let you know."

DeMarco could see that her attitude needed a slight adjustment. "What's your first name?" he asked.

"Agent," she said.

Tough cookie. "Okay, Agent, let me explain something to you. Right now, as far as John Mahoney is concerned, *you* are the Federal Bureau of Investigation when it comes to Sarah Johnson. But Mahoney isn't going to talk to you. He's going to talk to your boss's boss's boss. In other words, Mahoney, who is a good friend of the president of the United States, is going to call the director of the FBI and tell him that he—meaning me—isn't satisfied with your performance in solving the murder of the granddaughter of a man who saved his life in Vietnam."

"Are you threatening me, DeMarco?"

"Well, yeah. I thought I was being pretty clear about that. I'm threatening to destroy your career if I don't get the sense that you're busting your ass on this case. I liked Sarah and I admired what she was trying to do, and I think it may have been my fault she was killed. So this is personal for me—and I'm making sure you understand that it's personal for you, too."

DeMarco stood up. "I'll be calling you, Agent."

"Now what's going on?" Marjorie said. When Heckler called, she had been trying to get a grass stain out of a pair of Bobby's jeans that had cost seventy bucks. She was going to wring her son's neck if he didn't change out of his good clothes when he got home from school.

"I don't know," Heckler said. "About an hour ago he met with a tough-looking old guy and had a drink with him. I ran the plates on the guy's truck and he's from Montana and his name is Doug Thorpe. Thorpe is a fly-fishing guide. I have no idea why he was talking to DeMarco but based on the way they both looked, they weren't talking about fly fishing. I'm trying to get more info on Thorpe, and when I do, I'll let you know. Then after he met with Thorpe, he met with a tough-looking gal in the Pirogue Grille."

Marjorie rolled her eyes: everybody DeMarco met with according to Heckler was *tough-looking*, like DeMarco was the leader of some kind of street gang.

"So he met a woman in a bar," Marjorie said. "Maybe he was trying to get laid again, like he did with the teacher."

"I don't think so," Heckler said. "I couldn't hear what they were saying to each other, but judging by the body language, it wasn't a friendly conversation. I think she could be a cop."

"Why would you think that?" Marjorie said.

"Because when DeMarco first sat down with her, I caught a glimpse of a gun she's packing in a shoulder holster. So I think she could be a cop, but I don't know for sure. DeMarco left the bar before she did and I followed him, but I'll go back to the bar later and see if I can find out who she is."

15

Marjorie hadn't seen Bill all day yesterday, the day they discovered Johnson's body. She was concerned that he was off on a bender but when she called him, he told her he was in Belcourt. He'd driven up there to talk to Buchanan, the state senator who needed his septic system fixed and a contractor who could fudge the necessary permits. Marjorie had forgotten about Buchanan with all the stuff going on with Sarah Johnson.

Bill finally dragged himself into the office at ten thirty, unshaven, bloodshot eyes, obviously hung over.

"How'd it go with Buchanan?" she asked.

"Okay, I think."

"You think?"

"It went okay. He's our new best friend."

Bill dropped down in his chair but then just sat there, looking like he didn't know what to do next—and Marjorie snapped. "Hey! You have to get back on track. You need to knock off the boozing and the moping and get refocused. Johnson's out of our hair, and Curtis will be happy about that, but . . ."

"Out of our hair, Marge? She's dead."

"I don't wanna hear it. Did you send Murdock the rest of his money?"

"Hell, yes. You think I want him coming up here to collect?"

"Then we're done with that whole . . . thing. Now get to work."

Men were just useless! Which reminded her: she needed to call Dick and tell him to get a guy over to do the annual maintenance on the air conditioner before it got hot. She went outside to have a smoke and call her husband but Heckler called her before she could.

"DeMarco just took off in an airplane," Heckler said.

"Thank God," Marjorie said.

"No, you don't understand. I followed him to the Bismarck airport but he didn't catch a commercial flight. He caught a charter flight. Naturally, I couldn't follow the guy after the plane took off. It cost me fifty bucks, which I plan to expense to you, to find out where the plane's going. It's headed to Great Falls."

"Great Falls, Montana, or Great Falls, Virginia?"

Marjorie knew, the way her luck had been going, that that was a really dumb question.

"Montana," Heckler said. "DeMarco left his rental car in the parking lot here at the airport so I'm guessing he's coming back. The only thing I can do at this point is wait for him to return."

———◆———

To DeMarco's relief the plane landed on its wheels, on a runway, instead of upside down in a wheat field. Small planes made him nervous.

That morning, he'd woken up early and driven to the Bismarck airport where he discovered that the woman with the deep voice who'd booked the charter flight for him was also his pilot. She had dark hair streaked with a lot of gray, wore no makeup, and looked harder than granite. He handed her his government credit card and signed a bunch of papers without reading them or looking at the amount she charged to his card. He imagined the papers were an insurance waiver that said if she crashed the plane and killed him, his estate couldn't sue her company. He didn't care.

They flew from Bismarck to Great Falls in some kind of small jet. DeMarco didn't pay any attention to the type of plane it was. The only thing he did was buckle his seat belt and say a silent prayer that the lady knew how to fly. She asked him if he wanted her to point out the sights as they were flying and he said, "Sure."

"Well, that's North Dakota down there," she said and then didn't say anything else until they crossed into Montana.

He took a taxi from the Great Falls airport to Janet Tyler's house. Tyler was the lawyer who had dropped a water contamination lawsuit against Curtis to get her son out from under various robbery and assault charges. Sarah had told DeMarco that Tyler expressed remorse for what she'd done but refused to tell Sarah exactly what had happened or how Curtis had gotten to her. DeMarco's plan was to hit Tyler right between the eyes with Sarah's death.

When Tyler answered the door, DeMarco held up his Congressional ID like it was a badge and said, "Ms. Tyler, I'm from the United States Congress. My name's DeMarco."

"Congress?"

"Yeah. Sarah Johnson's dead. You know, the young lady who came to see you a couple of days ago? Someone shot her twice in the heart."

"Oh, my God," Tyler said, holding her hands to her mouth, her eyes going wide with shock.

"May I come in?"

Tyler was so thin that DeMarco thought she might be anorexic. Sarah had said the woman was in her fifties, but she appeared to be at least a decade older. There were dark half-circles under her eyes from lack of sleep and because her face was so pale, it looked as if the skin under her eyes had been smudged with charcoal. Her hair was blond and brittle, like dried-out straw.

She backed into the living room and pointed DeMarco to an overstuffed chair. The blinds in the room were closed but enough light entered through the slats that they could see each other. He wondered why she didn't let in the sunlight; he wondered if she ever ventured out into the sunlight. There were at least a dozen photographs of a handsome young man in the room; the young man had Tyler's eyes.

"Like I said, Sarah Johnson's dead. And I think the reason she's dead is because she came to see you, and even though you didn't tell her anything, whoever killed her didn't want her asking more questions." That was a lie and not fair to Tyler, but DeMarco didn't care. "But now I want the answer to the question she asked you, and you're going to tell me. When you dropped that lawsuit to keep your son from going to jail, who got to you? Who was the person who talked to you?"

Tyler started shaking her head.

DeMarco shouted, "Don't you give a shit that someone killed that girl?"

"Yes, of course, but . . ."

"Let me explain something to you, Janet. The FBI is investigating Sarah's death. The Bureau is also looking into the claims she made in her blog about Curtis bribing and blackmailing people to get his way. In other words, *you're* going to be investigated. But the thing is, I don't care about you and I can make the FBI back off if you cooperate."

Now Tyler was weeping softly, but DeMarco didn't know if she was weeping for herself or Sarah.

Speaking more softly, DeMarco said, "Janet, I know you're a decent person. I know all you were doing was trying to save your son, and I have no desire to see you disbarred. I just want to find the person responsible for killing Sarah. If you give me what I want, you'll never see me again and the FBI won't come after you."

"Do you have children, Mr. DeMarco?"

"No."

"Then you can't possibly understand. The chances of me winning that suit against Curtis were small to begin with and even if I'd won, his lawyers would have appealed. But my son was going to go to jail and he didn't deserve to be in jail. He was sick. He wasn't a criminal. The damn laws in this country about drugs . . . Paul would have died in jail. The only time he was strong was when he was high. He would have committed suicide."

"I understand," DeMarco said. He didn't know what else to say.

"Then my son died anyway. After I turned my back on the people who hired me to sue Curtis, Paul relapsed again and killed himself behind the wheel of a car."

"I'm sorry," DeMarco said, "but Sarah . . ."

"Bill Logan," she said. "Or that's what he said his name was. He was the one who came to see me and told me that if I dropped the suit he could guarantee my son wouldn't serve time."

Finally. "What else do you know about Logan? What does he look like?"

"He was about your age. A tall, nice-looking man with dark hair. He was very polite, not threatening at all."

"Do you know where he lives or where he works? Did he give you a card or a phone number?"

"No. All I know is his name. I'll never forget it because my life ended the day I talked to him."

When she said this, DeMarco had the impression that she was being literal: her life really did end after she betrayed her clients and her son died. That she was still breathing was almost accidental.

"You said I could be disbarred. Well, I don't practice law anymore. After Paul died, I hardly ever leave this house. The only reason I'm co-operating with you is because I feel terrible about that young woman, but I don't care what happens to me."

As DeMarco was leaving her dark house, he wondered what the odds were that Janet Tyler would eventually commit suicide. He figured the odds were high.

When he reached his car, he called Westerberg. It was nice having the Federal Bureau of Investigation at his beck and call.

"Agent," he said when she answered, "I got a name. Bill Logan. I need to find out who he is and if he has any connection to Leonard Curtis."

"That's all you got? Bill Logan? No address, no DOB, nothing else."

"Just the name. What you could do is—"

"Don't tell me how to do my job, DeMarco."

"Fine. Just get me some answers. And I need them quick. I've got a plane at my disposal and I'll be back at the airfield in half an hour and I want to tell my pilot where to go next." DeMarco liked saying *my pilot*.

DeMarco arrived at the airfield to find *his* pilot reading a magazine with a picture of a horse on the cover. "I want to wait here for a while before flying back," he told her. "I'm waiting for a phone call."

The pilot shrugged. "It's your money," she said.

He noticed the magazine she was reading was called *American Quarter Horse.* He thought a quarter horse was the kind cowboys used to cut cattle out of the herd, to brand them or something, but wasn't sure. DeMarco had only been on a horse twice in his life and both times he'd felt like the horse was the one in control. Yanking on the reins of a beast that weighed a thousand pounds and had big teeth had never made sense to him.

"You own quarter horses?" he asked the pilot.

"Yeah, I've got two. I like 'em better than my husband and my kids. In fact, I'm thinking about selling one of my kids so I can buy another one."

Half an hour later—as DeMarco was still learning why quarter horses were better than thoroughbreds, big-footed Clydesdales, and every other four-legged critter on the planet—his phone rang. It was Westerberg.

"There's a Leslie William Logan in Bismarck," she said.

"Leslie?" DeMarco said.

"Yeah. He's self-employed and the co-owner of D&L Consulting. His partner is a woman named Marjorie Dawkins. Logan and Dawkins are also registered lobbyists in the state of North Dakota. But if you look at D&L Consulting's website, you can't figure out what the hell they do. It says they work on creating "partnerships committed to integrity"—whatever that means—and "developing uncommon approaches to solving problems." Their website says they've worked with trade associations and numerous small businesses—but doesn't name a single business they've worked with. I mean, you couldn't get any more vague if you tried and the address for the company is a post office box."

"Are you saying you couldn't find a connection between this Leslie Logan and Leonard Curtis?" DeMarco said.

"No, I'm not saying that," Westerberg said, "because in addition to looking at D&L Consulting's website, I called a guy at the IRS and asked him to take a peek at the company's last tax return. One hundred percent of D&L's business income, based on the 1099s in their return, comes from companies owned by Leonard Curtis."

"This is good, Agent. In fact, this is great. Give me Logan's home address," DeMarco said.

"No. Not until you tell me why you're asking about him."

"I gotta think about that," DeMarco said.

"What? Let me tell you something, DeMarco. You don't have a badge. You're not in law enforcement. I don't know what you do for John Mahoney but you are not licensed or sanctioned to investigate people for murder or any other crime."

"Yeah, I know, which is why I gotta think about this whole thing."

If DeMarco hadn't disconnected the call he would have heard Agent Westerberg curse in a most un-agent-like fashion.

DeMarco told his horse-loving pilot that they could head back to Bismarck. He was genuinely relieved that that's where Logan lived. He didn't have any desire to see more of Montana or North Dakota.

DeMarco hadn't told Westerberg that he suspected Bill Logan was Leonard Curtis's fixer because he wasn't sure that he wanted the FBI involved in whatever he was going to do next—and he didn't know what he was going to do next. The problem with Westerberg was that while she might attempt to build a legal case against Logan and Curtis—and maybe Logan's partner, this lady, Marjorie Dawkins—she would follow the law. This meant that she would worry about due process and warrants and people's right to counsel—and DeMarco didn't care about any of those things. DeMarco's objective was to make someone pay for Sarah's death and he wasn't going to allow the niceties of the legal system to hinder him.

DeMarco frankly doubted that Logan could be convicted of bribery, at least not based on what he knew so far or based on anything that Sarah had been able to find. Like in the case of Janet Tyler: Logan had most likely convinced a prosecutor to go easy on Tyler's son in exchange for helping the prosecutor's political career. However, there would be no hard evidence that Logan had bribed the prosecutor and the prosecutor would maintain that he had the lawful authority to reach a plea bargain with Tyler's son that didn't include jail time. So if DeMarco was going to put Curtis or Logan in jail, he need something more than he currently had.

DeMarco also figured that Logan or Curtis didn't kill Sarah themselves—assuming they had anything at all to do with her death. Curtis certainly wouldn't have been directly involved in a murder; he was an executive who used his minions to do things for him. And although it was possible that Logan had killed her, it seemed more likely that Curtis or Logan would have hired a pro, a guy able to make an assassination look like a robbery gone bad—but if the FBI and the

Bismarck cops couldn't identify the hit man, it seemed pretty unlikely that DeMarco would be able to do so. The hit man was a ghost.

So DeMarco needed to figure out what he was going to do next and how best to use Westerberg. Agent Westerberg wouldn't appreciate this but as far as DeMarco was concerned she was a tool—and DeMarco hadn't decided if she was a sledgehammer he could use to pound on someone or a scalpel he could use with precision to remove a malignant political cancer.

Westerberg had peevishly refused to give him Logan's address but De-Marco figured he now knew enough to find the guy. After landing back in Bismarck, he returned to his motel, powered up his trusty laptop, and went online. He entered the names William Logan, Leslie William Logan, and Bill Logan into one of those Internet people search engines and, to his delight, found only three men in the city of Bismarck named Bill or William Logan.

One of the Bill Logans was too old; he was sixty-eight—and Janet Tyler had said that the Logan DeMarco wanted was about his age. The second Logan was a general contractor; he had a website, an ad in the yellow pages, and was esteemed by the Better Business Bureau. The Bill Logan who had convinced a prosecutor to go easy on Tyler's son wasn't a carpenter—which led to the Logan he wanted—the third Bill Logan—and his home address was listed in the white pages of the Bismarck phone directory.

DeMarco started to shut down his laptop, but then decided to check out the website Westerberg had found for D&L Consulting—and it was just like Westerberg had said: the website was a masterpiece of obfuscation. Logan and Dawkins claimed to be experienced political consultants but they went out of their way to be as ambiguous as they could possibly be regarding what they actually did and who they represented.

Since Logan was a registered lobbyist, however, Sarah should have been able to find a connection between Logan and Curtis, and the fact that she didn't—and considering how many hours Sarah had spent researching Curtis—could only mean that Logan and his partner made sure that there was no paper or Internet trail tying them to their master. Logan and Dawkins were people who deliberately operated in the shadows—which is what lobbyists often did so the public wouldn't be able to see how they were twisting the political process.

The one thing Logan and Dawkins had not been able to do was hide their fiscal connection to Curtis—but Sarah, unlike Agent Westerberg of the FBI, couldn't call up a pal at the IRS and ask about D&L Consulting's tax returns. DeMarco couldn't help but wonder if the night Sarah had called him—the last time he'd spoken to her—if she'd been about to tell him about D&L Consulting. Now he'd never know.

DeMarco turned off his laptop and drove to Leslie William Logan's house. It was made of brick, had a fancy front door, cedar shakes for a roof, a couple of chimneys, and a three-car garage. The landscaping was elaborate and looked like it was maintained by professionals. DeMarco figured the place had to be at least four thousand square feet, and had it been located in D.C., it would have sold for well over a million, maybe two—which made him wonder how much money Bill Logan made.

But DeMarco didn't stop. He returned to his motel for a good night's sleep. He wanted to be bright-eyed and alert when he began his campaign to destroy Bill Logan. By the time he was done, Logan's next home might be a cage.

16

The next morning DeMarco forced himself out of bed at six a.m. Feeling like the walking dead, he headed in the direction of Logan's place. On the way, he stopped at a convenience store, bought coffee and donuts for breakfast, a couple cans of Coke, and two nasty-looking sandwiches that looked like they'd been sitting in the cooler since Sandwich invented the sandwich. There was nothing DeMarco hated more than surveillance duty although he'd been required to perform this task a number of times while working for Mahoney.

DeMarco didn't have a plan, not at this point. His only objective today was to see Logan in person, find out where he worked, and maybe follow him to see whom he met with and what he did during his workday. After that he wasn't sure what he was going to do. Break into Logan's office and examine his files? See if he could find something that Westerberg could use as justification to get a warrant to tap his phones? He didn't know—but he had to start somewhere.

"You're not going to believe this," Heckler said. "Right now DeMarco is parked outside your partner's house. He's watching the house."

"Son of a bitch," Marjorie muttered.

"Yeah. Yesterday when he got back from Great Falls, he went to his motel, spent about an hour there, then he got in his car and drove around for a while and I couldn't figure out what he was doing. When he drove by Logan's place, I didn't think anything of it because he didn't stop. But then this morning, he gets up early and heads over here, and now he's just watching the house."

"Son of a bitch," Marjorie said again.

At nine a.m., DeMarco's patience was rewarded when Logan's garage door rolled up and a red Porsche Boxster backed out. It was a nice-looking set of wheels—certainly much nicer than DeMarco's Toyota—but DeMarco couldn't clearly see the man who was driving. For all he knew, Logan could be gay and the driver could be his partner. Nonetheless, he followed the Porsche and a few minutes later it pulled into the parking lot of a restaurant. A tall, good-looking, dark-haired guy about DeMarco's age stepped from the car. Based on the description Janet Tyler had given him, he was now fairly certain he was following Logan.

DeMarco sat in his car and enviously watched through the windows of the restaurant as Logan ate breakfast. The waitress—who looked like she was about nineteen—stopped at his table three or four times, and DeMarco could tell by the way she was laughing and touching him on the shoulder that she was flirting with him. So much for Logan being gay.

After an hour, Logan left the restaurant and DeMarco followed him to a small strip mall. There was a Subway shop, a HairMasters, and a FedEx-Kinko's in the mall. The fourth storefront had a sign near the door too small for DeMarco to read from where he was parked, and the fifth office wasn't identified in any way. It had a dark green door with a mail slot and a single large picture window but the blinds were closed so he couldn't see inside. Logan parked next to a black Jeep Cherokee and entered the unmarked office.

Now what?

<hr>

"Guess where he is now," Heckler said.

"I don't want to guess," Marjorie growled.

"He's parked across the street from your office. What do you want me to do?"

"I don't know. Just stay on him." Marjorie disconnected the call.

Now what? In the two years Sarah Johnson had been writing her pointless blog, she'd named Leonard Curtis and numerous lawmakers, lawyers, and judges—but Johnson had never, ever mentioned her or Bill. So Johnson, as near as Marjorie could tell, never had any idea that she and Bill worked for Curtis—but somehow this son of a bitch, DeMarco, had found them in less than a week.

DeMarco locating them obviously had something to do with his trip to Great Falls because right after he returned from there, he started following Bill. Marjorie tried to think who DeMarco might have talked to in northwestern Montana but no one immediately came to mind. There were at least a dozen folks in the Great Falls area that they'd done business with over the years.

In order to identify who DeMarco might have talked to, Marjorie would probably have to go through Johnson's fucking blog again—hundreds and hundreds of pages, probably a million goddamn words. Marjorie had always thought that Johnson's blog should have been used by the CIA to torture terrorists. She could envision some guy in a cell down there at Guantánamo Bay—strapped naked to a chair, dogs snapping at his nuts, a bag over his head—as Johnson's blog was read to him until he either confessed or went insane.

So what should she do? The right answer was probably: do nothing. If Johnson hadn't been able to build a legal case against Curtis in two years, then DeMarco probably couldn't, either. On the other hand, DeMarco was a guy who had some political clout. What if he got some law enforcement agency, or maybe the North Dakota attorney general, to start investigating her and Bill to see if they could be linked to any of the nonsense in Johnson's blog? They probably wouldn't be able to prove that she and Bill had done anything illegal, but if the cops were watching them and prying into their business then that could render them virtually useless insofar as working for Curtis—and then Curtis would fire them.

She needed to find out what DeMarco was up to—and she was beginning to believe that having Heckler follow him wasn't going to tell her what she needed to know. Then she thought: Why not just ask the damn guy what he was doing? What did she have to lose?

She told Bill—who was acting more like his old self this morning, alert and cheerful and not hungover—that DeMarco had followed him from his home to their office this morning. She thought for a minute that Bill might throw up.

"Do you think he knows what we did about . . . You know?"

Bill was asking if DeMarco knew that they'd hired Murdock to kill Sarah Johnson—but he was afraid to say the words out loud.

"Bill, if he knew anything the cops would be parked across the street, not him. So get a grip on yourself." Marjorie stood up. "I'm going to ask him what the hell he thinks he's doing, following you around."

"Marge, I don't think that's a good idea."

Marjorie didn't care what he thought. She said, "I'm going to invite him into the office and talk to him but I want you to keep your mouth shut. Your head still isn't screwed on right."

DeMarco saw a woman come out of the office that Logan had entered. She was about five foot four, busty, and had short brown hair. She was cute. She crossed the strip mall parking lot—she had a bouncy, energetic way of walking—stopped at the curb, looked both ways before she crossed the street, and came toward his car. She made a motion for him to roll down the window.

She smiled at him. "Hi. Why don't you come on into the office so we can talk, Mr. DeMarco? There's no point in you sitting out here in your car or following my partner around."

How the hell did she know who he was? And how did she know that he'd been following Logan? But instead of asking those questions, he said, "Sure. Let's talk."

He was thinking: This could actually be a good thing as he hadn't been sure what to do next. Plus, it would give him a chance to see how hard it would be to break into the office if he decided to do that.

He followed her into her office. Bill Logan was sitting behind a desk, and he raised his hand in a little hello gesture when he saw DeMarco. Logan was trying to act as if he didn't have a worry in the world, but DeMarco could see the tension in his eyes. His partner, however, seemed genuinely relaxed.

He noticed that the office was a lot like his office in the Capitol: cheap furniture, not much of it, and nothing fancy. The file cabinets they had were identical to the one in his office: four drawers, constructed of sheet metal, and the same shade of gunmetal gray.

When DeMarco first went to work for Mahoney, he apprenticed under a guy named Jake, an ex-Boston cop who used to do for Mahoney what DeMarco now did. Jake died of a well-deserved heart attack about six months after DeMarco was hired. One day, DeMarco discovered that the file cabinet in their shared office contained nothing but a bottle of

Maker's Mark and phone directories. When he asked why there wasn't anything in it, Jake's response was: "They can't subpoena air." DeMarco was willing to bet that the file cabinets in Logan and Dawkins's office were similar: there'd be nothing in them that would cause them a problem if the cops obtained a warrant to examine their contents.

DeMarco wondered how much else he might have in common with Logan and Dawkins.

"Would you like a cup of coffee, Mr. DeMarco?" Dawkins asked.

"Sure," DeMarco said.

Dawkins poured him a cup and said, "Well, you already know Bill and I'm assuming you know who I am as well. I'm Marjorie. And would you mind if I called you Joe?"

"Joe would be fine," DeMarco said.

"So, Joe, what's going on?"

"How do you know who I am?" DeMarco asked.

Marjorie smiled; she had a great smile. "Joe, as the sports guys say, you're in our ballpark. We're the home team. We have the home field advantage."

DeMarco nodded. "Okay, I'll tell you what's going on. There's a guy named Doug Thorpe over in Montana. He's a fly-fishing guide. He also served with John Mahoney in Vietnam and saved Mahoney's life a couple of times. I assume you know the John Mahoney I'm talking about."

"Yeah, but so what?" Marjorie said.

"Doug Thorpe is—or was—Sarah Johnson's grandfather. He called Mahoney last week and said that somebody had assaulted Sarah and made death threats against her because she was accusing Leonard Curtis—your boss—of bribing politicians."

"What makes you think we work for Leonard Curtis?" Marjorie said.

DeMarco laughed. "I can tell you I didn't find out from reading your website. What a pile of bullshit that is. So I had someone take a peek at your tax returns and found out that Curtis is the guy who pays your salaries."

"What authority do you have for looking at our returns?" Logan said and Marjorie whipped her head around to face Logan and said, "Bill!"—and to DeMarco that sounded like: *Bill, keep your mouth shut.*

DeMarco didn't answer Logan's question. Instead he said, "Anyway, Mahoney sent me out here to find out what was going on, and the only reason he did was because Thorpe's his friend. Then Sarah was killed, which was the stupidest thing you people could have done."

"Hey! You watch your mouth," Marjorie said. "We didn't have anything to do with that poor girl's death. We knew about all the wild accusations she'd made against Mr. Curtis, of course, and he sued her because she was saying things about him that were untrue. A couple other people sued her as well. But that's all Mr. Curtis did and nobody who works for Curtis, including me or Bill, made any death threats and we sure as hell didn't kill her."

Before DeMarco could speak, she lowered her voice and said in a calmer tone, "Joe, Bill and I are political consultants. We keep our eye on state politics. We advise Mr. Curtis about pending legislation. We try to convince politicians to support his businesses, and we support politicians who feel the same way we do about certain issues. And that's it. That's all we do. We don't go around killing people. We *talk* to people."

As if she hadn't spoken, DeMarco said, "The reason why killing Sarah was so dumb was because she couldn't prove anything. She had no evidence that any crimes had been committed. She couldn't get anybody with a badge to listen to her. But now things have changed. Drastically.

"Right now, thanks to Mahoney, I have my very own FBI agent looking into Sarah's murder. In other words, I have a pit bull with a badge and a gun. And Mahoney is going to call up the governor of Montana, who's a Democrat, and tell him to get his attorney general to take a look at what Curtis has been doing.

"Unfortunately, for Mahoney that is, the governors of North and South Dakota are currently Republicans, but all three states have U.S. senators who are Democrats, and Mahoney's going to talk to these senators and tell them to get engaged. And in the end, because of all the pressure being brought to bear on the local cops and the FBI, they're going to break someone."

"What the hell does that mean?" Logan said.

"With Sarah Johnson," DeMarco said, "you had a young woman with no professional credentials, who hadn't even graduated from college, and who couldn't get anyone to take her seriously. But now it's a whole different ball game. The FBI is now poring over Sarah's blog like it's the fucking *Warren Report*. They're going to start looking at people's finances and phone calls and emails because, unlike Sarah, they have the power to get subpoenas and search warrants. Eventually, they'll find somebody who's committed a crime and they'll break that person and he'll point the finger at you two to keep from going to jail. Then guess what's going to happen next?"

Neither Bill nor Marjorie guessed. Logan just sat there looking scared; Dawkins had a little smile on her face, as if she found DeMarco amusing.

"What's going to happen," DeMarco said, "is one of you is going to turn on the other one to keep from going to jail. That's what always happens because the FBI is a master at this sort of thing. They get one guy to give up the guy he works for, then that guy gives up the guy *he* works for. That's how they get all the mafia guys. That's how they get the guys who engage in insider trading and bank fraud and shit like that. And that's how they're going to get you. One of you is going to crack and give up the other one, and then that person is going to give up Curtis—unless Curtis has that person killed first."

DeMarco stood up. "Let me tell you one other little thing. The FBI and the Justice Department care about the law and they follow the rules when it comes to obtaining evidence and interrogating folks. Well, I don't give a shit about the law. The only thing I care about is that I liked Sarah and I like her grandfather, and I'm going to nail you two and I don't care how I do it. Thanks for the coffee, Marjorie."

17

"We're fucked," Bill said.

Marge had been sitting there, about to call Heckler to tell him to stick with DeMarco. Now she shot up from her chair like it was spring loaded. For just an instant, she considered picking up the stapler on her desk and flinging it at Bill's head as hard as she could.

"Listen to me, Bill." She almost said, *Listen to me, you idiot.* "That little speech that DeMarco just made was total bullshit, and the only reason he made it is because he's hoping one of us will panic. DeMarco has nothing! And the FBI will find nothing. The kind of things we do for Curtis are nowhere near as bad as the crap that goes on in D.C. They have more lobbyists in Washington than they have politicians, and they throw *millions* at those politicians. When was the last time a D.C. lobbyist was arrested? And what the hell have we done? Arranged for some guy to get his septic system fixed without a permit? Big fucking deal. Nobody's going to jail."

"Yeah, but he knows who we are."

"Shut up and come outside with me."

"Can't you wait until we've finished talking to have a cigarette?"

"That's not why we're going outside."

Once they got outside, Marjorie did light up a Marlboro, however. "We need to be careful about what we say in the office. Thanks to DeMarco, those FBI weasels might try to tap our phones or bug the office."

"But they'd have to get a warrant to do that."

Marjorie just looked at him for a moment, then shook her head. "Sometimes I wonder what planet you live on. The FBI will use the Patriot Act or anything else they can think of to get a warrant if John Mahoney is pressuring them. So I don't want you to say anything on the phone or in the office about Sarah Johnson or Murdock or Curtis or anything else that somebody could consider the least bit illegal. We're going to keep doing what we've always done but we're going to be as squeaky clean as . . . Well, as I don't know what, but squeaky clean. Do you understand?"

"Yeah. But what do we tell Curtis?"

"I don't know. I have to think about that. But at some point, we need to let him know about DeMarco." She dropped her cigarette on the ground and crushed it out. "It's Curtis's fault we're in this mess. We never would have done anything about Johnson if he hadn't forced us. But that's water under the bridge, so you get your head on straight. You don't do anything out of the ordinary. You just go about your business. If the FBI tries to talk to you, you don't talk. They can't force you to talk to them. If they drag you in for questioning, you say you want a lawyer, then you call me and after that you keep your mouth shut."

Bill went back inside looking uncertain and queasy. Marjorie lit another cigarette—she was smoking way too much lately—and called Heckler. She told him to stick with DeMarco then asked, "You know anybody who can tell if our phones or our office is bugged?"

"Maybe. There's a guy I know in Minneapolis who used to do stuff like that. I mean, he used to bug phones and offices for the cops. He was a contractor, I guess. You want me to call him?"

"Yeah, do that."

Marjorie knew, however, that their office being bugged wasn't her biggest problem. Even DeMarco and the FBI weren't her biggest problems. The big problems were Bill and Curtis. Bill was a weak link. He was drinking too much and he was a nervous wreck because he was an accomplice to Johnson's murder and was terrified he might get caught.

Curtis was a different story. There wasn't anything weak about him. He might call Murdock himself if he thought she and Bill had become liabilities.

18

"Agent, it's Joe DeMarco. I was thinking maybe we could meet for lunch and compare notes."

"Is that right?" Westerberg said. "Does this mean you're going to tell me why you wanted Bill Logan's address?"

"Yeah, sure," DeMarco said, like he was the most reasonable guy in the world.

"Well, we may as well meet because if I keep reading this blog my eyes are going to start bleeding."

DeMarco met Westerberg at a place called the Blarney Stone Pub on Main Street, about a mile from the Capitol. The Blarney Stone had redbrick walls, old hardwood floors, a long, dark bar, and twenty different beers on tap. Behind the bar was a painting of a cheerful-looking bearded Irishman wearing a red beret and toasting the patrons with a frothy pint of Guinness.

DeMarco arrived before Westerberg, took a seat at a table near the bar, and she arrived five minutes later. As she came toward him,

DeMarco couldn't help but appreciate that she had a nice, trim figure and outstanding legs. She was probably a jogger. She also looked tired, and DeMarco suspected she was working hard because she wanted to go home. She was wearing the same clothes she'd been wearing the evening DeMarco first met her: dark suit, white blouse, except the tie-like scarf was absent. She was probably wearing the same clothes because when she flew or drove to Bismarck from Minneapolis she hadn't been expecting to stay for long.

DeMarco ordered a cheeseburger for lunch; Westerberg asked for a chicken salad. As much as DeMarco wanted to sample one of the many beers the Blarney Stone offered, he followed Westerberg's lead and had an ice tea. After the waitress had taken their order, she said to DeMarco: "So? What's going on?"

DeMarco told her about Janet Tyler and how Logan convinced her to stop pursuing a lawsuit against Curtis in return for keeping her son out of jail, and that Tyler was the one who gave him Logan's name. He concluded, saying: "Bill Logan and Marjorie Dawkins are Curtis's go-to guys. They're the ones who have been going around bribing people."

"Yeah, I figured that might be the case when I found out they were lobbyists and worked for Curtis. But what Tyler told you isn't proof that Logan did anything illegal or that he conspired in Johnson's death?"

"I realize that," DeMarco said. "But I talked to Dawkins and Logan, and I told them that you were going to find some proof."

"You what! Goddamnit, DeMarco! If by some remote chance we—and by *we*, I mean the FBI—can actually build a criminal case against these people, you could screw things up by talking to them. I told you before: you are *not* law enforcement."

"Yeah, yeah," DeMarco said, then went on to tell her about his conversation with Bill and Marjorie. He didn't tell her that he'd referred to her as a pit bull with a badge. He concluded by saying that Logan and Dawkins naturally denied being anything more than innocent political consultants, but Logan had looked particularly nervous, like he was about ready to come out of his skin.

"So in other words," Westerberg said, "all you did was forewarn them that they're being investigated."

"What have you got?" DeMarco said to change the subject. "Do the Bismarck cops have anything on Sarah's murder?"

"No. There was no incriminating evidence at the crime scene. One thing that was a bit unusual was that the shooter didn't leave any brass behind. I mean, it's possible he used a .22 revolver, but folks don't usually buy .22 revolvers. And what this means is that whoever killed Sarah had the presence of mind to pick up the shell casings before he left, which is not what you'd expect if the shooter was some hopped-up meth addict. The other thing is, I thought we might be able to find Sarah's phone. What I'm saying is, if a tweeker stole her phone he would have started using it or sold it to somebody and that person would have used it. But we couldn't locate the phone so whoever stole it disabled or destroyed it, which again, isn't typical meth-head behavior. So this shooting has the earmarks of a professional hit but there's no evidence leading to the shooter."

"Okay, but that's not exactly big news," DeMarco said. "I never did think she was a victim of a random home invasion. Did you get anything else?"

"Yeah, two things. The first is that Logan took a trip to Denver a few days before Sarah was killed."

"What made you look at his travel records?" DeMarco asked.

"I was just checking him out after you gave me his name, looking at credit card records, tax returns, criminal records, whatever I could look at."

"So what about this trip to Denver? Why's that significant?"

"Because in looking at Logan's travel history, he doesn't usually go to Denver. In fact, until last week, the last time he'd been in Denver was six years ago. Normally he flies to Houston, where Curtis has his headquarters, a PR firm in LA, and Washington D.C."

"Could you figure out what he was doing in Denver?"

"No. He checked into a hotel, spent one night there, and flew out the next day. His credit card charges were just for normal things like dinner and booze and snacks. If I had to guess, I'd say he went there for a quick meeting."

"By any chance, was anybody connected to Curtis killed right after Logan went to Denver the last time?"

"Not that I could find," Westerberg said.

"Huh," DeMarco said. He sat there for a moment, turning his ice tea glass in his hands. "Can you get a warrant to tap Logan's phones?"

"Are you crazy? No judge is going to give me a warrant because the man flew to Denver. I have nothing to indicate that Logan has committed a crime. And what good would tapping his phones do anyway?"

"I'll tell you what good it would do," DeMarco said. "I think if you lean on Logan, you'll scare the shit out of him. You handcuff him, drag him into an interrogation room, read him his rights, then you tell him that Janet Tyler is willing to testify against him and . . ."

"Testify to what?"

"That Logan said he could keep her son from going to jail if she dropped the lawsuit against Curtis. In other words, she can testify that Logan admitted to her that he could influence her son's prosecutor."

"Yeah, but . . ."

"Then you start lying. You lie like a son of a bitch. You say that the prosecutor who Logan paid off to make sure Tyler's son didn't go to jail, confessed. You say he confessed because you nailed him on some other bullshit and he gave up Logan for a reduced sentence. You say that you've also got two or three politicians—people named in Sarah's blog—who've admitted that they took bribes from Logan. They admitted this because you're a badass federal agent and scared them."

Before Westerberg could interrupt him, DeMarco continued. "Then you hit Logan between the eyes with his Denver trip. You say you know he went to Denver and he hired somebody to kill Sarah. You say that you're about ready to arrest the killer, who you can prove was in Denver at the same time as Logan. In other words, you lie some more and say you found evidence at the crime scene or a picture on a surveillance camera. Whatever you can think of. I mean, you're going to need a pretty good script before you interrogate Logan, but I think you can write one and maybe he'll fall for it."

"And you think if I tell him all these lies, he'll confess?"

"Probably not. His lawyer will tell him to keep his mouth shut. But after you interrogate him and tell him the lies, Logan might panic and call somebody and say something that will incriminate himself or Curtis. So. Let me ask again: do you think there's any way you might be able to get a warrant to tap Logan's phones?"

"Forget it. No judge will give me one unless I lie to the judge, which I'm not about to do."

"Well, then—and I mean hypothetically—could you tap his phones without a warrant?"

"DeMarco, there is no way in hell that I am going to break the law, no matter who you work for."

"Okay, be that way," DeMarco said. "But I'm curious about something. Didn't you need a warrant to find out that Logan flew to Denver?"

Westerberg looked away—and she looked sheepish. She cleared her throat before she said, "There are a lot of databases out there, databases that legally collect information on people who purchase things—like airline tickets. I just happen to know somebody who has access to the right database."

"All right, Agent! I'm proud of you."

"Shut up, DeMarco."

"You said you learned two things. The first was Logan's trip to Denver. What was the second?"

"When Sarah was assaulted by those three men in April, she called the cops and I talked to the two cops who responded to the call. They told me that Sarah couldn't positively identify her attackers because they wore ski masks, but she said one of the men had full sleeves."

"Full sleeves?"

"Tattoos covering his arms, from shoulder to wrist. She couldn't see his face but she could see the tattoos because he was wearing a T-shirt. And his arms were right in her face because he sat on her chest, holding his hand over her mouth so she couldn't scream. The problem is that she couldn't remember anything distinctive about the tattoos: no image of a screaming eagle or a skull and crossbones or anything like that. The other thing was, this same guy was wearing beat-up old cowboy boots and the boots had silver caps on the toes."

The image of Sarah being pushed to the ground and three goons in ski masks, standing over her and threatening her, made DeMarco want to kill somebody. "So how are the tattoos and the boots important if Sarah couldn't ID her attackers?"

"Bismarck isn't a big city, and this means that the local cops know most the local assholes. As soon as Sarah said full sleeves and silver-tipped cowboy boots they thought of a guy named Roy Patterson."

"Did they question Patterson?"

"Of course. Patterson's alibi for the time Sarah was attacked was another asshole named Mark Jenkins. Jenkins and Patterson said they were sitting in Patterson's double-wide watching a ball game when Sarah was attacked. And the cops couldn't break Patterson's alibi and you can't arrest somebody for having tattoos and cowboy boots. The other thing was their attitude. Patterson and Jenkins both acted smug when the cops questioned them, like they knew they were getting away with something. But you can't arrest anyone for attitude, either. At any rate, based totally on cop instinct and a couple of tattooed arms, the Bismarck cops think that Patterson and Jenkins may have been two of the men who attacked Sarah but they can't do anything about it."

"Are there any surveillance cameras you can look at to see if Jenkins and Patterson were running around town during the time they were supposedly watching this ball game? You know, maybe a red-light camera that might have taken their picture."

"There aren't all that many public surveillance cameras in Bismarck. This isn't London. And the cops here aren't complete idiots. They actually did check out places between Patterson's trailer and the parking lot where Sarah was attacked. You know, a couple convenience stores and bars where these mutts might have stopped for a beer after they did the job—but they couldn't find anybody who saw them and the surveillance cameras in those places didn't show anything."

"But the cops are sure these guys were involved?"

Westerberg shrugged. "Are they sure? Well, they'd tell you that they're sure but as Denzel said in that movie: It's not what you know, it's what you can prove."

"Yeah, I guess," DeMarco said, as if he agreed with Westerberg—which he didn't. But rather than argue with her—and maybe tip his hand—he decided to change the subject. "Did you find anything in Sarah's blog you might be able to pursue?"

Westerberg laughed. "Let me tell you about the last thing I read in Sarah's blog. There was a North Dakota state senator who changed his vote on a bill related to disposal of wastewater from fracking. This got Sarah's attention because the guy had always been on the right side of environmental issues in the past and his vote was inconsistent with his voting pattern. So Sarah . . . .. She was really good, DeMarco. I wished she'd applied for a job at the Bureau. Anyway, Sarah somehow found out that the sewer line from the senator's house got clogged up by tree roots, and the sewer backed up and flooded his basement. Well, the senator's insurance company, being a typical insurance company, refused to pay for the water damage, which amounted to eight thousand bucks. Then, low and behold, this insurance company—who coincidentally provides insurance for a whole shitload of things connected to Leonard Curtis—has a change of heart.

"Sarah concluded, of course, that somebody paid the senator a visit and said they might be able to get his insurance company to pay his claim if he quit being such a pill about this wastewater legislation. Then this person—who we now suspect was Logan or Dawkins—made a call to the insurance company, telling them that Curtis was going to find somebody else to insure his many homes and businesses, and the insurance company decided to pay the claim.

"I mean, everything in her damn blog is like that, DeMarco! Like in this case: An insurance company paid off on a claim they probably should have paid in the first place, and a politician simply changed his mind. There's no way to prove the guy was bribed. You remember that congressman in Louisiana we busted with ninety thousand bucks in cash in his freezer? Now you can *do* something with ninety grand in a freezer. You can't do anything with an insurance company that just decides to do the right thing for once."

Westerberg stood up. "I gotta go, DeMarco. I have work to do." She turned to walk away, then turned back to face him. "I don't like the situation I'm in right now. I don't like it at all. Mahoney's got his boot on my boss's neck and my boss won't assign me to another case until I can convince him that there's nothing I can legally do to catch Sarah's killer. The operative word there being *legally*. And then my boss will have to convince Mahoney and Mahoney will probably ask you if I've done everything I can. So I want you to know that I'm busting my ass on this case, but at some point you and Mahoney may have to accept the fact that I can't find the evidence needed to convict someone. I also want you to know it really pisses me off that I have to satisfy you that I'm doing my job."

"Sorry, Agent," DeMarco said, not sounding sorry at all. "By the way, are you ever going to tell me your first name so I don't have to keep calling you Agent? With all this clout you seem to think I have, I can probably find out on my own if you won't tell me."

"My name is Bertha. Okay? Are you satisfied? And if you ever call me Bertha, I'll shoot you."

"So what do your friends call you?"

"You're not my friend, DeMarco."

19

Mark Jenkins and Roy Patterson.

Westerberg had finally given him something he could use. And in this case, Denzel was wrong: DeMarco didn't need proof, he just needed to know he was right.

The question was: Was he willing to accept the consequences if he failed? It took him about two seconds to decide that yes, he was. Twenty-two-year-old Sarah Johnson, a woman with her whole life ahead of her, had been willing to risk her life to get Leonard Curtis—and DeMarco was willing to risk the possibility of going to jail.

So he didn't spend much time agonizing over whether he would do it. He spent the time instead thinking about how to do it, and concluded he needed some help and some equipment he didn't have. If he'd been near New York, he could have called up a couple of mafia-connected lowlifes—guys who used to work with his father—and paid them to do the job for him—but he was sixteen hundred miles from New York.

He thought about logistics for another minute, then called Doug Thorpe.

"Mr. Thorpe, it's Joe DeMarco."

"What do you want, DeMarco?"

"Do you have any guns?"

"What? Yeah, of course."

"I don't mean rifles or shotguns. Handguns."

"Yeah, I got a couple. Why are you asking?"

DeMarco told him, and then told him what he planned to do. He concluded by saying, "You understand you could end up in jail if you help me."

"I couldn't care less about jail," Thorpe said.

"Okay, as long as you understand." Then he hesitated and asked, "When's Sarah's funeral?"

"Friday," Thorpe said.

------◆◆◆------

After speaking to Thorpe, DeMarco called Mahoney and told him that he needed Roy Patterson's address. He said that Patterson was a tattooed thug who might have a criminal record and that he lived in a double-wide, but that's all he knew. DeMarco might have been able find Patterson's address using the Internet and without Mahoney's help, but he didn't feel like spending hours on a computer. And Mahoney had the sort of connections in D.C. that could find the guy if he lived in a cave.

After speaking to his boss, DeMarco got into his rental car and drove slowly through the streets of downtown Bismarck, checking his rear-view mirror to see if he could spot whoever was following him.

When DeMarco met Dawkins and Logan in their office yesterday, it became apparent to him then that they'd been having him followed. If they hadn't had someone tailing him how else would Dawkins have known that he'd been following Logan? He didn't buy that you're-playing-in-our-ballpark crap that Dawkins tried to feed him.

The more startling conclusion he came to was that maybe Logan and Dawkins had someone start following him the day he arrived in

Bismarck or, more likely, they'd been following Sarah, and when Sarah met with him he was identified. This also meant that maybe they knew he and Sarah were seeing people like Janet Tyler, trying to get evidence to use against Curtis. DeMarco also remembered Doug Thorpe telling him that Sarah had been concerned that her phone calls were being monitored, something Thorpe had chalked up to paranoia—and a possibility DeMarco had completely ignored. So it was even possible that Dawkins and Logan, in addition to having him followed, had listened in on calls Sarah and DeMarco had made to each other. And what all this meant was that DeMarco felt more convinced—and more guilty than ever—that he could have been the catalyst for Sarah getting killed.

After driving for about fifteen minutes, DeMarco was pretty sure he was being followed by a man in a gray Honda sedan. He got on the I-94 interstate, in the middle lane, and the Honda got in the same lane, staying two cars behind him. At the next exit he came to, DeMarco waited until he was almost past the exit, then turned the wheel hard to the right, cutting in front of a sixteen-wheeler, almost clipping the semi's front bumper, and took the exit. Whoever was driving the gray Honda was blocked by the semi and didn't stand a chance of following him off the highway.

Satisfied that he'd lost the guy, DeMarco consulted his phone for directions to the nearest Walmart. He'd picked the Walmart for one reason: he was sure it would have self-checkout and, therefore, no one would witness his purchases. He found two black ski masks in the sporting goods section, paid in cash at the self-checkout machine, dumped the ski masks into a plastic bag, and never had contact with another human being.

As he was driving out of the Walmart parking lot, a man called, didn't give his name, but gave DeMarco Roy Patterson's address. DeMarco's last stop was a RadioShack, after which he returned to his motel to wait for Doug Thorpe. He didn't see the gray Honda.

Thorpe knocked on DeMarco's motel room door just before sunset. The expression on Thorpe's gaunt face was grim and determined.

"Are you sure you want to do this?" DeMarco asked him again.

"If I wasn't sure, I wouldn't be here," Thorpe said.

"Okay. We'll take my rental car. I don't want to take the risk of someone getting your license plate number."

Thorpe just shrugged.

"You got the guns?" DeMarco asked.

"Yeah. They're in a sack in my truck. A .45 auto and an old .38 revolver. I haven't fired the .38 in thirty years. The last time I fired the .45 was five years ago when I had to put down a deer that got hit by a car."

"Well, get the guns. But take the bullets out. Leave the bullets in your truck."

"What?" Thorpe said.

"I'm not going to take the chance of accidentally killing someone. For that matter, I'm not going to take the chance that you might intentionally kill someone."

Thorpe just looked at DeMarco for a moment than said, "Okay." It was impossible to read the guy. He was obviously angry. Angry at whoever had killed his granddaughter. Angry with DeMarco, who he probably blamed for Sarah's death. Angry at the whole damn world. But aside from anger, DeMarco couldn't detect any other emotion. Thorpe certainly wasn't nervous about what DeMarco was planning.

"The first thing we have to do is see if we're being followed," DeMarco said. "Look for a gray Honda."

"Followed?" Thorpe said.

"Yeah. I think someone's been following me from the day I met with Sarah."

He then told Thorpe what he knew about Logan and Dawkins, and how he'd come to the conclusion that they'd been having him followed. "So start looking behind me to see if you can spot a tail. I'm going to start making a bunch of random turns."

Four random turns later, Thorpe said, "The blue Camry. The guy must have changed cars."

"Yeah, I see him," DeMarco said. He'd spotted the Camry also.

DeMarco stomped on the gas, committed a few minor traffic infractions, made a couple of high-speed turns, and five minutes later said, "I think I lost him," feeling proud of himself.

Thorpe said, "I'm not so sure you lost him, as he just gave up. He figured out that you knew you were being followed, and he didn't see much point in trying to stick with you."

"Hmpf," DeMarco said. He liked his version better.

They arrived at the trailer park where Roy Patterson lived and DeMarco found Patterson's trailer. The once-white siding was covered with grime and mildew, there was a blue tarp on the roof to keep the rain out, and one of the windows was patched with plywood. There was a trash can in front of the trailer—a rusty fifty-five-gallon drum—that appeared to serve no purpose as the ground around the trailer was littered with beer cans. A battered blue Ford pickup squatted in front of Patterson's trailer.

As they were sitting there, the sun went down and the lights came on in Patterson's trailer, as did the lights in the trailers adjacent to his. The mobile homes in the park were less than ten yards apart, and DeMarco could see an overweight woman in the trailer on the right side of Patterson's. She was sitting at a table, shoveling food into her mouth, as she watched television.

"We need to wait for him to leave or for his neighbors to go to bed," DeMarco said.

Thorpe just nodded.

About nine p.m., Patterson—or at least DeMarco thought it was Patterson—emerged from his trailer. According to the information DeMarco had been given Patterson didn't have a wife, but DeMarco didn't know if he lived alone or not. The man he assumed was Patterson was wearing a dark-colored baseball cap and a green letterman's jacket with white sleeves. He got into the blue pickup.

DeMarco followed the pickup to a bar that had a silhouette of a big-busted, long-maned woman on a sign over the door. The bar featured exotic dancers, who turned out to be not so exotic. After Patterson went into the place, DeMarco said, "I'm going to go in for a quick beer to make sure we're following the right guy."

Thorpe grunted. A man of few words—or no words.

The bar was dimly lit and very warm, both conditions necessary to accommodate the dancers: the high temperature kept them from getting chilly as they were almost nude and the dim lighting made it less easy to see what they looked like nude. There was a short, six-stool bar along one wall and behind the bar was a bald-headed behemoth who was probably the establishment's bouncer as well as its bartender. In the center of the room was a small stage with a pole in the middle and a U-shaped bar that ran along the perimeter of the stage, close enough that the most nearsighted customer could get an eyeful. On the stage was a woman in her forties wearing nothing but a G-string and high heels, and her movements seemed to have no connection whatsoever to the music playing. There were seven men seated near the stage, one of them wearing a blue ball cap and a letterman's jacket. The guy was also wearing cowboy boots and the boots had silver toe caps.

DeMarco took a seat to the left of the man he assumed was Patterson so he wouldn't be directly in the guy's line of sight. A moment later, the man stripped off his jacket and placed it on the stool beside him. A sleeveless T-shirt displayed two thick arms—more fat than muscle—covered with red, green, and blue ink. DeMarco took a sip of his beer, used the restroom, and left the bar. When one is on a stakeout, it's always smart to use a restroom when one is available.

"It's him," he said to Thorpe as he got back into the car. "And I'll bet you he sits in that place until it closes or he runs out of money."

For the next three hours, DeMarco and Thorpe sat in DeMarco's car, mostly in silence. In an attempt to make conversation, DeMarco asked Thorpe what John Mahoney had been like as a young man in Vietnam.

"Like most everybody else. He was scared when we were out in the boondocks, but he did his job. He wasn't a coward. He looked out for his buddies. He was a city boy so he didn't really know how to shoot or move through the jungle, but he learned fast. If he hadn't, he would have died right after he got there. When we were back at the base, he drank a lot, smoked dope, and chased what few women there were to chase. He probably got the clap half-a-dozen times. Thank God this was before all the AIDS shit. Anyway, he was a good guy. We got along."

An hour later, DeMarco asked, "What was Sarah like when she was little. Was she always so driven?"

Thorpe smiled slightly. "Sarah was hell on wheels when she was a kid. Hardheaded, mouthy, thought she had all the answers by the time she was twelve. She didn't do all that well in school but it wasn't because she didn't have the brains. If she liked a subject or a teacher, she'd get straight As. But if she didn't like it, she just didn't bother.

"I'll tell you one thing, though: Sarah could cast a fly. I started taking her fishing with me when she was about five, and by the time she was sixteen, she was better than me—and I'm pretty darn good. I remember once—" Then his voice broke and he looked away from DeMarco and out the car window so DeMarco couldn't see the tears welling up in his eyes. "I don't want to talk about Sarah," he said.

DeMarco had a sudden image of Sarah as a little girl of five— butterscotch curls, skinny legs, jabbering nonstop as she stood beside her tall grandfather fishing—and he could almost understand how miserable Doug Thorpe felt.

MIKE LAWSON

Patterson left the bar a little after midnight. DeMarco had parked his car next to Patterson's pickup and he was hoping they'd be able to take Patterson before he got into his vehicle. But Patterson was followed out of the bar by another guy, and they bullshitted with each other as Patterson walked over to his truck and got inside. Patterson didn't notice—or was too drunk to notice—the two men sitting in the car next to his.

"Shit," DeMarco said.

They followed Patterson back to the trailer park and DeMarco was glad that a cop wasn't nearby. Patterson drove like a man who would blow two thousand on the Breathalyzer. Patterson pulled into the trailer park and DeMarco was relieved to see that the lights were out in all the trailers except for one at the far end of the park.

"Let's do this," DeMarco said. As Patterson was trying to extract himself from his vehicle, DeMarco pulled the ski mask down over his face and Thorpe did the same, then DeMarco gunned the engine and pulled his car in right behind Patterson's truck. DeMarco and Thorpe got out of DeMarco's car quickly and ran toward Patterson: two masked men pointing guns.

Patterson said, "Whoa, whoa," backing up rapidly as DeMarco and Thorpe came at him, then he stumbled and landed on his back. "Don't hurt me," he said. "Tell Monty I'll get him the money next week."

"Shut the fuck up," DeMarco said. "Now get up. We're going inside your trailer."

"Yeah, but—"

"You don't move in the next two seconds, I'm going to shoot you in the head," DeMarco said.

Patterson got to his feet, pulled keys from his jacket, and struggled to unlock the trailer door. As drunk as he was, he took an inordinate amount of time to get the key into the lock. "Hurry up," DeMarco said. If one of Patterson's neighbors happened to look out a window at one in the morning, the Bismarck cops would be there in the next ten minutes.

Patterson finally got his door open and DeMarco shoved him hard in the back to get him inside. The trailer was a pigsty with unwashed dishes, fast-food cartons, and empty beer cans on every flat surface. There was a galley-like kitchen with a two-burner stove and half-size refrigerator. A frying pan encrusted with burnt eggs was on the stove. Along one wall was a small dining room table that had a bench seat on one side and a single, freestanding folding chair on the other.

"Sit down," DeMarco said, pointing at the folding chair, then he reached into a pocket and turned on the tape recorder he'd purchased at RadioShack.

"What do you guys want?" Patterson said.

"I want to know who was with you the night you roughed up Sarah Johnson."

"Who?" Patterson said—and Doug Thorpe smashed a fist into Patterson's face, knocking him off the chair. Thorpe may have been in his seventies but he could still throw a punch.

"That's enough," DeMarco said to Thorpe.

DeMarco helped Patterson back into the chair. His mouth was bleeding and his eyes were glassy.

"Sarah Johnson was the young woman you and two of your friends assaulted a couple weeks ago in a parking lot. You threatened to rape her."

"Oh, I know who you mean now. We didn't hurt her. We just scared her."

"Who was with you?"

"Who are you guys?"

DeMarco placed the muzzle of the .45 against Patterson's forehead, right over the bridge of his nose. "If you don't answer my question in the next two seconds, I'm going to put a bullet into your brain. I think one of the assholes with you was a guy named Mark Jenkins, the guy who alibied you when the cops came to see you. So I don't really need you and after I kill you, I'll go talk to Jenkins. One. Two."

"Okay! It was Tim Sloan! It was me and Mark and Tim."

"Why did you do it?"

"Because Tim gave me and Mark a hundred bucks. He said he just wanted to scare the girl."

"Why?"

"Tim said she was a big-mouth reporter and was writing shit that was going to cost people their jobs."

"What does Sloan do? Is he involved in natural gas?"

"Tim? He doesn't do anything. He gets a disability check for his back."

"Did someone tell Sloan to assault Sarah?"

"I don't know. He didn't say. Mark and me, we was just having a drink down at Shorty's and Tim comes up to us and says he wants some help making this chick back off. But he didn't say anything about anyone telling him to do it."

"Then where'd he get the two hundred bucks he paid you and your buddy?"

"I don't know. We've both known Tim since high school and he just said it would be fun."

"Fun?" Thorpe said. "Did you say fun?"—and he hit Patterson on the right side of his head with the .38 he was holding and knocked Patterson off the chair again. A trickle of blood was now running down the side of Patterson's neck.

"Goddamnit," DeMarco said to Thorpe. "Knock it off. Once was enough."

Patterson was on the floor moaning, holding a hand over the place where Thorpe had hit him.

"Where does Sloan live?" DeMarco asked.

"Jesus Christ, that hurt," Patterson said.

"Tell me where Sloan lives or I'm going to let him beat you to death."

"Over on the east side of town. He lives with his girlfriend."

"What's the address?"

"Hell, I don't know."

DeMarco again pressed the muzzle of the .45 against the top of Patterson's head.

"What's Sloan's address?" DeMarco said.

"I'm telling you, I don't know. I swear to God."

DeMarco believed him. "What's his girlfriend's name?"

"Debbie something. I don't know her last name. I've only met her a couple of times."

"Okay, Roy," DeMarco said, "we're leaving now. But if you call Sloan and he isn't home when I get to his place then I'm going to come back here and kill you. Do you understand? You call Sloan, you better get in that piece of shit you drive and just keep driving until you fall off the edge of the earth, because I'll find you."

"Let's go," DeMarco said to Thorpe.

As they were leaving, Patterson said. "Who are you guys?"

"CAA," DeMarco said.

"CIA?" Patterson said.

"CAA. Citizens Against Assholes."

———◆———

Back in DeMarco's rental car, DeMarco said, "It's too late now, but tomorrow I'll call Mahoney and have him get Sloan's address."

"Okay," Thorpe said.

"You got a place to stay tonight?"

"I'll find something."

"You don't need to do that. There are two beds in my motel room. Stay with me."

DeMarco actually wanted Thorpe to stay with him because he was afraid Thorpe might go back to Patterson's trailer and beat him to death.

20

DeMarco had set the alarm for six a.m. and that's when he woke up—
even though getting up at that time of day almost killed him. Nobody
—not farmers, fishermen, or even roosters—should be required to rise
at such an ungodly hour. He used the bathroom, then noticed that
Thorpe's bed was empty. "Goddamnit," he muttered.

He woke up so early because he wanted to get Tim Sloan's address as
soon as possible and again decided to let Mahoney use his connections
in D.C. to get what he needed. He knew Mahoney wouldn't answer
his phone at seven a.m. EST—Mahoney might not take a call from
the president at seven a.m.—but Mahoney's secretary would already
be at her desk.

"Mavis, tell the boss I need an address for a guy named Tim Sloan
who lives on the east side of Bismarck, North Dakota. He gets some
kind of disability check for his back so maybe he's got a file with Social
Security or the VA. He's got a girlfriend named Debbie. The only other
thing I know about him is he went to high school with a full-blown
asshole named Roy Patterson. Tell Mahoney I also need to know if
Sloan has any sort of connection to a man named Leonard Curtis, another man named Leslie William Logan, and a woman named Marjorie

Dawkins. Did you get all that? Tell him I need the information right away."

DeMarco took a shower wondering the whole time where Thorpe could be. He didn't have a cell phone number for Thorpe; he didn't know if Thorpe even owned a cell phone. All he could do was pray that Thorpe hadn't killed Patterson. He dressed and thought briefly about shaving, then said screw it. As long as he was acting like a thug he might as well look like one.

DeMarco stepped outside the motel room and was relieved to see Thorpe's pickup parked where it had been the night before. He went back into the motel room and scratched out a note for Thorpe to call him and placed the note under a windshield wiper on Thorpe's truck. A block from the motel was a diner that was open twenty-four hours a day and DeMarco decided to go there and get a cup of coffee. He desperately needed coffee; his heart was barely pumping blood because of the hour.

When he walked into the diner, he saw Thorpe sitting alone in a booth. DeMarco sat across from him, and said, "Couldn't you sleep?"

"No. Did you call John?"

"No, but I talked to his secretary and she'll get to him. I don't know who Mahoney's using to get information from, but last time I got what I needed in a couple of hours."

DeMarco had breakfast—a cholesterol-laden plate of eggs, hash browns, and link sausages—and felt almost human by the time he was finished. Thorpe hardly spoke while DeMarco was eating. He just stared out the window at the parking lot. At one point he did say, "I can't imagine how people can live in a place like this."

"A place like what?" DeMarco said.

"An ugly city. I've lived next to a Montana river my whole life. I couldn't imagine living anywhere else."

DeMarco and Thorpe walked back to the motel. They couldn't really do anything until Mahoney's guy called him back. DeMarco thought briefly about calling Agent Westerberg to see if she'd learned anything more, then decided not to. He certainly had no intention of telling her what he'd been doing. Not at this point.

At eight a.m., DeMarco's phone rang. He didn't recognize the number on the caller ID, just saw that it was a 202 area code.

"Hello," DeMarco said.

"I have Tim Sloan's address for you," a soft-spoken man said. DeMarco wondered what organization employed the man: FBI, IRS, Justice? Hell, he could be CIA or NSA.

"Hang on," DeMarco said. "Let me get a pen and paper."

The guy rattled off Sloan's address and DeMarco wrote it down.

"Did you find out if Sloan had any connection to—"

"He was married to Leslie William Logan's sister for four years. She divorced him three years ago. Sloan's not married now. I couldn't find any connection between Sloan and Dawkins or Curtis."

"You gave me what I needed, masked man. I thank you."

———◆◆◆———

Marjorie was not happy. Last night Heckler had informed her that Doug Thorpe, Sarah's grandfather, came to DeMarco's motel. Then DeMarco and Thorpe got into DeMarco's car and DeMarco deliberately shook Heckler. This meant three things: One, DeMarco now knew he was being followed. Two, he most likely knew that whoever was following him worked for her and Bill Logan. And three, since DeMarco shook the tail, he was probably up to something sneaky.

Marjorie couldn't think of anything DeMarco could do to cause them a problem but it was worrisome that he was still in Bismarck, running around.

She called Heckler. "What he's doing now?"

"He just had breakfast with Thorpe. Last night, after he lost me, the only thing I could do was go back to his motel and wait for him. DeMarco returned to the motel about two in the morning and Thorpe spent the night in his room. This morning, Thorpe left the motel before five and went to a restaurant, and DeMarco joined him an hour or so later. DeMarco and Thorpe are back at the motel now. I've had about two hours of sleep, Marjorie. I can't keep this up."

"Well, you're gonna have to keep it up. Or hire someone to help you."

"If I can get DeMarco's phone number," Heckler said, "and find out the type of cell phone he uses, maybe Gordy can download that spyware shit onto his phone so I can use GPS to track him."

"Gordy's not here this week," Marjorie said. "He went to some video game conference in Vegas." She was pissed at Gordy. Technically, Gordy didn't work for her—he was an independent businessman, not her employee—but as she and Bill were his best paying customers, she was annoyed that he hadn't told her in advance that he was going to Vegas. Instead, he'd just left a message on Marjorie's office answering machine saying he'd be gone for a few days and wasn't sure when he'd return. She was going to ring his dope-smoking neck when he got back.

"Anyway," she said to Heckler, "I don't want to just know *where* DeMarco is. I want to know what he's doing."

"Well, shit," Heckler said.

"Yeah. So you do whatever you gotta do to stick with him," Marjorie said and hung up.

Goddamnit, what the hell was DeMarco up to? And why was Johnson's granddad hanging out with him?

She wondered, for about two seconds, if she should make Bill contact Murdock and tell Murdock to make DeMarco disappear. No murder, no accident, DeMarco just vanishes. Then she immediately decided it would too risky to do something to DeMarco. He claimed to have his own FBI agent assigned to the case and Heckler had seen him with a woman packing a gun who looked like a cop. So DeMarco was probably telling the truth about the FBI being involved in Johnson's death and if something happened to him, they might end up with an entire FBI task force in Bismarck.

No, she wouldn't do anything and she wouldn't panic. There was no reason to panic. Neither DeMarco nor the FBI would find anything because there wasn't anything to find. Her biggest fear at this point was still Bill. Bill made her nervous. Bill was barely holding it together. When they had to deal with the swing judge, Wainwright, six years ago, Bill went through a period where he couldn't sleep and drank too much, but he eventually got over it. The same thing was happening again, but he seemed even worse this time. Maybe she'd make him go on vacation. He could go sit on a beach in Hawaii, drink mai tais, and chase after sluts.

Yeah, it might be smart to get Bill out of town

DeMarco told Thorpe what he'd learned from Mahoney's guy, that Tim Sloan was Logan's ex-brother-in-law.

"So I guess we go see Sloan next," Thorpe said.

"No," DeMarco said. "I mean, we don't go see him like we saw Patterson. Beating information out of Patterson was okay as it led us to Sloan and now I know Sloan's working for Logan."

"But you don't know for sure," Thorpe said.

"I know," DeMarco insisted. "That's the only thing that makes sense. But I don't want a forced confession out of Sloan. In the long run, that won't do any good. What I want is for Sloan to agree to testify against Logan in court. Then I'll have something I can use to squeeze Logan."

"You won't have shit," Thorpe said. "Even if Sloan can be forced to testify, all you'll get is him saying that Logan paid him and his pals to scare Sarah. Since they didn't really hurt her, it's not like you can put Logan in jail for years."

"I don't know what kind of prison sentence you can get for threatening to kill someone, but whatever it is, it'll be something."

"So what's the plan?"

"I'm going to make my FBI agent arrest Sloan. But I need to talk to her alone. You can't be there."

Before Thorpe could debate the issue, DeMarco said, "You should head back to Montana. I'll give you a call after I meet with the FBI and Sloan and let you know what happened. Do you have a cell phone?"

"Yeah, got one in my truck for emergencies."

"Good. Write down the number, and I'll call you later."

"Okay, but I'm not leaving, DeMarco, until after I see what happens with Sloan."

DeMarco nodded. He should have known that. "All right. And if you want to save the expense of a room you can stay in my room again tonight."

Thorpe laughed, although it didn't sound like a laugh. "DeMarco, the least of my worries is money. I'm the beneficiary of Sarah's will. I could buy that motel where we're staying. One of the things I need to do is have my will changed. My will says everything I've got goes to Sarah. With her dead, the goddamn state of Montana will get the money."

"So call a lawyer while you're waiting to hear from me and get a new will drawn up."

"Yeah, but who do I leave all that money to?" Thorpe asked.

21

Agent Bertha Westerberg was not amused. DeMarco figured the only reason she didn't take out her Glock and pistol whip him was that they were in a Starbucks and there were a dozen people nearby.

He'd called her and told her that he had information that would advance the case against Bill Logan and asked her to meet him. When she arrived at the coffee shop, he said, "You told me the cops suspected a guy named Roy Patterson of being one of the people who assaulted Sarah. I have Patterson on tape admitting that he was hired by a man named Tim Sloan, and Sloan is Bill Logan's ex-brother-in-law."

"You what?" she said. "How did you . . . Let me hear the tape."

DeMarco took his RadioShack recorder from a pocket and hit PLAY—and a moment later Westerberg went berserk. "Jesus Christ! I should arrest you right now. You attacked a man with a gun, hit him at least twice, and threatened to kill him. I'm not even sure how many crimes you've committed. And who was with you?"

"Nobody was with me," DeMarco said. He was not about to get Thorpe in trouble.

"I could hear you talking to someone other than Patterson on that tape," Westerberg said.

"Never mind what you heard. The big thing is, I got the guy on tape admitting Sloan paid him to assault Sarah. What we need to do next is go see Sloan and get him to admit that Logan paid him, except with Sloan I won't point a gun at him. I won't have to use a gun because I'll have you with me."

Since Westerberg didn't appear to know what to say—her lips were moving but no words were coming out—DeMarco kept talking, "The other thing is, if you play with that recording a bit, all you'll hear is Patterson confessing. I mean, we can probably fix it so you won't hear me telling him I'm going to shoot him."

"Good Lord," Westerberg muttered.

It took some time for DeMarco to convince Westerberg to go along with his plan. She didn't like it at all but could see the logic in it, and since she didn't have a better idea, she finally agreed. She knew that if she didn't make progress on the case, she'd never get Mahoney's big boot off her boss's neck. It took him a while longer to convince her to let him go with her when she interviewed Sloan. DeMarco basically said that it was his football—meaning the recording—and she couldn't play with his football unless she let him join her team.

They drove in Westerberg's car to Sloan's place in silence. He could see that Westerberg was still fretting over the legal position he'd put her in. Tough shit. He'd noticed that she was wearing different clothes today: she had on the jacket from the suit she'd been wearing the night he met her, but was wearing a T-shirt under the jacket and tight-fitting jeans that looked good on her long legs. It appeared that she'd found time to go shopping. DeMarco was wearing the one suit he'd brought with him to Montana and a white dress shirt but no tie. He was wearing the suit because the FBI guys he'd seen always wore suits.

Sloan lived on the second floor of a dilapidated apartment building. Westerberg knocked hard on the door, hammering on it with her fist like she was trying to wake the dead. They finally heard someone inside the apartment say, "Christ, hold on, I'm coming." An emaciated blonde in her thirties—one who looked as if she might enjoy a bowl of crystal meth for breakfast—finally opened the door.

Westerberg held up her identification and said, "FBI. We're here to see Tim Sloan."

"What?" the woman said.

"Let us in," Westerberg said.

"What?" the woman said again.

Westerberg pushed past the woman without waiting for an invitation, and said, "Where's Sloan?"

At that moment a man walked out of a bedroom wearing faded jeans with a rip in one knee and a soiled white T-shirt. He was barefoot. Like his girlfriend he was short and skinny and his dark hair was long and disheveled, springing away from his head in all directions. His mouth hung open and his eyes seemed to have a hard time focusing. He didn't look like the brightest guy in the world.

"Mr. Sloan," Westerberg said, "I'm arresting you for assaulting Sarah Johnson."

"What?" Sloan said—and DeMarco was starting to wonder if these two people had another word in their vocabulary.

Westerberg marched over to Sloan and said, "Turn around." When he just stood there, still confused, she grabbed his left arm, spun him around, and slapped the cuffs on him. "Let's go," she said.

Sloan's brain finally caught up to what was happening to him. "Can I put my shoes on?" he said.

Before Westerberg could answer, DeMarco said, "No. They'll give you flip-flops at the jail." It was May; his feet weren't going to freeze.

They led Sloan out to Westerberg's car and put him in the backseat. On their way to the Bismarck Police Department on Ninth

Street—Westerberg's temporary headquarters—Sloan asked several times: "What's going on? Why are you guys doing this?" Westerberg and DeMarco pointedly ignored the questions, saying nothing, letting Sloan's anxiety increase on the short ride to the station.

They marched Sloan into the police station, DeMarco gripping his upper arm. The sergeant at the desk in the lobby appeared to know Westerberg and when she told him she needed to use an interview room, he didn't ask why, he simply directed her to one. Inside the interview room, Westerberg removed the handcuffs from Sloan's thin wrists and pointed him to a chair on one side of a scarred wooden table. She and DeMarco took seats across from him.

Sloan said, "I want to know what's . . ."

Westerberg said, "I'm Special Agent Westerberg of the Federal Bureau of Investigation and . . ."

"FBI?" Sloan said.

". . . and this is DeMarco." That was good, DeMarco thought: she didn't say that DeMarco was FBI—he was just DeMarco.

"As I told you at your apartment," Westerberg continued, "you've been arrested for assaulting Sarah Johnson on the night of April—"

"Hey, I didn't assault anyone."

"Sloan," DeMarco said, "your buddy, Roy Patterson, gave me a recorded statement that you paid him and another moron named Mark Jenkins two hundred bucks to rough up Sarah. You knocked her to the ground. You touched her in inappropriate places. You threatened to rape her and kill her—and Patterson has testified that you did all those things. You're looking at five years in prison."

DeMarco had made up the number. He didn't know how long Sloan would serve but he doubted it would be that long. But Sloan didn't know that.

"I think I need a lawyer," Sloan said.

Before Westerberg could answer, DeMarco said, "You definitely need a lawyer. But we might cut you a break if you admit that Bill Logan paid you to assault Johnson."

"What kind of break?"

Westerberg said, "You're in no position to negotiate, Mr. Sloan. All I can say is that we want Logan more than we want you, so it's possible you won't serve time if you cooperate."

"I don't know. I think I should talk to a—"

"Do you want to spend five years in prison?" DeMarco said. "And do you think Logan wouldn't give you up if he was in your position?"

"He didn't pay me to *assault* her," Sloan said. "You keep using that word. He told me not to hurt her. He just said to scare her, and that's all I did."

"It was an assault," DeMarco said, and took out his handy-dandy RadioShack recorder. "Now I'm tired of fucking with you. I want you to say, for the record, that Logan paid you to assault Sarah Johnson. If you don't, you're going to be formally charged and you'll spend tonight in a cell. Tomorrow you'll be arraigned and released on bail. That is, you'll be released if you have money for the bondsman. Do you have five or ten grand in cash?"

"No," Sloan said. "I'm flat broke."

"I want you to say: Bill Logan paid me to assault Sarah Johnson," DeMarco said. He hit RECORD and held the recorder near Sloan's mouth. After swallowing a couple of times, Sloan said, "Bill Logan paid me to assault Sarah Johnson."

"How much did he pay you?" DeMarco asked.

"Five hundred. I gave a hundred each to Roy and Mark."

"That's Roy Patterson and Mark Jenkins. Is that right?" DeMarco said.

"Yeah," Sloan said.

"And why did Logan pay you to assault Ms. Johnson?"

"He said she was causing him problems by writing a bunch of lies about his business or something. I guess she was a reporter."

"Did you kill Sarah Johnson for Bill Logan?"

"What!" Sloan screamed. "I didn't kill anybody."

DeMarco hit the STOP button on the recorder. "Okay," he said. "Because you've been cooperative, we're not going to charge you. But if at a later date you retract the statement you made today or refuse to testify against Logan, you're going away for five years. And don't even think about calling Logan. We're going to arrest him shortly and if he's not where he's supposed to be, I'm going to assume you called him and then we'll haul you back here and charge you. Now get out of here."

"How am I supposed to get back home?"

"I don't know and I don't care." DeMarco said.

"It's too far to walk, plus I don't have any shoes."

"Tough shit," DeMarco said.

"And I don't have any money to catch a cab or a bus."

"Once again, tough shit," DeMarco said.

"Call your girlfriend," Westerberg said, "and have her come and pick you up."

"I could, but her license has been suspended," Sloan said.

"Get out of here. Now," DeMarco said, and Sloan shuffled out of the room.

"Well, I thought that went pretty well," DeMarco said to Westerberg.

"I'm going to lose my job," Westerberg said.

"Nah. Mahoney won't let them fire you. And if we get the people who killed Sarah, you'll probably get promoted."

"I don't know what DeMarco's up to," Heckler said to Marjorie.

Marjorie was still in the office, she'd been there all day, working on a dozen different issues, but the whole time she'd been working she'd been thinking about DeMarco and her partner.

"This morning I followed DeMarco from his motel to a Starbucks where he met up with that tough-looking gal," Heckler said, "the one I told you about with a gun who looks like a cop. And by the way, DeMarco didn't do anything to shake a tail like he did last night. I changed cars so if he was looking for the car I was driving last night, he wouldn't see it."

"The woman he's with is probably FBI," Marjorie said. "DeMarco told me and Bill he had an FBI agent working on Johnson's murder."

"FBI?" Heckler said.

"Yeah," Marjorie said. She could tell by the sound of Heckler's voice that he didn't like the idea of following an FBI agent. "Anyway, continue with what you were saying. What happened after DeMarco met her at Starbucks?"

"They drove in her car to an apartment building on the east side, and a few minutes later they came out with a guy in handcuffs."

"So who was he?" Marjorie asked.

"I don't know. Some little raggedy-ass doofus who wasn't wearing shoes. He looked like a homeless guy."

"A homeless guy?"

"Yeah. Anyway, they took him to the Bismarck police station on Ninth and DeMarco and the gal have been inside the station the last half an hour. Maybe they're interrogating him, but I have no way to know."

"A homeless guy?" Marjorie said again. "But they picked him up from an apartment building?"

"Maybe he was loitering around the building, sleeping in a stairwell or something. I don't know."

Then Marjorie had a horrible thought: What if the homeless guy was a witness to Johnson's murder? What if he'd seen Murdock leave Johnson's house after he killed her? That would not be good. But if he were a witness, why would they arrest him? None of this made sense. "Find out who he is, Heckler, but stick with DeMarco."

A moment after she'd disconnected the call with Heckler, Bill walked into the office. He'd shown up for work at ten that morning, looking hungover and as if he hadn't slept much the night before. To give him something to do, she'd sent him over to the state capitol to take the temperature on a bill that was winding its way through the senate. She was pretty sure the bill would pass—which was what Curtis wanted—and she'd told Bill to go see if it looked like they still had the votes.

"How are you doing?" she asked him.

"Fine," he said. "And everything's on track with the bill."

He went on to tell Marjorie who he'd spoken to over at the capitol and the number of votes it looked like they had for the bill. He seemed to be okay—not all mopey and listless like he'd been this morning—and from what he was saying it sounded as if he did his job the way he was supposed to. Still, making him take a vacation might be the best thing for both of them right now.

About five minutes after he spoke to Marjorie, Heckler watched the raggedy-looking barefoot guy come out of the police station. He stood on the curb, hopping from one foot to another like his feet were cold on the concrete. He appeared to be waiting for someone. A few minutes later an old Mazda sedan with a dent in the left front fender, driven by a woman with wild-looking blond hair, pulled up next to where he was standing and he got into the car. Heckler jotted down the license plate number.

Heckler called a guy he used in the DMV to find out who the car was registered to, but his DMV guy didn't answer his phone. Heckler left a voice message giving the license plate number, said he pay the usual amount, and asked the guy to get back to him as soon as possible.

A short time later, DeMarco and the good-looking FBI agent came out of the police station and got into the agent's car. Heckler let them get a one block lead on him before he pulled out of his parking place. Marjorie would be pissed if he lost DeMarco but he didn't care. He didn't like the idea of following an FBI agent at all.

———— ◆◆◆ ————

DeMarco and Westerberg drove to Logan's house.

"Nice place," Westerberg said.

"Yeah, crime pays," DeMarco said. DeMarco rang the doorbell a couple of times but no one came to the door. "He's probably at his office," DeMarco said.

Half an hour later, they were parked half a block from the strip mall where Logan and Dawkins had their office. "That's his Porsche," De-Marco said, "so he's there, but I don't want to talk to him in front of his partner. She's sharp, and she struck me as being a lot tougher than Logan. I think if we talk to him with her there, she'll insist that he lawyer up immediately. Let's wait until she leaves."

"Yeah, all right," Westerberg said.

———— ◆◆◆ ————

Marjorie's phone rang and she saw it was Heckler calling. She didn't want to talk to Heckler with Bill close enough to hear, although Bill was on the phone. She told Heckler to hold on a minute, and then made a gesture at Bill that she was going outside for a smoke. Bill shook his head, meaning: *That's bad for you.*

"Now what?" she asked Heckler.

"Well, if you look across the street, about half a block north, you'll see a dark blue Taurus. DeMarco and the FBI lady are in the Taurus."

"Goddamnit. How long have they been there?"

"They just got here. After they left the police station they drove to Logan's house—"

"Aw, shit."

"Yeah. They knocked on the door and when nobody answered they came here."

What in the hell did they want with Bill?

"Did you find out who the homeless guy was?" Marjorie asked.

"Not yet. I'm waiting for a call back on him."

"Call me when you know something but stick with DeMarco," Marjorie said.

Marjorie went back inside the office. She looked over at Bill. He was still on the phone. She didn't know what to do next. It was apparent that DeMarco and his pet FBI agent wanted to see Bill, and she hated the idea of them talking to him without her being present. But she had things to do this afternoon, and she couldn't stay glued to Bill's side twenty-four hours a day.

She had to pick up Bobby from school and take him to the orthodontist. Normally her husband would have picked up Bobby, but she'd given Dick permission to play golf this afternoon with some of his buddies who were just as useless as him. She could call him at the golf course and make him go get Bobby, but it might take him half an hour to get back to the clubhouse, then another half hour to get to the school. She didn't want her son hanging around outside the school by himself for an hour. There were too many twisted creeps out there who preyed on kids.

Bill was still on the phone and she heard him say, "I'll see you about seven." She wondered if he was making a date. She made an impatient gesture for him to get off the phone, and he did, saying "Honey, I gotta go now, but I'll see you tonight. What's up?" he said to Marjorie.

"You need to listen to me, Bill. DeMarco's parked outside, just down the street, and he's with a woman who's probably FBI. Heckler said DeMarco went to your place today and knocked on your door, and when he found out you weren't home, he came here. So I think he's waiting for you."

"Aw, shit," Bill said. "What do I—"

"Listen to me! If he tries to talk to you, you tell him to take a hike. If the woman tries to talk to you, even if she's a cop, you tell her to take a hike. If she arrests you—"

"Arrests me!"

"I'm just saying, if she arrests you, don't say anything. You ask for a lawyer, then you call me. Got it?"

"Yeah, but why would she arrest me?"

"I don't know. I can't imagine that she would, but I can't be sure. Most likely she just wants to question you, but like I said, if she or DeMarco tries, you tell 'em to go to hell. You got it?"

"Yeah."

"I'm counting on you to hold it together, Bill. Now I gotta go, but I'll call you later."

God, she hated to leave; Bill looked like he was going to be sick.

DeMarco watched Dawkins drive off in a big black Jeep Cherokee. She looked too small to be driving a car that size. "I think we should wait until Logan leaves the office in case she comes back," he said to Westerberg.

"Yeah, all right, but I have to use the restroom. My bladder's about to burst."

"So go into Subway. They'll have a restroom. But make it quick."

He could see that Westerberg was about to snap at him, but then she didn't, and just left the car. While Westerberg was relieving herself, DeMarco called Thorpe and gave him an update on where things stood. He was terrified that if he didn't make progress on the case that Thorpe was going to do something on his own to avenge Sarah—like track down Tim Sloan and shoot the man.

Westerberg returned from Subway with a big chocolate chip cookie; she was kind enough to bring one for DeMarco. As they sat munching their cookies, waiting for Logan to leave his office, DeMarco told her what he wanted to do next. He was pleased Westerberg agreed; Westerberg was more of a pragmatist than he'd expected. An hour later, Logan left his office, got into his Porsche, and they followed him to a bar a half mile away.

They parked next to Logan's Porsche and DeMarco said, "I think it would be best if I talked to Logan by myself. I mean, maybe it would be best for your career. You just sit off to one side and look like a pissed-off fed, and when I signal, you call the cops." Westerberg nodded.

Logan was sitting at the bar drinking what looked like scotch. DeMarco walked up to him with Westerberg at his side, and said, "Bill, let's you and me go sit in a booth and talk. Oh, this is FBI Agent Westerberg, by the way. She's going to wait until we're finished talking before she arrests you."

Logan surprised DeMarco by smiling at him. "Nice to meet you, Agent, but I don't think you're going to arrest me for anything. I haven't committed any crimes. So I'm just going to finish my drink, then I'm going to go home, take a shower and shave, and then I'm meeting a nice-looking young woman for dinner."

"Logan," Westerberg said, "I have all I need at this moment to arrest you for the assault committed on Sarah Johnson on April twenty-fifth. I'll drag you out of here in handcuffs if you don't march over to that booth right now, and listen to what DeMarco has to say."

"You're bluffing," he said—but he wasn't smiling anymore.

"Do I look like I'm bluffing?" Westerberg said, and DeMarco had to admit that she did a pretty good impression of a badass federal agent—and maybe that's because she really was a badass federal agent.

Logan hesitated a moment, then said, "Okay," and picked up his drink and stood.

DeMarco waved a hand at the bartender and said, "How 'bout bringing a Stoli martini over to that table. Easy on the vermouth. Would you like anything, Agent?"

"No," Westerberg said, glaring at DeMarco. Well, hell, he thought: she might have some requirement not to drink on duty but he certainly didn't. In fact, drinking on duty was pretty much standard operating procedure when working for Mahoney.

Westerberg took Logan's seat at the bar and DeMarco joined Logan in the booth.

"I'm going to play you a recording first," DeMarco said, "so you can get over the notion that anyone's bluffing about anything. The man speaking is your buddy, Tim Sloan."

"Tim?" Logan said. Before Logan could ask why his former brother-in-law would be making a recording, DeMarco hit PLAY.

"Bill Logan paid me to assault Sarah Johnson."

"How much did he pay you?"

"Five hundred bucks. I gave a hundred each to Roy and Mark."

"That's Roy Patterson and Mark Jenkins. Is that right?"

"Yeah."

"And why did Logan pay you to assault Ms. Johnson?"

"He just said she was causing him problems by writing a bunch of lies about his business or something. I guess she was a reporter."

"Did you kill Sarah Johnson for Bill Logan?"

DeMarco hit the STOP button. "Okay, let me tell you where things stand right now, Bill." Logan looked stunned, like he'd just been told that he had cancer.

Before DeMarco could speak, the bartender placed DeMarco's martini on the table. DeMarco thanked the bartender and took a sip. "That hits the spot. Now where were we? Oh, yeah, I was about to tell you how I'm going to destroy your life."

"Sloan's lying," Logan said, finally reacting to the recording.

DeMarco laughed. "Don't even try to go there, Bill. First, you're going to be convicted for paying Sloan and two other knuckleheads to assault Sarah. That's a slam dunk. I got Patterson to give me Sloan and you just heard Sloan give you up, and you know Sloan was telling the truth. The next thing I've got is a lawyer over in Great Falls who will testify that you fixed a case so her son—who's now dead—would get off on a robbery-assault charge in return for her dropping a lawsuit against Curtis. I'm not sure how that will play with a jury, but the lawyer in Great Falls is just one brick in the wall."

"Brick in the wall?" Logan said.

"You remember what I told you when I met you and your partner in your office the other day? You remember me saying how you were no longer up against a girl with a laptop? You're now dealing with the Federal Bureau of Investigation, Bill. I'm talking about an agency that has Justice Department lawyers coming out of its ass, an agency that can get all the warrants it wants.

"Agent Westerberg and her ten thousand friends at the Bureau are now reading Sarah's blog—a blog that up until now only a few people ever bothered to read. Federal agents are going to investigate every accusation Sarah made and start scaring the shit out of the politicians you bribed. And what this all means is that the lawyer in Great Falls won't be the only person testifying against you. Like I said, she's just one brick in the wall."

Logan started to say something, but DeMarco held up a hand.

"I'm not finished. Why did you go to Denver the week before Sarah was killed?"

———◆◆◆———

Marjorie walked out of the orthodontist's office, Bobby trailing along behind her. She was thinking about how Bobby's braces were going to cost over eight grand—the damn dentist was a thief!—when her phone rang. It was Heckler.

"Go get in the car," she told Bobby. "What is it now?" she said to Heckler.

"The guy who wasn't wearing shoes?" Heckler said. "The guy I thought was a homeless guy? His name is Tim Sloan. After he left the police station a woman picked him up and I got the plate number on the car she was driving. Then I called a pal at the DMV and he just got back to me a little while ago. He said the car was registered to Sloan, then he emailed me Sloan's driver's license photo. It was a bad photo but I'm ninety percent sure it was the barefoot guy."

"Tim Sloan?" Marjorie said. Then it clicked. "Aw, shit," she said. Sloan was Bill's idiot ex-brother-in-law, the guy Bill paid to try to scare Sarah Johnson.

"What's DeMarco doing now?" Marjorie asked.

"I was just getting to that," Heckler said. "Right now he and his FBI pal are sitting in a bar with Logan. They followed him after he left your office."

"Goddamnit!" Marjorie screamed—and her son inside the car looked at her with big eyes. She immediately disconnected the call with Heckler and called Bill's cell phone. She had known this might happen and she wanted to make sure Bill wasn't talking to DeMarco. But Bill's cell phone rang only twice then went to voice mail. "Call me. Now!" she screamed into the phone.

DeMarco had just said "Why did you go to Denver the week before Sarah was killed?" when Logan's cell phone rang.

"Don't answer that," DeMarco said. "Why did you go to Denver, Bill?"

"I'm not going to answer that question without an attorney present."

"Well, I'll tell you why you went. You went there to hire somebody to kill Sarah. Which brings me back to the FBI. What the FBI is also doing right now is looking at suspected contract killers who operate out of Denver. They're looking at passenger manifests to see if any of these guys took a trip to Bismarck. They're looking at credit card records to see if any of them slept or ate in Bismarck. The other thing they're looking into is a trip you took to Denver six years ago. So far they haven't found anybody connected to you that was murdered at that time, so now they're looking at folks who died under mysterious circumstances. It's just amazing what the largest federal law enforcement agency in the country can do when it sets its mind to it."

Logan's cell phone rang again. "Don't answer that," DeMarco said.

"I'm leaving," Logan said.

"No, you're not," DeMarco said. "If you don't agree to cooperate right now, Agent Westerberg is going to arrest you for assaulting Sarah. Actually, she's going to call the Bismarck cops and have them arrest you. But I'm going to give you a chance. I want two things from you. I want you to confess that your partner and Curtis were involved in a conspiracy to kill Sarah and I want the name of the killer. The second thing I want is for you to spend the next several days with Agent

Westerberg and tell her all the things you've done to undermine the political system for Leonard Curtis."

"I'm not going to do either of those things," Logan said. "And I had nothing to do with Johnson's death."

"Okay, have it your way," DeMarco said. Then he yelled over to Westerberg, "Make the call." To Logan, he said, "While we're waiting for the cops to get here—"

Logan's cell phone rang again.

"Don't answer that," DeMarco said. "While we're waiting for the cops to get here, I want you to think about something. You're going to be tossed into a cell tonight, arraigned tomorrow, and then given bail. In other words, you're going to be back on the street tomorrow where your buddy Curtis can find you. If Curtis was willing to have Sarah killed when she didn't have any evidence that could hurt him, what do you think he might do to a guy like you who can actually cause him some damage?"

⸺

Westerberg and DeMarco followed the Bismarck squad car containing Logan to the police station, and Westerberg went inside to assist the local cops. DeMarco returned to his car and drove until he spotted Famous Dave's Bar-B-Que. He was starving. The only thing he'd eaten since breakfast was the chocolate chip cookie that Westerberg had given him.

Before going inside the restaurant, he called Thorpe again and told him that Logan was in jail. "You need to go home, Doug. I'm going to get these guys. I'm not leaving Bismarck until I do, and right now there isn't anything you can do. "

Thorpe didn't say anything for a moment. "Okay. But I'm telling you right now, DeMarco, if all that happens is that Logan spends a couple months in jail, that's not going to be good enough for me. I want the guy who killed her. Somebody has to pay."

"Somebody will pay, Doug. That's a promise. I'll keep calling to tell you what's going on. Now go home. And I'm sorry, but I probably won't make it for Sarah's funeral."

———————◆———————

It was ten p.m. and Marjorie was getting ready for bed. She usually went to bed early because she was an early riser. And God help Dick and the boys if they made a bunch of noise and kept her up. She was dressed in an old flannel nightgown that was ten years old and wash-faded, but she couldn't bring herself to throw it away because it was her favorite nightgown. She was brushing her teeth when her cell phone rang.

She didn't recognize the number on the caller ID, only that it was a Bismarck area code. She thought briefly about ignoring the call but since she hadn't heard from Bill in the last five hours, and after calling him a dozen times, she decided to take the call.

"Hello," she said.

"It's me," Bill said.

"Where in the hell have you been? Why haven't you returned my calls?"

"Shut up. This phone is probably being monitored. I'm in jail. I was arrested for the assault on Sarah Johnson. They fingerprinted me, took mug shots, and generally just fucked with me. This is the first chance I had to call. I'm being arraigned at nine a.m. tomorrow. You need to get me a lawyer and get that lawyer down here to see me right now."

"Okay, but don't you say a goddamn thing to anybody, not to the cops and not to the guys you're in a cell with, either."

"Yeah, I've seen the movies, too, Marge. Get me a lawyer."

"You just keep your mouth shut," she said, but Bill had already hung up.

She thought for a minute. She and Bill didn't work with attorneys who represented common criminals. The lawyers they worked with dealt with property and business issues. They knew dozens of lawyers who specialized in mineral rights and environmental law, but she couldn't remember ever using the kind of lawyer that defended thugs who beat people up. Finally she called a woman who was a senior partner in a fair-sized firm in Bismarck; Marjorie was pretty sure she had a couple of criminal lawyers working for her. She was feeling kind of hysterical and almost laughed, thinking "criminal lawyers" was probably an oxymoron.

After she talked to the lawyer, telling her to send the best guy she had down to the jail tonight to talk to Bill, she put on her slippers, grabbed her phone and her cigarettes from her purse, and left the bedroom. She walked through the living room where Dick was sitting on the couch looking at his laptop—probably visiting porn sites. She opened the hall closet and put on a long coat over her nightgown.

"Where are you going?" Dick asked.

"Just outside," Marjorie said.

He knew that meant she was going out for a smoke. She never smoked in the house and never in front of the boys. "You gotta knock that shit off," Dick said as she was walking through the door.

She walked down the driveway and stood on the curb to smoke, hoping none of the neighbors would see her. She'd been thinking about calling Curtis to let him know Bill had been arrested, but in the short distance from the front door to the curb, she realized that would be stupid. There was no point getting Curtis all upset until after she'd talked to Bill and found out what kind of case the cops had against him. Plus, there was nothing Curtis could do tonight, anyway. She would have to call him after the arraignment, however. It wouldn't do for Curtis to learn from some other source that Bill had been arrested.

Okay, that was it. She wasn't going to panic and she wasn't going to do anything tonight. She'd get a good night's sleep and deal with all this crap in the morning after she had more information. She didn't know exactly what the cops had on Bill, but she was almost positive that whatever they had, the likelihood of them having anything that could hurt her or Curtis was almost infinitesimal.

She dropped the cigarette butt in the gutter, feeling like a litterbug, and walked back into the house. She put her coat back in the closet and turned to see Dick still sitting on the couch, looking at his laptop. What a pervert. Then, knowing that she was going to have a hard time falling asleep, she said, "Instead of looking at naked ladies on your computer why don't you come to bed and look at a real naked lady?"

"Okay," Dick said, and closed the laptop.

22

Marjorie took a seat in the last row of the courtroom. Bill's arraignment was scheduled for nine, and it was ten minutes before the hour.

She didn't know which lawyer was representing Bill, but he was probably one of the dozen guys wearing suits all bs-ing with each other near the courtroom rail. There were a few other people scattered about the room, mostly women who looked like they might be the mothers or wives of the guys who were going to appear in court that morning.

At that moment, DeMarco and a slim woman with dark red hair walked into the courtroom and sat down at the end of the row where Marjorie was seated. She bet the slim woman was the FBI agent who was working with DeMarco. She was pretty, but as Heckler had said, she was also sort of hard-looking. DeMarco noticed Marjorie at that moment and smiled at her, a big shit-eating grin. Asshole!

Eventually the judge appeared and six or seven guys, including Bill, came out one of the side doors. When Bill's name was called, his lawyer—a man with a really bad comb-over—joined him at the defense table. A clerk rattled off the charges against Bill, Bill pleaded not guilty, and the judge set his bail at fifty grand. Bill's lawyer started to argue that the bail was too high, that Bill was a respected member of the community and . . . The judge told the lawyer to shut up and set a trial date that was six months away.

After Bill was taken away, Marjorie spoke to his lawyer to get his understanding of the case against Bill. When the lawyer said the cops had a recording of a man named Tim Sloan admitting that Bill had paid him to assault Sarah Johnson, Marjorie said, "Are you serious?"

"I'm afraid so," the lawyer said.

Marjorie made sure the lawyer was dealing with all the bail stuff and told him to tell Bill to call her as soon as he was released. As she was leaving the courtroom, she was wondering how that damn DeMarco had found Sloan and forced him to testify against Bill. She pushed open the door to leave—and there was DeMarco, waiting out in the hall, leaning against the wall opposite the door.

"What do you want?" she said to him.

DeMarco smiled. "Your boy looked a little green around the gills to me. Are you sure he's a stand-up guy?"

"A stand-up guy? What the hell does that mean?"

"It's like I told you the day you invited me in for coffee, Marjorie. Eventually, one of you is going to give up the other one, and right now my money's on Logan giving you up. And if the FBI can tie Logan to Sarah's murder, he'll sing like Pavarotti to avoid life in prison. But if you're as bright as I think you are, you'll make the first move."

"Nobody's giving anybody up. And Bill's going to get out from under these false charges against him."

"False charges?" DeMarco echoed and smiled.

"That's right."

"Okay. But I'm telling you, Marjorie, I'm not leaving Bismarck until somebody is in jail for killing Sarah." DeMarco turned to leave, then turned back to her and said, "By the way, you got a guy following me, a fat guy who thinks if he changes cars and wears different hats I won't notice him. I'm going to have my FBI agent arrest him if I see him again."

Marjorie stood there watching as DeMarco walked away. It seemed to her like he was *swaggering*, he was so fucking pleased with himself. She doubted that the FBI could arrest Heckler—she doubted that following somebody was a federal crime—but on the other hand, she didn't want the FBI questioning Heckler, either. If Heckler admitted that she'd paid him to follow Sarah Johnson, that might cause her problems.

Another thought was also beginning to form in the back of her mind—although she wasn't ready to go there yet—and having Heckler watching DeMarco could complicate things later. On the way to her car she called Heckler, told him his services were no longer required, and that he should send her a bill. She almost told him that he ought to use the money to take a class on how to tail people and not get spotted.

———◆◆◆———

Marjorie met Bill an hour later at Denny's. Bill had said he was hungry but when his breakfast arrived, he didn't take more than two bites before he pushed the plate away.

He looked like hell. Hair mussed, unshaven, his clothes all wrinkled like he'd slept in them, which he most likely had. And he smelled, some smell Marjorie couldn't identify. She wondered if it was a generic jail smell—what you get when you put a bunch of men together in a cage.

It took Bill fifteen minutes to tell her everything that had happened, the big news being what she already knew from the lawyer: how his idiot ex-brother-in-law had admitted, on tape, that Bill had paid him to assault Johnson. When Bill said that the FBI knew that he'd been to Denver just days before Johnson was killed and was now looking at suspected contract killers who operated out of that area, Marjorie dug her fingernails into the palm of her hand so hard she was surprised she didn't bleed.

"Now you listen to me, Bill," she said. "They don't have anything. They don't have shit! They don't know why you went to Denver. You just made a trip there and we'll come up with a plausible explanation if we have to. They can't prove you talked to Murdock, and Murdock sure as hell isn't going to tell them. As for these contract killers who operate out of Denver, that sounds like total bullshit to me."

"I don't know. DeMarco looked like he was telling the truth."

"He was bullshitting you! He specializes in bullshit! And they're not even going to convict you on the assault charge."

"The hell they're not," he said.

Marjorie had figured out how to deal with the assault charge on the way from the courthouse to Denny's. "Bill, all they have is your lowlife ex-brother-in-law saying you paid him. It's your word against his. If this thing actually goes to a trial, which I doubt it ever will, they'd never convict you based on that dumb shit saying you ordered him to do anything. The other thing is, if this goes to trial, we'll just buy Sloan off."

"Buy him off?"

"That's right. We'll pay him to retract his statement and take the fall. I mean, how much jail time could he possibly get for *yelling* at some girl? They didn't hurt her. They didn't hit her. And nobody can prove they made any death threats against her because she isn't alive to testify. All they have is the statement a hysterical girl made to the cops after her so-called assault. Sloan wouldn't even get six months, if he gets anything, but most likely he'd get a suspended sentence. But whatever he gets, we'll pay him enough to make it worthwhile. So, like I said, they don't have zip and you're not going to jail."

Bill didn't say anything for a moment, then smiled hesitantly. "I think you're right. I just hadn't thought it through, particularly the part about paying Tim. After they put those handcuffs on me, it was like my brain locked up. But what do we tell Curtis?"

"Yeah, Curtis is the real problem," Marjorie said. "Not DeMarco or the FBI or the Bismarck cops."

"Do you think Curtis might contact Murdock to have me—"

"Oh, hell no! You think we're in that movie *Fargo*? Curtis isn't going to have Murdock come up here and feed you through a wood chipper. Curtis is a businessman and killing you doesn't make sense."

"He thought killing Sarah Johnson made sense."

"No, he didn't. He just got emotional about Johnson, which he doesn't normally do. Curtis isn't going to kill you but what he might do is fire us both. He'll think that we can't be much use to him if we've got the FBI breathing down our necks, watching every move we make. And he'll be right. What I need to do is convince Curtis that this is just a minor speed bump in the road and won't affect his business or our effectiveness."

"So do you want to call him or should we go see him?"

"*I'll* go see Curtis. I think it would be best if I talked to him without you there so he can rant a little about you, and then I'll calm him down. What you need to do is go see Sloan. Don't yell at him, don't hit him. Be calm with him and tell him you don't blame him for talking to the cops, that it was understandable that he was scared, but now what he has to do is look toward the future."

"I can do that," Bill said.

"I know you can."

Bill rubbed a hand over his face. "I don't know about you, Marge, but I don't know what I'd do if Curtis fired me."

"I'm in the same boat you are, Bill. Plus I've got two kids and a husband who's basically no better than a kid. So I'm going to make sure he doesn't fire us."

"What we could do—I mean if push comes to shove—is remind Curtis that we know a lot of things about him that could cause him big problems if we—"

Marjorie slapped her hand on the table. "Are you out of your fucking mind? Don't even think about blackmailing Curtis. You'll get us both killed. Now you go home and take a shower and get some sleep. Then maybe you should go out to the driving range after you've had a nap and smack a few balls around. That always relaxes you. So tomorrow, you go talk to that moron your sister married and I'll go see Curtis, wherever he is."

"Yeah, okay," Bill said, and left the restaurant a few minutes later.

Marjorie ordered another cup of coffee, then decided she wanted a cigarette. That was really becoming a problem: it was like she couldn't think these days if she wasn't smoking. She told the waitress she was just stepping outside for a moment and would bring the coffee cup back.

She left the restaurant, lit a Marlboro, then saw a sign that said she couldn't smoke near the door and the damn ash can was about fifty yards away, next to a bench covered with bird shit. What a bunch of crap. If the scientists were right, people oughta be more worried about all the fossil fuels that guys like Leonard Curtis sucked out of the earth and burned, overheating the entire planet, instead of a little second-hand cigarette smoke.

She took out her phone and called Curtis's office in Houston, having no idea where he might be. She told his secretary that she needed to see him in person, wherever he was, and right away. There was a serious problem, she said, and she didn't want to talk to Curtis about it over the phone.

Half an hour later, she was back at the office, hoping Curtis would call back soon so she could make travel plans. As she waited she thought some more about Bill.

She'd told Bill the truth, that if he handled Tim Sloan correctly, she was sure he wouldn't be convicted for assaulting Johnson. She'd also been telling him the truth when she'd said that it was damn unlikely that the FBI would find Murdock just because Bill had taken a trip to Denver. What she wasn't sure of was how Curtis might react to the current situation.

Curtis had been willing to kill three times that Marjorie knew of to protect his interests. There'd been the swing judge, Wainwright, in South Dakota and Sarah Johnson, but there was at least one other person he'd ordered killed. How else would he have known about Murdock if he hadn't used him before? But would he kill Bill because he'd been arrested and was being hounded by the FBI? She didn't think so—unless Bill did something stupid.

She hadn't liked what she'd seen this morning after Bill left the jail. She didn't like the way he'd looked, all sweaty and scared. She didn't like, as he'd admitted, that his brain froze up when they arrested him. And what she *really* didn't like was the dumb comment he'd made about threatening Curtis, which could get her killed as well.

What she'd always admired about Bill, and what made him so good at his job, was that he had the ability to make people like him. He was charming and funny and he was really good at acting sincere—which also explained why he got laid so much. The trick to convincing a politician to take a bribe was a lot like trying to talk some woman into the sack: the politician had to be romanced, he had to be *wooed*—and Bill Logan was a master at that.

But in all the time they'd worked together, she'd never seen him in a situation where he was under as much pressure as he was now. He'd never before been in a go-to-jail situation much less a life-threatening situation—and from what she'd seen this morning, he didn't handle pressure well at all. Bill could be a major liability.

There was one bit of good news: all the heat was on Bill. Bill was the one who'd made the trip to Denver. Bill was the guy who'd been arrested for assault. But Marjorie . . . She was pristine. No one had accused her of doing anything. So one possible outcome was that she might have to find a new partner or work without a partner, and Bill . . . Bill just might have to go away.

Curtis's secretary finally called her back and said Mr. Curtis would see her at eight a.m. tomorrow at his office in Houston. Marjorie got online, booked a flight, and then went home to pack a bag.

Dick was sitting in the living room, watching the *Ellen DeGeneres Show* when Marjorie walked through the door. He was turning into a regular housewife. When she said she had to fly to Houston that evening, he whined, "But tonight's my poker night."

"I don't want to hear it, Dick," she said. "And don't even think about taking the boys with you to your poker game." She didn't see any point in reminding him that he was no better at poker than he was at day trading.

23

Bill Logan went home after having breakfast with Marjorie at Denny's, took a shower to get the smell of the Bismarck jail off his skin, then tried to sleep but couldn't. He was too anxious to sleep but was actually feeling better about his situation after talking to Marjorie. She might be right about him winning at trial if they tried to convict him for assaulting Johnson based on Tim's testimony, but he didn't want to take the risk and end up with a felony record. He really liked her idea of paying Tim to recant his testimony and take the fall for him.

He also thought about DeMarco's one-brick-in-the-wall speech, how Janet Tyler was going to testify that he'd fixed her son's case so her son wouldn't go to jail. All he had said to Tyler was that if she dropped the lawsuit against Curtis, he *might* be able to help her son—and she wouldn't be able to prove otherwise, and she sure as hell wouldn't know about the deal he'd made with the Great Falls prosecutor. As for the FBI squeezing politicians mentioned in Johnson's blog, they could squeeze as hard as they wanted. Those politicians weren't going to incriminate themselves.

Last night in jail, surrounded by drunks and thieves and meth addicts, he'd been more depressed than he'd ever been in his life. He could just see himself spending months in jail for the assault, surrounded by violent thugs. And he would obviously lose his high-paying job; Curtis wasn't going to employ a felon. But worse than the assault charge and the possibility of unemployment was DeMarco saying how the FBI was using all its considerable resources to prove he'd committed bribery and been an accomplice to murder. Then it wouldn't be months in jail, it would be years, maybe even life. But now, after talking to Marjorie and thinking things through . . . It was like that old saying about how it was always darkest before the dawn. Last night had been his darkest hour, but today . . . Well, things didn't seem so bad now. Thank God, Marjorie was on his side.

He thought about going to see Tim this afternoon, but then decided to put it off until tomorrow. Right now what he needed to do was relax so he could get some sleep. He thought about going for a walk, then decided to take Marge's advice and go to the driving range.

— ◆◆◆ —

DeMarco was feeling okay about the way things stood, but knew that he needed to do more and he needed to do something soon.

He'd been bullshitting Logan about the FBI having a list of suspected contract killers who operated out of Denver. There was no such list. And maybe Logan, to avoid a jail sentence, would give up Curtis and whoever had killed Sarah—but that seemed unlikely. First, the case against Logan was weak because the person who would be testifying against him was a loser who was currently defrauding the government out of a disability check for a nonexistent medical condition. So maybe Logan wouldn't be convicted at all. And if he was convicted, DeMarco doubted that he'd be given a long prison sentence as Sarah hadn't been hurt. So unless the judge sentenced him to years in jail, DeMarco doubted Logan would want to incur Leonard Curtis's wrath by testifying against Curtis.

In an effort to make a stronger case against Logan, DeMarco told Westerberg that he wanted her to pursue a couple of other angles. He wanted her to see if Bill Logan had wired a substantial amount of money to someplace that looked funny the week before Sarah's death. An offshore account, for example. Then DeMarco wanted her to see if six years earlier, the last time Logan went to Denver, if money went to the same place.

Westerberg said she'd need warrants to do what he wanted, and DeMarco gave her the same answer he'd given her once before: *That's your problem. Figure it out.*

The second thing DeMarco wanted was for Westerberg to pressure the IRS to audit Dawkins and Logan's business tax returns. If he was lucky, the IRS might be able to get them for income tax evasion, which would place more pressure on Logan and maybe result in more jail time than an assault charge. The other purpose of the IRS audit would be to see if Dawkins and Logan's so-called consulting firm distributed cash to various people—or simply couldn't account for income or cash that had been disbursed. DeMarco figured that in their line of work, they were paying off some politicians with good old-fashioned greenbacks instead of some complicated, under-the-table deal that no one could prove was illegal—like forcing an insurance company to pay off a claim as a method of bribery. So DeMarco wanted D&L Consulting audited, hoping the IRS might find the start of a money trail that could lead to something bigger.

Westerberg agreed and said she'd try to get the IRS to do what DeMarco wanted, but as the IRS was a large, practically immoveable federal bureaucracy that didn't work for the Justice Department, that might not be possible.

Westerberg also told DeMarco that, whether he liked it or not, she was returning briefly to Minneapolis. She was going home to talk to her boss face-to-face about the case and to pack up some more clothes so she wouldn't have to wear the same thing almost every day. Her last reason for going home, she said, was to get laid. This comment actually shocked DeMarco, as Westerberg had struck him as being somewhat of a prude, or if not a prude exactly, too much of a straight arrow to talk about her sex life. He did tell her that she didn't have to drive all the way to Minnesota if she had an itch that needed scratching. Nice guy that he was, he'd be happy to do the scratching. This almost made Westerberg smile. Almost.

The bottom line was that DeMarco needed to put more pressure on Logan and he wasn't satisfied that anything he'd done or that Westerberg might do in the future was going to be sufficient. He needed to think of something else. Something big.

He finally decided that the best thing he could do was go play golf. Maybe something would occur to him while walking about, whacking a little white ball. Before going to the golf course, however, he called Mahoney and gave him an update so Mahoney would think he was actually working. While driving to the course he looked to see if someone was following him, but couldn't spot anyone.

<hr />

DeMarco rented clubs—he wished again that he had his golf shoes so he wouldn't have to play in tennis shoes—and walked over to the driving range. He'd hit a small bucket of balls before he teed off. And who should he see on the driving range but Bill Logan.

He watched Logan for a while. Logan was taller than him, in good shape, but DeMarco figured that he was stronger. Logan drove the ball about two hundred yards, most of the time fairly straight. DeMarco could drive the ball farther than Logan but more of his shots sliced right than Logan's. Then he watched Logan pitch a few balls at a flag about fifty yards from where he was standing, and he came fairly close to the flag on almost every shot. Pitching was DeMarco's biggest weakness. He was okay with a driver, good with the irons, not bad with his putter, but his pitching sucked. Nonetheless, he figured he might be able to beat Logan—not that beating him at golf mattered. It was just a guy thing.

He walked up to Logan and said, "Want to play a round? My tee time is in twenty minutes."

Logan was shocked to see him, but then he recovered and smiled. "Are you still following me, DeMarco? I might have to get a restraining order against you."

DeMarco didn't like that Logan sounded relaxed and wondered if Dawkins had convinced him that he didn't have anything to worry about. That wouldn't be good.

In response to Logan's question, DeMarco said, "No. Honest. I wasn't following you. I just came here to play a round while I was thinking about other ways to screw you."

Logan laughed.

"So. You wanna play?" DeMarco said.

Logan hesitated. "Yeah, okay, why not? But on one condition. We don't talk about the assault case or Sarah Johnson or anything like that."

"Deal," DeMarco said.

It turned out that he and Logan played at about the same level. DeMarco outdrove him, they were even with the irons, Logan was better at pitching. After nine holes, DeMarco was eight over par and Logan had two strokes on him mostly due to two extraordinary pitches where he landed about a foot from the cup.

DeMarco couldn't help it, but he actually kind of liked Logan. The guy had a sense of humor—told him two golf jokes he hadn't heard before—and he didn't come across as a total asshole. He certainly didn't come across as a murderer. He found out that Logan, just like himself, was divorced and had spent his whole life on the fringes of politics. Again, DeMarco was struck by the fact that Logan was a guy a lot like him: single, easygoing, and engaged in a similar business. In a different universe, Logan might have been a friend.

On the eighteenth hole, Logan was a one stroke ahead but DeMarco figured he still had a chance of winning because the eighteenth was a long par four and his driving ability gave him an advantage. They ended up with Logan lying four, sixty yards from the pin, and DeMarco lying three, thirty yards from the hole. Logan, once again, made a magnificent pitch, and ended up two feet from the pin. DeMarco pitched up onto the green, but his ball rolled fifteen feet past the hole—and DeMarco figured he was screwed.

Then, whichever god is in charge of golf, decided to kiss DeMarco on the head—and he made a putt he couldn't have made again if his life had depended on it. Logan sank his putt easily.

"Well, I guess it's a draw," Logan said.

Which pretty much summed up where things stood in general between DeMarco and Logan—unless DeMarco could come up with something that was equivalent to a fifteen-foot putt.

24

The first thing Curtis said when Marjorie walked into his office in Houston at eight a.m. was, "Why did you guys kill that girl? That was a stupid thing to do."

Marjorie's started sputtering. "But, but, but you told us—"

"Hey!" Curtis said, "I didn't tell you to kill her. I just told you to make her quit writing about me."

Marjorie took a breath to calm herself. Technically, what Curtis had just said was true: he hadn't ordered them to kill Sarah Johnson. On the other hand, he'd made it pretty damn clear that if they didn't do something about her, he was going to replace them. But arguing with Curtis about whose fault it was that Johnson was dead wasn't going to help. Her whole purpose in coming to Houston was to tell Curtis where things stood—and things did not stand well—and then convince him that she had everything under control.

Curtis sat like a gnome behind his big desk, dressed in one of his cheap suits, scowling at her, as she laid out the whole story: how Bill had been arrested, how DeMarco had gotten the FBI involved, and that the FBI knew that Logan had taken a trip to Denver before Johnson was killed. "Son of a gun," Curtis muttered.

"I came here," Marjorie said, "so you'd know what was going on but also to tell you that you don't have anything to worry about." She then told him that she'd gotten Bill a good lawyer and her plan was to pay off Tim Sloan so he wouldn't testify against Bill. As for Johnson's murder, DeMarco and the FBI didn't have a snowball's chance in hell of finding Murdock and proving that Logan had anything to do with her death. One thing Marjorie did intentionally was make sure that Curtis understood that Bill was the one who was in trouble and not her.

When she finished, Curtis said, "I don't like this one damn bit."

"I don't like it either, Mr. Curtis. But you need to understand that you don't have a problem and Bill and I can still do our jobs. We'll take things slow for a couple of months, being very careful, and then it will be back to business as usual. You have my word on that."

"Are you sure Logan isn't going to talk?"

"Yes. Why would he talk? The very worst thing that could happen to him is that he gets probation or a couple months in jail for this assault on Johnson, but even that's not going to happen. He's not going to talk about anything he and I have done for you, and he sure as hell isn't going to talk about Murdock."

"Yeah, maybe," Curtis said, "but the thing about Logan is that boy's never really been tested, he's never been under fire. I almost wish *you* were the one who was in trouble because I know you got the grit to hang tough. But Logan . . . He's all bullshit and blarney and good at schmoozing folks, and I'm not too sure about the size of his balls."

"His balls are big enough," Marjorie said. "And I'll make sure they stay that way." But she was really thinking that it was pretty amazing how Curtis had instantly come to the same conclusion that she had about Bill, and Curtis hadn't even seen the way Bill looked after he got out of jail. She was also flattered that Curtis recognized that she was stronger than Bill.

"All right," Curtis finally said. "You did the right thing coming here."

"I know. And one other reason I came, instead of calling you, is that we need to be careful for a while about what we say on the phone. I don't think the FBI can get a warrant to tap our phones, but we need to be cautious."

"Okay. You keep me informed." Then he added, "Oh, and one other thing. If you and Logan have to buy off this Sloan character to keep him quiet, that's coming out of your pocket, not mine."

Why you cheap son of a bitch, Marjorie thought.

She had a taxi take her back to the Houston airport, called Dick to make sure everything was okay with the boys and to tell him when to pick her up at the Bismarck airport. She also asked him if he'd remembered to call the guy to come look at the washing machine, which was squealing like somebody had stepped on a cat. She was going to go ballistic if he'd forgotten again. But he hadn't. He said the guy was coming tomorrow.

She had a glass of Chablis while she waited for her flight and thought about old man Curtis's reaction to everything she'd told him. The problem with Curtis was that he was hard to read. He hadn't been happy but he'd *seemed* satisfied that she was managing things. She was willing to bet, however, that he'd have somebody in Bismarck watch Bill's case closely to see how things were progressing. She also knew that if he got even a whiff that Bill might point the finger at him for Johnson's murder, Curtis was very likely to contact Murdock and have Bill disappeared. And maybe her, too. She had to make sure—she just *had* to—that Bill didn't buckle under the pressure. Which made her think: the guy who was causing all the problems was DeMarco. There had to be some way to neutralize that slick bastard.

Curtis sat there after Dawkins left his office, wondering if he should take some sort of independent action or trust Dawkins to handle things. He liked the woman, and she and Logan had done well in the ten years they'd been working for him. Including their salaries, their operation cost him two, three million a year, but they'd made or saved him a hundred times that amount. It would be a shame to lose them, especially Dawkins. It would be hard to find anybody who knew the playing field in Montana and the Dakotas the way those two did.

He wished they hadn't killed that girl. He hadn't really expected them to do that—and he sure as hell hadn't ordered them to. He thought they'd come up with something more creative than murder. On the other hand, he was glad that pain-in-the-ass girl was gone and there was no way they could tie him into what Logan and Murdock had done. Logan may have used his money to pay Murdock but Curtis could show that he didn't control every dime he paid Logan and Dawkins as consultants.

So the problem wasn't the girl's death; that was unfortunate but not a game changer. The game changer was this guy, DeMarco, who had gotten the FBI involved. A couple dozen FBI agents looking at everything he was doing could grind things to a halt and tie him up in court for years on all sorts of bullshit.

He called a lawyer in Bismarck and told the lawyer he wanted him to stay on top of Bill Logan's assault charge and he also wanted the lawyer to sniff around to see if a judge had granted the FBI a warrant to tap phones and such. Then he stood and looked out the window, and thought some more.

Like he'd told Dawkins, he was worried about Logan. People were like lumps of coal. Some lumps turned into diamonds under pressure; others just crumbled. He had the feeling that Logan was a crumbler. He wanted Logan watched to make sure he didn't start taking meetings with the FBI—and if he did start doing that sort of thing, he wanted to be able to act quickly.

He looked at his watch. It was already nine a.m. He'd spent an hour talking to Dawkins and then stewing about what to do. But nine was plenty early enough to set up a meeting with the man he needed to see. He took out a cell phone he used when he didn't want calls traced to him and punched in a number.

———————◆◆◆———————

Ian Perry could hear a phone ringing in his office; there were four cell phones there. He thought for a moment about ignoring the call, but then he thought about the house next door. He wanted that house gone. He padded in stocking feet toward his office and the ringing phone. He never wore shoes in his house.

He picked up the phone and said, "Yes?"

The caller said, "This is Longhorn. I need to see you today. You still using the same place for meeting people?"

"Yes," Perry said.

"Can you be there in three hours? I'll pay top dollar for the job and give you ten just for taking the meeting."

"Okay," Perry said. "I'll see you at noon."

Perry stood for a moment looking out at his garden. He had a house in Colorado Springs, the second-largest city in Colorado, sixty-some miles south of Denver. The house sat on a hill, and from the front of his house, he had an unobstructed view of the chapel at the United States Air Force Academy. The academy chapel was one of the most striking works of architecture in the state of Colorado with its seventeen rows of spires that rise one hundred and fifty feet into the sky. The spires were like silver hands joined together in prayer, the fingers raised to God.

The view from the back of Perry's home was, in his opinion, just as magnificent. Perry had been stationed in Japan for a while and although he didn't particularly like the Japanese, their food, or their culture, he'd fallen in love with their gardens. His backyard garden was identical to one he'd seen in Kyoto. It was enclosed by a bamboo fence, and had winding, crushed gravel walkways. Two ponds were connected by a small stream that burbled over boulders. There were Japanese maples and cedars, holly leaf osmanthus, partridge berry, black mondo grass, Kyushu azalea, small empress trees, and one lone Japanese black pine. It was simple yet stunning, and he spent hours tending to the plants and hours more simply sitting on a stone bench in the garden. It was the most serene place on earth. The only flaw was that he could see his neighbor's house looming over his fence and he wanted to destroy that house. He'd asked the neighbors if they would be willing to sell and they'd smirked and said they would for eight hundred fifty thousand—which was why he'd agreed to meet Longhorn in Denver.

Curtis's father-in-law had introduced him to the man he knew as Murdock.

Curtis had never liked his father-in-law and his father-in-law hadn't liked him much, either. His father-in-law was a man named Jim Baker—who they called Big Jim, of course. He'd been born and raised in Arkansas but developed into a caricature of a Texas oilman: a tall, heavy-gutted man with a loud voice who wore cowboy boots and Stetsons and smoked cigars. He had a Texas twang like a country western singer. Curtis had worked for Big Jim early in his career and ended up marrying his daughter—which was the main reason Big Jim tolerated him and later helped him out. Curtis was a good husband to Big Jim's daughter and a good father to his grandchildren, and unlike Big Jim, he didn't screw every whore in Houston.

About fifteen years ago, near the end of Big Jim's life, Curtis found himself in a bad situation, the kind of situation where he could go to jail, and the only one he felt he could go to for advice was his father-in-law. What Curtis had done had been done by many men before him: he was short of cash but had the opportunity for an incredible investment—one which would provide the funding to launch his own company—and he stole from the men who were his partners at the time. Actually, the way he looked at it, he didn't really embezzle from the company, he just borrowed some money for a short period then paid it back.

The problem was an accountant/auditor discovered what he'd done and instead of telling the police or Curtis's partners, he decided to blackmail Curtis. And that's when Big Jim told him about Murdock and how to contact him. He had no idea how Big Jim knew Murdock.

Curtis called his pilot and told him to be ready to fly to Denver in half an hour. As he walked out of the office he told his secretary where he was headed and she said, "Don't forget it's your wife's birthday today, and there's a party for her at seven. Your children are coming for the party."

"Doggone it," Curtis muttered. He'd forgotten all about the party. "Did I buy her a birthday present?"

"Yes, sir. You bought her a nice pearl necklace."

Meaning his secretary had bought the necklace.

"I hope it wasn't too expensive," Curtis said.

"I'm sure you can afford it, sir."

It always pissed him off the way people assumed that just because he was rich he should squander his money.

Curtis hated meeting Murdock in the damn steam room. Although he appreciated the man taking precautions to make sure there was no record of their conversation, being naked made him feel vulnerable and less powerful. He knew he looked like a scrawny chicken with its feathers plucked off.

Murdock hadn't changed much since the last time Curtis had seen him. His hair was thinner and he had the muscle tone of a man who didn't do a lot of manual labor, but he hadn't gotten fat. The most surprising thing was that he was still working and not dead or in jail, which was a testament to his competence. Or his luck.

"I want you to keep tabs on a man named Logan up in Bismarck. You met with him recently. He had you deal with a young woman in Bismarck. But now I want him watched. I want to know if he's talking to the FBI."

"So hire a detective," Murdock said. "That's not what I do."

"I know that," Curtis said, "but the thing is, I want you on the ground up there, ready to move at a moment's notice in case I need you to take care of Logan. And Logan has a partner. You may have to deal with her, too."

They settled on how they would communicate and Murdock's compensation. He'd be given a lump sum for watching Logan plus a per diem rate depending on how long he was required to stay in Bismarck. If he had to do more than watch Logan, the lump sum would double. If he had to take care of Dawkins, it would double again. Curtis thought the amount Murdock asked was pretty doggone steep—and another example of people gouging him just because he was rich.

As they were about to leave the steam room, Curtis said, "I'm curious as to how you got into this business."

Murdock smiled slightly. "I guess you'd say that the U.S. government gave me a certain skill set and this is a line of work where those skills are useful."

Well, aren't you the cryptic SOB.

25

While Marjorie Dawkins was meeting with Leonard Curtis in Houston, DeMarco drove to Montana. As he was driving, he checked his tail continuously. He wasn't being followed.

When he arrived at Thorpe's cabin, he saw Thorpe's pickup in the driveway and the old dog, Daisy, sleeping on the front porch, but Thorpe didn't answer the door. DeMarco knew Sarah's funeral had been yesterday and he wondered if Thorpe was inside, sitting in the dark, drinking. That's what DeMarco would have been doing if his granddaughter had been killed.

He walked down to the river, trying to decide how long he should wait for Thorpe when he saw a man fly fishing a few hundred yards away. It looked like Thorpe: tall, gray-haired. DeMarco walked along the bank, glad he'd worn jeans and tennis shoes, until he was close enough to call out to Thorpe—but he didn't. Watching the man cast was a thing of beauty: a green-colored line looping out about thirty yards and then dropping softer than a butterfly on the water. Thorpe would let the fly drift downstream a ways, then with an effortless motion, he'd bring it back, the line curling behind him, and he'd cast the fly out again. Each time, the fly appeared to land in exactly the same spot. On the fifth cast, Thorpe pulled back hard and the rod bent practically in half, and a trout that must have been two feet long came out of the water, its tail twisting as it tried to shake the hook. Thorpe fought the fish calmly, taking his time, and when it was close enough to touch, he reached down and flipped it off the hook.

"That was a hell of a trout," DeMarco said.

Thorpe turned around to face him. There were tears streaming down his cheeks. He'd probably been thinking about his granddaughter who he'd said could cast even better than him.

"What are you doing here, DeMarco?" Thorpe said.

"I need something."

DeMarco told Thorpe where things stood with Logan and what he wanted as they walked back to Thorpe's cabin.

"This better work," Thorpe said. "If it doesn't, I'm going to solve this in my own way."

After DeMarco had what he'd come for, he began the five-hour trip back to Bismarck.

While DeMarco was driving to Montana to see Thorpe, and while Marjorie was meeting with Curtis in Houston, Bill Logan was still sleeping; he didn't wake up until ten a.m. He was anxious to talk to Marjorie to see how her meeting with Curtis had gone but figured she wouldn't be back until late in the afternoon or early evening. Overall, though, he was feeling pretty good. Marjorie had been right: the assault charge could be made to disappear and the cops would never connect him to Johnson's death.

He smiled thinking about his golf game with DeMarco. He was glad he'd done that—shown DeMarco that he wasn't worried at all. He just wished that he'd won the game, and knew the only reason he didn't was that DeMarco got lucky on his last putt. He hoped DeMarco's luck didn't extend beyond the golf course.

He shaved and took a shower, dressed in a gray sport jacket, black slacks, a black polo shirt, and black loafers. He didn't have any meetings today; he just liked to look good. The first thing he was going to do was go see Tim Sloan and put that problem back in the box.

On the way to Sloan's place he stopped at his bank and it was a little after eleven when he rapped on his ex-brother-in-law's door. A couple minutes later a sleepy voice said, "Who is it?"

"Tim, it's Bill. Let me in. I need to talk to you."

This remark was greeted with silence.

"Come on, Tim. Open the door. I'm not going to hurt you. I'm not mad at you. Really. Now open up. "

Finally Tim opened the door, then stood in the doorway looking leery, as if he was ready to spin on his heels and run if Bill showed the slightest sign of aggression. He was dressed in a once-white T-shirt that was now almost gray and red boxer shorts with small white dots. Bill wondered where Tim's skanky girlfriend was, but didn't ask.

"Why don't you get dressed and we'll go get some breakfast," Bill said. "I don't know about you, but I'm starving."

When Tim just looked at him suspiciously, Bill clapped him on the shoulder and said, "Timmy, I'm not mad at you. Honest. That goddamn DeMarco had you by the balls and you did the only thing you could do. Now go put on some pants, and let's head over to Denny's and get one of their giant breakfasts."

While they were having coffee, waiting for their food to arrive, Bill chatted about everything under the sun: the weather, sports, a movie he'd seen, and the local economy. The economy in North Dakota was booming thanks to oil and gas; unemployment was at an all-time low.

Tim responded by saying that the economy wasn't so good as far as he was concerned, and Bill could understand why. A guy like Tim was too lazy to get a real job, and because of the natural gas boom, merchants were raising their prices and rents were skyrocketing. This meant that Tim had to pay more for food and booze and probably drugs, and Tim was on a fixed income—like a retired guy—since his Social Security disability check was his only steady source of income. Bill sympathized with Tim and by the time their meal arrived, Tim was relaxed and not worried that Bill might beat him to a pulp for telling the cops who had paid him to assault Sarah Johnson.

"Now about this legal thing," Bill said as Tim was stuffing steak, eggs, and hash browns into his unshaven face. "This could actually be a good thing for you. I mean, considering how you always need money."

"What?" Tim said.

"I'm thinking twenty thousand," Bill said. "Ten today and the rest when they drop the charges against me."

"What?" Tim said again.

Bill explained to Tim that he was going to get a good lawyer, which Bill would pay for, and when Tim was subpoenaed to testify against Bill at Bill's trial, he'd recant everything he'd told DeMarco. He would say that DeMarco had confused and threatened him, and that was why he'd said that Bill had paid him to scare Johnson. He would say that harassing Johnson—and that's all he did—he just harassed her—he didn't assault her—he didn't hurt her—had been his own idea. He'd say that Johnson's blog just pissed him off, telling lies about politicians, writing things that could cost his friends their jobs.

"But that means I'll go to jail," Tim said.

"Nah, you won't go to jail," Bill said. "You just yelled at the girl, who, by the way, isn't around to contradict whatever you say. And right now, not only is business booming but so is crime. The jails are full of real criminals. They'll give you a suspended sentence—the lawyer will make sure of that if you agree to plead guilty and save them the expense of a trial. And hell, even if you did go to jail, you wouldn't serve more than a couple of months. I'd say that twenty grand isn't a bad paycheck for sitting on your butt for two months."

Bill pulled an envelope out of his pocket and opened it so Tim could see the cash in the envelope. "There's ten grand. You'll get the other ten when the case is settled and provided the charges against me are dropped." Tim just stared at the envelope; Bill doubted that Tim had ever seen ten thousand dollars all in one place before.

It took a while, but by the time Bill was finished, Tim agreed to do what Bill wanted. Bill had spent his entire career convincing folks a lot brighter than Tim to do things he wanted.

Bill dropped Tim off at his apartment after breakfast—he was guessing that Tim and the skank would go out to celebrate tonight—then he called Marjorie. He was desperate to know how things had gone with Curtis and he wanted to tell Marjorie about Tim. But the call went to voice mail, and he figured she might be on a plane coming back to Bismarck. He also figured she'd probably go straight home after she landed, so he'd give her a call later this evening.

Bill headed toward the office and it started to rain as he drove. In fact, it started to come down hard. The rain was okay, though, as far as Bill was concerned; he wasn't planning on doing anything outside. His plan was to stay in the office and work his ass off for the rest of the day and long into the night if necessary.

Curtis wanted to purchase a small parcel of land in McKenzie County near Watford City, North Dakota (population 1,744). Watford City was about an hour south of Williston and in the Bakken oil field. Bill's first problem was that Curtis didn't want anyone to know he was buying the property. Curtis had learned that whenever folks discovered he was buying land, a whole lot of hoopla usually followed with the anti-gas crackpots leading the pack. Bill wasn't too worried about buying the land, however. He had done this sort of thing before, and a couple of Curtis's lawyers would be assisting him, and by the time he was finished it wouldn't be impossible to find out that Curtis owned the property but it would take some hard digging.

The other problem Bill had was that the property was currently zoned for agricultural use but Curtis planned to store a few chemicals used for fracking on the site. As near as Bill could figure, a structure for storing chemicals on agricultural land wasn't specifically prohibited by the town's zoning regulations. Farmers, after all, stored fertilizers and pesticides and God knows what else. But it wasn't clear that storing fracking chemicals was permitted—and no way in hell did Curtis want to ask for permission because some of the chemicals . . . Well, the energy companies' scientists would tell you they weren't toxic but the nuts at the EPA, who would classify sunshine as toxic, were inclined to say otherwise. What Bill needed to do was get this one guy on the city's planning commission to sign off on the building permits that storing a few thousand barrels of chemicals didn't violate any zoning ordnances. The fact that the guy on the planning commission was a young guy who had political ambitions—and who would one day need some help financing his campaign for the state legislature—gave Bill some leverage.

Normally, making this all happen—acquiring the land and dealing with the zoning issue—would be a tough but doable problem, but this time, because of the whole Sarah Johnson mess, Bill needed to be especially careful. He just couldn't risk getting caught doing anything that some small-minded nitpickers might consider illegal.

So Bill needed to roll up his sleeves and get to work. He wanted to impress Curtis. He knew—no matter what Marjorie might have told Curtis—that Curtis would be having some doubts about his effectiveness at this point, and he wanted to make sure Curtis understood that he was still at the top of his game.

At five p.m., while Bill was still toiling away, Marjorie called him. She was at the airport waiting for her husband to pick her up. She said things had gone well with Curtis and Bill told her that things had gone well with Tim Sloan, too. Bill concluded by saying, "It's going to cost twenty grand and whatever the lawyer charges, but Tim will play ball and keep me out of it."

"Uh, Bill, I hate to tell you this, but Curtis said taking care of Sloan is going to come out of your pocket, not his."

"What! That motherfucker!" Bill hesitated, then said, "You know, Marge, it seems only fair we split the cost. Like you said before, we're in this together."

"I don't think so, Bill. Hiring Sloan was your bright idea and I've got mouths to feed."

After he hung up with Marjorie, he kicked a trash can across the office—then told himself it could be worse. He could afford the twenty grand and spending it was better than spending time in jail and losing his job. It pissed him off, though, that Marjorie wasn't bearing some of the cost.

———————◆◆◆———————

After Marjorie finished talking to Bill—the nerve of the damn guy thinking she should split the cost with him!—she made another phone call.

While on the plane from Houston she'd come up with an idea for dealing with DeMarco. It wouldn't take him off the board completely but it would complicate his life and give him less time to screw with her and Bill. And if she was really successful, she might even be able to land his ass in jail.

What gave her the idea was a woman sitting across the aisle from her on the plane: the woman had these incredible long legs, and on her feet were sexy black stilettos. She wasn't really any better-looking than Marjorie, and she wasn't as stacked as Marjorie, but she had fantastic legs and with the high heels, she'd be about six feet tall. Marjorie had always wanted to be tall; short women—even when they were cute and busty like Marjorie—just don't turn heads the way tall girls do.

Thinking about the woman across the aisle got her to thinking about Bill and all the women he'd gone to bed with, which then made her mind ricochet to DeMarco, thinking about how he'd gone to bed with the same woman Bill had: the slutty schoolteacher.

And that's when the idea came to her.

The woman she phoned was a gal she'd gone to high school with. Her name was Christine, but everyone called her Christie. Like the woman across the aisle, Christie was tall. In high school she'd been a cheerleader of easy virtue; she got laid a lot. She ended up marrying a guy who looked good on their wedding day but eventually lost his hair, gained fifty pounds, and drank himself out of a job. Christie had divorced him three years ago.

Marjorie had run into Christie a few weeks ago. The woman still looked good; she was practically broke but she had a membership at a gym. She was now a cashier at Walmart, made less than minimum wage, and complained that she didn't know how she was going to pay her rent that month. Her only ambition in life was to find a rich guy to marry her—which was why she spent her salary on clothes and a gym membership instead of paying her rent.

Marjorie asked Christie if she could stop by her place this evening. When Christie asked why, Marjorie said she had a job for her and would pay five grand. Come on over, Christie said.

Dick finally showed up at the airport, the boys with him in the car, fighting in the backseat. Since it was raining outside, he'd been trapped with them in the house ever since they got home from school. She told Dick she had an errand to run before they went home, and naturally Dick wasn't happy to hear this as the boys were driving him nuts.

Christie let Marjorie into her apartment, which was small, cluttered, and shabby. Her TV set was a big, boxy, older model and had rabbit ears. Marjorie couldn't remember the last time she saw a television with an antenna, but then Christie probably couldn't afford cable on the generous salary the Walton family paid.

Nor did Christie look particularly ravishing tonight: she wasn't wearing makeup, her hair wasn't combed, and she was dressed in sweatpants and a too-big T-shirt that made her look flat-chested. But Marjorie knew that with hot-red lipstick, a short, tight cocktail dress, and a push-up bra . . . There was no doubt she'd turn DeMarco's head.

Marjorie told Christie what she needed: "I want you to meet a guy named DeMarco in a bar and pick him up. You know, seduce him."

"What?" Christie said. Christie had hair the color of a raven's wings but she acted so clueless that Marjorie always thought she should have been blond.

"I need for there to be witnesses that you left the bar with him."

"I don't understand," Christie said.

Ignoring her confusion, Marjorie continued. "Then you're going to take him back here and screw him—he's a good-looking guy, that part should be fun—then after he leaves, you rip your dress, punch your thighs a few times to make some bruises, maybe slap yourself in the face really hard—a cut lip would be good—then call the cops and say he raped you."

"Are you insane?" Christie said.

"No. This guy is causing me problems and I want him arrested. And you'll make five grand. I mean, I'd use a prostitute if I could, but I need somebody credible."

"I'm not going to—"

"Christie, it's not like you're a virgin and you couldn't possibly have thought that I was willing to give you five thousand dollars to give me a tip on the next big rollback at Walmart. The other thing is, I might have some more work for you after this guy's out of my hair."

Marjorie was being sincere about that. She actually had considered using Christie before when there was a politician they'd wanted to catch fooling around with someone other than his wife. Christie was shaking her head, but Marjorie could see the gears slowly turning inside the bimbo's not-so-big brain.

"But I'd have to commit perjury, or whatever it's called," Christie said. "Then I could go to jail."

"Nah, you won't have to commit perjury. They'll arrest the guy and then I'll go see him and tell him that if he leaves town, you'll retract your statement."

"I don't know," Christie said.

"Listen to me, Christie," Marjorie said. It took her fifteen more minutes to convince Christie that the risks were small in comparison to the reward, and that other than spending a night or two in jail, nothing too bad would happen to DeMarco—not that Marjorie cared what happened to DeMarco. Marjorie eventually had to raise the price to eight grand, but in the end Christie agreed. It really helped that Christie couldn't pay this month's rent.

Marjorie left saying, "For the next couple of nights you get all dressed up and be ready to go when my guy calls you. He's a private detective named Heckler. I'm going to have him follow DeMarco and as soon as he lands someplace appropriate—you know, a bar or a restaurant—you get your ass over there and make him fall in love with you."

When Marjorie got back into the car with Dick and the boys, they were all mad at her for making them wait so long. They just had no appreciation for the sacrifices she made for them.

———◆———

It was nine p.m. by the time Bill finished working for the day. All the paperwork had taken longer than he'd expected and one lawyer wasn't immediately available, and didn't call back until after seven. But now he was finished, and it was time for a drink and some dinner. He felt like being around people—particularly female people—so he'd go someplace that was lively and had a decent crowd, maybe a country western bar that served a good steak. There was nothing better than riding a cowgirl.

He powered down his laptop, put it inside the top drawer of his desk, and locked the desk. There wasn't anything incriminating on the laptop, he just didn't want to make it too easy for some loser who lived off food stamps to steal the thing. He put on his sport coat, checked to make sure he had his car keys and started to leave, but then stopped because he could hear it was still raining hard outside. He looked around to see if Marjorie had left an umbrella in the office; she hadn't. Oh, well, it was just a short distance to his car. He turned off the lights, opened the door, ready to dash to his car—and there was the guy, a black ski mask on his face, pointing a gun at him.

"Wait!" Bill yelled.

The man didn't wait. He pulled the trigger and blew out a chunk of the door frame above Bill's head. When the shot was fired Bill fell backward into the office and the guy fired again, and this time the bullet hit the wall behind him.

"Son of a bitch," Bill screamed.

Bill was now on his ass and the shooter was in a Weaver stance—legs spread, holding the pistol with two hands—still pointing the gun at Bill's head. So Bill did the only thing he could: he reached out with his right foot and swung the door shut, then scrambled to his knees and threw the deadbolt in the lock. He was terrified the man was going to shoot right through the door and hit him. The next thought he had was the guy might kick open the door—that's what they always did in the movies—and he needed a weapon. There wasn't a gun in the office and the only thing he could think to use for a weapon was the wooden coatrack next to the door. He picked up the coatrack and stood to one side of the door. If the shooter kicked it open, Bill might be able to hit him in the head with the coatrack as soon as he came through the door. Now he just hoped the guy didn't shoot through the wall next to the door.

Bill stood next to the door listening. He didn't hear anything outside—the rain didn't help—but he figured at least a couple of minutes had passed since the last shot. Maybe the guy had decided to leave. Or maybe he was still outside waiting for Bill to come out.

The office had one window, but the blinds were closed. He and Marjorie always kept them closed as they didn't want people to see them inside the office and bother them. If he pushed back the blinds he'd be able to see if the shooter was still there, but he was afraid to push on the blinds as the shooter might see them move and shoot him through the window.

So Bill did the only thing he could think to do: he called the cops. He dialed 911, whispered his name and address, and told the dispatcher he was hiding in the office.

As he waited for the cops, he thought about what had happened. He hadn't actually seen the guy. All he'd seen was the ski mask and the gun, and the hole in the muzzle of the gun had been enormous; it had looked like the entrance to a big black tunnel. But he hadn't noticed anything about the shooter: he couldn't say how tall he was, if he was fat or skinny, or how he was dressed. He just saw the ski mask and the gun. As for the gun, all he knew was that it was incredibly loud and fired a huge fucking bullet. The hole in the wall where the second bullet had hit was the size of a quarter. If one of those bullets had hit him in the head, it would have blown his brains through the back of his skull.

He didn't know how long ago he'd called the cops but it seemed like an eternity. They should have arrived by now. A long five minutes later, someone rapped hard on the door and said, "You inside the office, this is the Bismarck Police. If you're armed, put down your weapon before you open the door."

Bill wasn't going to just open the door. For all he knew, it could be the killer pretending to be a cop. He crawled over to the window, pulled down the slats on the blinds, and looked outside: flashing blue-and-red lights. Thank God.

Bill wasted the next hour at the police station, being questioned by two detectives. When they asked him if he could describe the shooter, he told the truth: No. All he'd seen was a black mask and a gun. Plus, it had been dark outside and raining so hard that visibility wasn't good.

"How did the shooter know you'd be in your office at nine thirty at night?"

"That's easy," Bill said. "I'm pretty sure I don't own the only Porsche in Bismarck but I've never seen a red Boxster like mine. The guy may have been following me or maybe he just saw my car sitting in front of the office and decided to wait until I stepped outside."

"Do you have any enemies?" one of the detectives asked.

"I can't think of anybody who hates me enough to kill me," Bill said. That was a lie. He knew who had tried to kill him.

But the other detective, who knew Bill from the Elks, said, "Come on, Bill. You got a reputation for screwing anything in a skirt. Have you been diddling some married woman and maybe her husband decided to blow your pecker off?"

"The guy wasn't aiming at my pecker," Bill said. He was being serious, but the detectives laughed. He thought about the detective's question, however. The last married woman he'd slept with was six months ago up in Minot. He doubted the woman's husband knew that his wife had committed adultery, and if he had known, it seemed pretty unlikely that he'd stew about the situation for six months before deciding to drive to Bismarck to kill him.

The detectives finally ran out of questions, which was a relief to Bill. He wanted to get out of Bismarck. He *needed* to get out of Bismarck. Then the detective he knew from the Elks said, "Bill, do you want a couple of guys to escort you home and make sure nobody is waiting for you inside your house?"

"Yeah," Bill said. "I'd really appreciate that."

Two uniformed cops followed him to his house and made Bill wait outside for ten minutes while they searched the place. As soon as the cops left, Bill rushed to his bedroom and packed a duffel bag with enough clothes to last a week. He tossed the duffel bag onto the backseat of his Chevy Tahoe, and backed out of the garage. He sure as hell wasn't taking the Porsche; the Porsche was like a mobile red sign that said: *Here I am. Come kill me.*

Bill was gong to hide out in a cabin on the Knife River, about an hour and a half from Bismarck. The cabin belonged to a married woman named Rachel Collins who he'd had an affair with seven years ago and he knew she still owned the cabin. Rachel had an extraordinary body and a sense of humor to boot, and the affair had lasted five months—which was a long time for Bill. They had gone to her cabin a couple of times when they were seeing each other and Bill knew where she hid the spare key.

Bill was almost positive that Rachel and her family wouldn't be at the cabin because Rachel's son would still be in school this time of year. In fact, her getting pregnant with her son was the reason they'd stopped seeing each other. Bill never knew if he was the child's father but he was confident Rachel would never claim that he was. She broke off their affair because with a child on the way, she said she didn't want to jeopardize her marriage; her husband was a good provider and—unlike Bill—she knew he wouldn't cheat or abandon her. Bill didn't disagree, but his feelings had actually been hurt when she told him that.

As he was driving to the cabin all he could think about was why did Curtis decide to kill him? He knew the shooter had to have been Murdock and that Curtis had sent him, but he had no idea why. Did Curtis believe that he was going to give him up to the feds? Or, another thought, did Marjorie convince Curtis that Bill was somebody they couldn't trust to keep his mouth shut?

Bill didn't have any answers. All he knew was that he had to go someplace where Murdock couldn't find him and figure out what he was going to do next.

He arrived at the cabin about two in the morning. He took a flashlight from the glove compartment of the Tahoe and found the spare key in the well house. He didn't turn on the lights in the cabin. He dropped his duffel bag by the front door and used the flashlight to guide him to the bedroom. Without undressing, he fell onto the bed but had a hard time falling asleep. It's hard to sleep when you know somebody wants you dead.

26

DeMarco called Westerberg. "Where are you?" he asked.

"I'm still in Minnesota. I'm—"

"Well, you need to get out of bed and—"

"I'm not in bed, goddamnit. I'm at the office and I'm . . ."

"Somebody tried to kill Bill Logan last night."

"What? How do you know this?"

"Because it was on the local news this morning. Somebody went to his office last night and took a shot at him. You need to call the Bismarck cops and find out what they know. According to the news, they don't know anything. But the main thing is, we need to find Logan. He seems to have disappeared."

"How do you know that?"

"Because I went to his home and his office after I heard the news, and he's not in either place." Before Westerberg could ask another question, he said, "This could be our chance, Agent. If somebody tried to kill Logan, it has to be related to Sarah's murder or Logan's arrest. What I'm saying is, maybe Curtis ordered him killed because he's afraid Logan will talk. I think Logan's running scared and he's hiding someplace, and if you offer him protection maybe we can turn him against Curtis and find out who killed Sarah."

Westerberg didn't respond immediately, like she was mulling over what he'd just told her—or like she was wondering if he was telling her the truth. Westerberg wasn't the trusting type. Finally she said, "Okay."

"Okay, what?"

"Okay, I'll contact the Bismarck cops."

"Are you coming back to Bismarck?"

"Yeah. I'll be there as soon as I can. In the meantime, don't do anything, DeMarco. You need to keep in mind that you don't have a badge. And if somebody is running around shooting at people, you need to be careful."

DeMarco was touched that Westerberg would be concerned for him.

———————

Bill Logan woke up at eight feeling like he hadn't slept a wink. He was exhausted. He was also hungry. There wasn't anything in the refrigerator that wasn't frozen so he pawed through the cupboards but all he could find were a couple cans of chili. He didn't feel like chili for breakfast. There was a small restaurant a few miles from the cabin and also a general store and a gas station. He'd go get breakfast and then pick up some food so he'd have something other than chili to eat. And some booze.

He hadn't been to the cabin on the Knife River in over six years, and when he used to come with Rachel, they hardly left the narrow bed in the cabin. So he wasn't worried about anyone local knowing or recognizing him. Nonetheless, he found a blue Nike baseball cap in a closet and he wore it and sunglasses to the restaurant.

After breakfast, he decided to call Marjorie. He started to punch their office number into his cell phone when he remembered Marjorie being concerned about the FBI tapping their phones. He still thought it pretty unlikely the FBI could obtain a warrant to tap their phones, but figured why take the chance. There was a pay phone by the general store adjacent to the restaurant. He walked over to it, called the office, and Marjorie answered.

"It's me," Bill said.

"My, God! Are you all right? Where are you?"

"Never mind where I am. Go to the pay phone we use, you know the one I mean, and I'll call you there in three minutes."

There was a pay phone next to the Subway shop in the strip mall by their office. He and Marjorie used it occasionally when they made calls they didn't want traced to them. Bill had used it often enough that he knew the number. He waited three minutes, called Marjorie at the Subway pay phone, and she answered immediately, saying again, "Where are you?"

"I'm not going to tell you. Why did Curtis send Murdock to kill me?"

"What are you talking about? Curtis didn't send anybody."

"Then who tried to blow my head off?"

"I don't know but it wasn't Murdock. Maybe it was some woman's husband. I mean, considering the way you—"

"It was Murdock."

"Bill, you need to get your head on straight. According to the cops— I talked to a guy I know—he said the shooter took two shots at you from a distance of five or six feet and both shots went high. Can you imagine a professional killer missing you from five feet away?"

"I yelled before he fired the first shot and that might have thrown off his aim. And then I fell back into the office when he was firing the second shot. The guy just missed."

"Bill, Murdock wouldn't have missed. And I talked to Curtis—"

"Yeah, I know you did."

"What the hell does that mean? Do you think I told Curtis to have you killed? That's not only paranoid, it's stupid. I explained to Curtis that you weren't going to have a problem with the assault charge and this whole thing was going to blow over in a couple of months. When I left his office, he was satisfied. I swear."

Bill didn't respond. He didn't trust Marjorie.

"Bill, I don't know what happened last night, but I'm telling you that Curtis didn't try to have you killed and you need to calm down. Now tell me where you are."

"Fuck you," Bill said and disconnected the call.

———— ··· ————

Marjorie walked back to the office, but instead of going inside she fired up a Marlboro. She spent so much time outside smoking these days, she ought to just move a chair out by the door. As she smoked, she glanced up at the door frame, which was all splintered and had a big hole in it—the bullet hole made larger when the cops dug the slug out. The good news was the door still shut and locked okay, but she'd have to call somebody to replace the chunk of wood at the top of the frame. They didn't get many visitors but it wouldn't do to have an office that looked like the scene of a drive-by shooting.

So who tried to kill Bill? It was possible, as she'd told him, that an irate husband had tried, but the timing made that unlikely. That is, at any other time an irate husband would have been the most logical suspect, but the attempt on Bill's life was so close to Bill's arrest that such a coincidence would be extraordinary.

Marjorie could only think of three people with a motive for killing Bill, the first of those being Leonard Curtis—even though she'd told Bill otherwise. Curtis had told Marjorie that he wasn't too sure about the size of Bill's balls. He knew Bill had the assault charge hanging over his head and that the FBI was digging into Johnson's death—so maybe Curtis was worried that Bill would buckle under the pressure and start talking to the feds about all the things they'd done for him over the years.

The problem with the idea that Curtis had ordered Murdock to kill Bill, however, was what she'd told Bill: Murdock wouldn't have missed. Murdock put two bullets in Sarah Johnson in a circle the size of a fifty-cent piece. He certainly wouldn't have missed Bill from a distance of five feet.

Which left two possibilities for who had tried to kill Bill: DeMarco and Sarah Johnson's grandfather. She knew from Heckler that DeMarco had met with Johnson's grandfather and maybe he'd told the man that Bill was responsible for Johnson's death. So the grandfather had the most compelling motive of all: revenge. She didn't know enough about Thorpe's personality to know if he was the kind of man who would kill, but she was willing to bet that an outdoorsman—a fly-fishing guide—probably owned guns and had been steeped in all the bloodthirsty, eye-for-an-eye attitudes of the old frontier West.

DeMarco, on the other hand, wouldn't have taken a shot at Bill for revenge, but what DeMarco might do was try to scare Bill. Which also explained why Bill hadn't been killed: DeMarco didn't want Bill dead. DeMarco wanted Bill thinking that Curtis had tried to kill him so Bill would testify against Curtis.

Hmmm. So which one did it, DeMarco or Grandpa? She had a hard time seeing DeMarco risking a jail sentence for attempted murder. Based on what Peach had told her, DeMarco was a political operator, basically a guy just like Bill—although maybe a harder, tougher version than Bill. It was hard to imagine him being so emotionally invested in Johnson's death that he'd be willing to risk ten or twenty years in jail.

Yeah, she liked Grandpa for the shooter.

She called Bill's cell phone—she had no other way to reach him—to tell him what she'd concluded, but the son of a bitch didn't answer his phone. She had to find the damn guy before he did something stupid.

She also needed to call Heckler. She needed to get Heckler back on DeMarco so she could execute her plan to have Christie seduce DeMarco and then accuse him of rape. She was going to nail DeMarco's slippery hide to the wall.

27

Westerberg picked up DeMarco at his motel. As soon as he was in the car, she said, "He's someplace on the Knife River, about an hour and a half from here."

"How'd you find him?"

"His cell phone."

"Didn't you need a warrant to use his phone to locate him?"

"Yeah. I told the judge that Logan was out on bail for assault, had disappeared, and that I was afraid that he might have decided to skip. I also told him that someone had tried to kill Logan, and I needed to find him for his own protection. So he gave me the warrant, but it's a one-time thing and I can't use it to track Logan indefinitely."

DeMarco *loved* having the FBI working for him, and he was glad to see that Westerberg was becoming more creative when it came to warrants. It also looked as if going back to Minneapolis and getting laid had been good for her. She seemed more relaxed than the last time DeMarco had seen her.

"What do the cops know about the guy who tried to kill Logan?" DeMarco asked.

"Nothing, really. He used a .45, so it wasn't the weapon used to kill Sarah. One of the slugs was in good enough shape that they can match it to the gun if they can find it. But that's about it. Logan couldn't describe the shooter and the police haven't been able to find any witnesses. All the businesses in the strip mall were closed when the shooting occurred, it was raining cats and dogs, and nobody driving by on the street in front of the mall has reported seeing anything. Where were you last night?"

"Me? I spent the night in my room, watching TV. I didn't feel like going out."

"Where's the gun you used the night you interrogated Roy Patterson?"

"I gave it back to the guy who loaned it to me."

"Who loaned it to you?"

"I'm not going to tell you that. And what's with all the questions?"

Westerberg's cynical brown eyes stared at him for a long heartbeat, then she said, "Just curious about what you were up to last night when Logan was almost killed."

"Are you serious?" DeMarco said. Before Westerberg could answer, he asked, "Have the Bismarck cops made any headway at all on Sarah's murder?"

"No. They've reached a dead end."

"Well, when we see Logan, I'm going to ask him again what he was doing in Denver. I almost asked him when we were playing golf."

"You played *golf* with him?"

"Yeah. The day before yesterday, the day you headed back to Minnesota. I didn't have anything better to do so I went to a course to play a round, just to think about what to do next, and I saw him there on the driving range. I wasn't following him or anything like that. It was just a coincidence. Anyway, I asked if he wanted to play and he said yes. The guy was completely relaxed, like he didn't have a worry in the world. But we didn't talk about Sarah's murder or anything related to Curtis—he said he wouldn't play if I started questioning him—so we just played a round."

"Who won?"

"We tied."

"Huh. What's your handicap, DeMarco?"

"Do you play?"

"Yeah. I played on the women's team at Northwestern and I'll bet I can kick your ass. So what's your handicap?"

———◆———

"That's his SUV," Westerberg said, pointing at a dark blue Tahoe sitting in the driveway next to a cabin that looked as if it might have been there when Custer passed through the Dakotas. Except for the satellite dish on the roof, that is.

"Who does the cabin belong to?" DeMarco asked.

"I don't know. Let's find out," Westerberg said.

Westerberg got the address off the mailbox, called somebody, and fifteen minutes later somebody called her back. "It belongs to a Mrs. Rachel Collins," Westerberg told DeMarco. "She lives in Bismarck. She's married to a man named Harvey Collins, who's a dentist, and has a six-year-old son named Aaron. There's nothing in any database, however, to show how Collins is connected to Logan."

"Let's go talk to Bill," DeMarco said.

As they approached the door, Westerberg said, "Stand off to the side of the door when I knock. The guy's probably scared and he could have a deer rifle in there."

"After you, Agent," DeMarco said.

Westerberg knocked hard a couple of times, then called out, "Logan, it's Agent Westerberg. FBI. I know you're in there. Open the door."

There was no response from inside the cabin.

Westerberg pounded on the door again. "Logan, open the door."

DeMarco saw a face briefly appear in a window—Logan looking out to make sure it really was Westerberg—then the door opened. Logan was dressed in jeans, a wash-faded red sweatshirt, and heavy wool socks. He wasn't wearing shoes. He hadn't shaved in a day or so and looked tired and frazzled.

"How did you find me?" he asked Westerberg.

Before Westerberg could respond, DeMarco said, "A drone. We've had a big-ass Predator drone tracking you ever since you were released on bail."

"Oh, bullshit," Logan said—to which DeMarco shrugged, like: *Hey, believe what you want.*

"Never mind how we found you, Mr. Logan," Westerberg said. "We're here to help you and we need to talk."

Logan shook his head.

"Logan," DeMarco said, "a guy with a few billion dollars wants you dead. You can't hide from a man with that much money. You can't run from him. What you need to do is start playing offense instead of defense."

"What the hell does that mean?" Logan said.

"It means you need to get Curtis before he gets you. It means, you let the FBI take you into custody and you spill your guts about Curtis. The bureaucrats in the Justice Department would much rather prosecute Curtis than a low-level player like you because Curtis will get their names in the news. But if you keep pretending you didn't do anything illegal for Curtis, then the next guy Curtis sends to kill you won't miss."

"I don't know that Curtis tried to kill me."

"Then you're an idiot," DeMarco said. "Who else would want you dead?"

"I'm not saying anything. And you people need to get out of here."

"Let me remind you of something, Mr. Logan," Westerberg said. "You're on bail for an assault charge. If you run, the government's going to assume you're trying to flee before your trial and then, after we find you, just like we found you today, your bail will be revoked and you'll be tossed into a cell. How hard do you think it's going to be for Curtis to kill you if you're in jail?"

"I want to know how you found me," Logan said. "Nobody knows about this place."

"A drone," Westerberg said.

"Now what do we do?" Westerberg said.

"You need to tap his phones. He's going to talk to somebody about what's going on—his partner or Curtis or maybe even the guy they hired to kill Sarah—and you might hear him say something we can use."

"I don't have justification for a warrant to tap his phones," Westerberg said. "I was lucky I was able to get a warrant to use his cell phone to locate him, but no way is a judge going to let me eavesdrop on him."

"Come on, Agent. Use your imagination. Invent some probable cause if you have to. There's gotta be something in Sarah's blog that ought to be enough to convince a judge. Or call up your pals at the NSA. Those guys obviously don't worry about warrants."

"The FBI does not work like the NSA," Westerberg said, sounding righteous.

"Well, then I don't know what to do next," DeMarco said, "but I was serious when I told Logan that Curtis has the resources to kill him."

Bill Logan put on his boots, then took a seat at the kitchen table. He needed to run—but before he ran, he needed to think.

He'd figured out how the FBI had found him: his cell phone. He'd been so panicky last night after someone tried to kill him, and tired by the time he arrived at the cabin, that he didn't even think about the damn phone being used to track him. A cell phone these days was like gluing a locator beacon to the top of your head. What he didn't know was how the GPS technology in a cell phone worked. If he turned off the phone, could they still track him? He didn't know. He should probably throw his phone away to be safe, but he hated to do that. He might need it for something urgent and wouldn't have time to drive around and find a pay phone. He almost wished that he hadn't dumped the prepaid phone he'd bought to communicate with Murdock, but he'd tossed that phone right after Johnson's death. Yeah, the smart thing would be to get rid of his cell phone. If the FBI could use it to find him, so could Murdock.

But did Murdock really try to kill him? One thing Marjorie had said that made sense was that Murdock probably wouldn't have missed shooting from less than six feet away. But if Murdock had tried to kill him, then DeMarco was right. If he wanted to survive he'd have to put himself under the government's protection and become the star witness against Curtis—which would effectively destroy his life. He could just see himself spending months helping the FBI develop a case against Curtis, then Curtis's trial would drag on for years and, in the end, Curtis might get off scot-free. But Bill Logan—assuming he didn't spend time in jail—would be flat broke by the time it was all over and would have a hell of a time getting a job.

So what should he do? How could he keep Curtis from killing him and at the same time not testify against Curtis? Then he figured it out. There was a way, even though it meant his life was going to change drastically.

He took out his cell phone and spent about an hour looking at the calendar, jotting down notes. When he was finished, he tossed his duffel bag into his car and took off, doing his best to make sure no one was following him. He stopped on a bridge near Stanton—a town with a population of three hundred sixty-six—long enough to fling his cell phone into the Knife River, then stopped again at the next gas station he saw. At the gas station, he used a pay phone to call a lawyer in Fargo.

After he talked to the lawyer, he began to feel a sense of hope.

Marjorie had to find Bill. The other thing she had to do was call Curtis. By now Curtis would know that somebody had tried to kill Bill, and it would look funny if she didn't call him. The one thing she absolutely had to do, no matter what happened to Bill, was make sure that Curtis trusted her.

She called Curtis's office and, as usual, was told that he'd call her back. She couldn't remember one time when she'd called Curtis and he'd been available to take her call. It was like every second of his day was scheduled out.

Two hours later, Curtis called her. The first thing he said was: "Be careful what you say on the phone."

"Yes, sir," she said. "I just wanted to tell you something that's already been on the news. Somebody tried to kill Bill Logan last night."

"Yeah, I heard. Where's Logan now?"

"I don't know," Marjorie said. "He got scared and ran, and I don't know where he is. Bill thinks that . . . I don't want to say more on the phone. Is there any chance you might be coming here soon?" Marjorie didn't want to fly to Houston again.

"Yeah, as a matter of fact I'm on my way there right now," Curtis said. "I've been invited to a party the governor's throwing tonight. I'm calling you from the plane. I'll be at the Radisson in about three hours. Meet me there."

Marjorie called Bill again—about the tenth time she'd called him—but the call went to voice mail. Where the hell was he? What was he doing? She had to find him.

———————◆◆◆———————

Curtis thought for a moment, then texted Murdock. The phones he and Murdock used to communicate were prepaid cells and not traceable to either man, but Murdock had told him to send text messages and not call. The phones had an encryption program installed for texting.

Using one finger, Curtis typed: Where's Logan?

I don't know.

Somebody tried to kill him.

I know. Heard on the news.

You mean it wasn't you?

Don't be stupid. I wasn't even here when it happened.

Curtis figured Murdock was telling the truth. He wouldn't have tried to kill Logan unless Curtis ordered him to, and if he had tried, he would have succeeded. This also meant that Murdock must not have been able to get to Bismarck before Logan took off. He knew that Murdock preferred not to fly because he didn't want there to be records of him traveling by plane, so by the time he drove from Denver to Bismarck, Logan had disappeared.

Curtis typed: Find him.

———————◆◆◆———————

Marjorie was on her way to the Radisson to see Curtis when her phone rang. She didn't recognize the number, just the North Dakota area code. She decided to answer the call anyway.

"Hello," she said.

"It's me," Bill said.

"Where are you?"

"Never mind where I am. Have you talked to Curtis?"

"I'm on my way to see him right now. He's here in Bismarck. What do want me to tell him, Bill?"

"You tell him that if anybody tries to kill me again, the guy had better succeed next time."

"What the hell does that mean?"

"It means, I have no intention of talking to anybody about the things we've done for Curtis but if somebody tries to kill me again, then I will."

"You listen to me, Bill, and you listen hard. You don't want to threaten Curtis and he didn't try to kill you. I think the guy who took those shots at you was Johnson's grandfather."

"What?"

"It's like I told you. I'm not going to mention his name on the phone, but the guy you think tried to kill you wouldn't have missed. I think what happened is DeMarco told Johnson's grandfather that you were responsible for killing Johnson, and the grandfather, who's your typical Montana redneck cowboy, tried to kill you. He missed because he's an old man."

"Huh," Bill said. "I hadn't thought of that."

"That's right, you didn't. And the reason why is because you've got your head up your butt and you're not thinking at all. Now you need to settle down and come back to Bismarck so we can straighten everything out."

"Yeah, maybe. But I want to take a day or two to mull things over. There's just been a lot of stuff going on. Getting arrested, somebody shooting at me. I just need a little time."

"No! You don't! You get your ass back here and—"

"I'll call you in a day or two, Marge. And you may be right about Johnson's grandfather but pass on the message to Curtis anyway."

Bill hung up.

———◆◆◆———

Marjorie knocked on the door to Curtis's room at the Radisson. He was wearing a tuxedo for the governor's party and it was shiny from age and the pants were about two inches too long. It looked as if Curtis had shrunk since he bought the tux probably twenty years ago.

He was sipping a Coke, but didn't ask if Marjorie wanted a drink. He said, "So what's the story on Logan?"

"Mr. Curtis, right now he's scared and he's hiding someplace. He thinks you tried to have him killed."

"I didn't," Curtis said.

"I know that, sir. But he's scared and he's not thinking straight. And there's something else you need to know. He called me while I was on my way here and he told me to tell you that if another attempt is made on his life, he'll talk to the FBI."

"He said that, did he?"

"Yes, sir. But he won't."

"Well, if he does talk, the only person that will have a problem is you. I don't commit crimes. It's like this party I'm going to tonight. I'll shake the governor's hand and tell him if he runs for reelection, I'll contribute to his campaign. But that's all I'll tell him and that's all I'll do. The only ones who've been bribing and blackmailing people are you and your partner, and no one can prove I ordered you to do anything illegal. And don't forget that one of the best law firms in Houston will be defending me if I have to go to court. What law firm is going to defend you and Logan?

"So you have a problem, young lady, and I'd suggest you resolve it quickly. And until you do, my company is not going to be paying your consulting fee."

Curtis took her arm and walked her to the door. "I've got to get over to the governor's place. Don't call me again until this mess is settled."

After Marjorie left, Curtis pulled out the phone he used to communicate with Murdock.

28

DeMarco had been hoping that after someone made an attempt on Bill Logan's life that Logan would buckle. The guy had been arrested for assault, was looking at jail time, and then someone tries to kill him. That should have been enough to make Logan want to testify against his partner or Curtis, but it didn't work—and DeMarco couldn't figure out what to do next, other than harass Westerberg.

After confronting Logan at the cabin on the Knife River and getting nowhere, Westerberg went back to work in earnest. She pushed again on the IRS to audit Logan and Dawkins—but the taxmen said that wasn't going to happen. They were still feeling the tongue lashing they got from Congress for auditing Tea Party organizations and were avoiding any audit that might appear to support someone's political agenda. Westerberg said she didn't *have* a political agenda—but the stubborn bean counters remained obdurate.

Next Westerberg, even though she knew it was an exercise in futility, started contacting people that Sarah named in her blog as having been bribed. Westerberg told these people that if they didn't admit that they'd been bribed and agree to testify against Logan, Dawkins, or Curtis, the federal government was going to huff and puff and blow their houses down. No one, however, was sufficiently intimidated by the government's big bad wolf to admit to anything.

Finally, Westerberg went through Sarah's blog again, looking for things that, with some really creative legal spin, could be used to obtain a warrant to monitor Logan's and Dawkins's phone calls. She'd told DeMarco that there was no valid justification for a warrant—and she knew there almost certainly wasn't—but Westerberg was getting desperate. So she spent twenty-four sleepless hours putting together an affidavit for a warrant based on Sarah's conclusions—doing her best to make it sound like Sarah's assumptions were the same as evidence—and then she and a fast-talking assistant U.S. attorney paid a visit to a federal judge, laying out their case.

The judge told them to go shit in their hats.

Since Westerberg was doing all the work and DeMarco couldn't think of anything better to do, he decided to expand his cultural horizon by visiting one of North Dakota's more bizarre tourist attractions: the Enchanted Highway. The Enchanted Highway is a thirty-two mile stretch of road eighty-five miles west of Bismarck where a local artist named Gary Greff had assembled the world's largest collection of scrap-metal sculptures.

There was *Geese in Flight*, consisting of ten metal geese with wingspans of thirty feet. The sculpture weighted seventy-eight tons and was listed in *Guinness World Records* because of its size. There was *Pheasants on the Prairie*, five birds constructed of pipe-and-wire mesh, one pecking the ground, the largest fowl being forty feet tall and weighing thirteen thousand pounds. And then there was DeMarco's favorite: *Grasshoppers in the Field,* showing a number of grasshoppers made from fuel-oil tanks, one of them sixty feet long, sitting in a field of wheat also made from metal.

That night, he went to the American Grill for dinner. He took a seat at the bar, ordered a martini, and started to watch the ball game on the TV over the bar. Mariners versus Yankees. Go Mariners. He hated the Yankees.

About fifteen minutes after he arrived, a tall, raven-haired woman took a seat at the bar, a few stools away from him. She was wearing a short cocktail dress; she had legs that went on forever. She smiled at DeMarco and he smiled back. Things were looking up.

The brunette ordered a drink and looked over at DeMarco again. She was definitely coming on to him. He stood up, planning to walk over and say hello to her, when a voice said, "Hi. Remember me?"

Aw, Geez, it was the fifth-grade teacher he'd spent the night with. He said, "Hey, how you doin'? It's good to see you." He then explained that he hadn't lied to her, that he really had been planning to leave town, but something happened and he had to stay a couple more days.

"So you gonna buy me a drink?" the teacher asked. DeMarco was trying like crazy to remember her name. What the hell was it? Amy? Amanda? No! It was Amelia. Thank God, he remembered.

He looked down the bar. The brunette was staring at him, a pretty pout on her face, making it clear she was disappointed. DeMarco gave her a little *Hey-what-can-you-do?* shrug.

The teacher was actually a lot of fun. She knew about a thousand dirty jokes and she cracked him up talking about the fifth-graders she taught. She said every kid in her class had a cell phone and when they had math problems to solve, they used the calculators on their phones. She didn't think there were two kids in her entire class that could actually do long division. She started to tell him a story about this one kid—a kid who was certain to be a future member of the United States

Congress—using his phone to email pictures of his little weenie to girls in the class. As she was talking, DeMarco noticed the long-legged brunette had left.

Oh, well, maybe he'd get lucky and see her again before he left Bismarck. In the meantime, another night with the teacher wasn't the worst thing in the world.

Marjorie didn't tell her husband that she'd been fired and that he might have to find a job. One reason she didn't tell him was because Curtis hadn't actually fired her—it was more like he'd suspended her until she had Bill Logan back under her thumb.

She didn't bother to go to the office. She stayed home and spent the time thinking, almost nonstop, about what to do about Bill and waiting for the gutless bastard to call again. While she was waiting, she harassed her husband into cleaning up the garage and fixing the back gate that was falling off the hinges, then sent him to Walmart to stock up on things they needed. She screamed at her sons about the state of their bedrooms and playing video games and the sorry-ass report cards they brought home. Sometimes she wished she'd had a daughter.

Marjorie's mood didn't improve when Christie called and informed her that she'd struck out with DeMarco. Christie said that Heckler had called her the night before, told her that DeMarco was at the American Grill, and she hustled right on down there to seduce him. But then, just when DeMarco was about to come over and talk to her—he actually was sort of hunky, Christie said—this short blond woman sat down next to DeMarco and it was obvious that she and DeMarco knew each other.

Damn it all, Marjorie thought. That fucking teacher! Did she spend every night at the American Grill? It seemed like nothing was going right these days. Marjorie told Christie to stay home the next couple of nights, that maybe there would be another chance to get DeMarco.

———◆◆◆———

While Marjorie was terrifying her family and Westerberg was working and DeMarco was enjoying artwork on the prairie and getting laid, Bill Logan checked into a motel in Washburn that would take cash and didn't ask for a credit card. He went to a nearby store, bought a Big Chief tablet like grade-school kids use, a couple of pens, a bottle of Glenlivet, half a dozen sandwiches, and returned to his shitty motel room. Then he wrote down five of the most incriminating, underhanded things he could think of that he and Marjorie had done for Leonard Curtis—with two exceptions. He didn't include in his manifesto that he'd contracted Murdock to kill Judge Wainwright or Sarah Johnson. The idea was to incriminate Curtis, not himself.

The reason he documented only five instances of bribery, blackmail, and political corruption was because those were instances when he and Marjorie had met with Curtis to discuss the issues. Bill had checked the calendar in his smart phone before he'd dumped the phone and copied down the times and dates when they'd met with Curtis so Curtis couldn't claim to have been somewhere else. He'd also, to the best of his ability, wrote down exactly what Curtis had said on those occasions. Okay, he did embellish the quotations a bit to make Curtis sound more guilty. He also wrote down the amounts of money paid to certain politicians so the FBI could squeeze them as necessary to corroborate Bill's statements.

When he finished, he'd filled thirty pages in the tablet. In places it was hard to read his handwriting as the legibility of his writing was directly proportional to the amount of scotch he'd consumed.

He checked out of the motel and drove back to Bismarck. The first place he stopped was a FedEx store. He made a copy of his thirty-page masterpiece, placed the original in a manila envelope he bought there in the store, and then wrote a note to his big brother, George.

George was an engineer who worked for Alcoa in Cleveland. Bill liked George well enough, but he didn't have a damn thing in common with the guy and the last time he'd seen him was three years ago. But George was the only one he could trust and, more important, George was named as the executor of his will. In the note, Bill said, "George, I know this is going to sound weird but if I die or disappear any time in the near future—even if my death looks accidental or I have a heart attack or something—there's a document in an envelope in my safe deposit box at the Wells Fargo bank on Broadway in Bismarck. I want you to deliver it to the FBI if anything happens to me. As my executor, you'll be able to get into the deposit box. Your brother, Bill."

After he'd FedExed the note to George, his next stop was the Wells Fargo bank, where he placed the original of the document in his safe deposit box. He kept the copy with him. He wanted to go home but he was afraid to in case Murdock or Sarah Johnson's grandfather or anybody else was still looking to kill him. He checked into a motel in Bismarck and took a shower for the first time in two days. He thought about calling Marjorie to set up a meeting with her, but then decided he needed a nap. He'd call her later when he was rested—but he was feeling pretty good about where things currently stood.

Bill had come to a conclusion in the last two days. He'd decided to quit working for Leonard Curtis and at the same time he was going to protect himself against Curtis. Working for Curtis—and working with Marjorie—had become too dangerous and stressful. Not only that, Bill felt terrible about what had happened to Sarah Johnson, and he didn't ever want to have to do something like that again. The way he looked at it, it was *Marjorie's* fault that Johnson had been killed. She was the one who forced him to contact Murdock. So he wanted to be done with both Curtis and Marjorie Dawkins—but at the same time, he wanted to maintain his lifestyle and keep doing the kind of work he enjoyed.

The lawyer in Fargo that Bill had called from the pay phone at the gas station near Stanton was a man named Clarence Penrose. Penrose worked for Concordia Oil, an independent that was rumored to be two to three times bigger than Curtis's company. Penrose did the same sort of things Bill and Marjorie did for Curtis, and Bill and Penrose had crossed paths numerous times in the last ten years when Concordia's interests coincided with Curtis's.

Penrose was a lot older than Bill, about Curtis's age, but he and Bill had always hit it off and Penrose was impressed by some of the things he knew Bill had done. The last time Bill had dinner with Penrose in Fargo, Penrose had said that he was thinking about retiring in a few years and Bill would be a good man to replace him.

So Bill had called Penrose, said he'd decided to part ways with Curtis, and asked if the job offer was still on the table. Penrose said it was. Bill asked about the salary and Penrose told him that he made three to four hundred grand a year depending on his annual bonus, but Bill would start off at seventy since he'd basically be acting as Penrose's helper. Bill said that seemed kind of low, but Penrose said, "Kid, I'll be retiring in exactly two years. My wife wants to move to Florida. She's sick of Fargo. So in two years, the job will be yours." Bill decided that he could live off seventy grand for a couple of years because it sounded like if he did the job well, he'd eventually make more working for Concordia than he'd been making working for Curtis.

Once again, Marjorie didn't recognize the number on the caller ID. She was in the garage, with all the doors shut, smoking. "Hello," she said.

"It's me," Bill said.

"Where the fuck are you?" she screamed.

"Here in Bismarck. We need to meet."

"No shit," Marjorie said. "But I don't want to meet at the office. I'm worried because of all the, you know, stuff going on that the FBI could be bugging us or something."

"So where do you want to meet?"

"Let me think about that for a minute," she said, although she didn't really have to think about it at all. "You remember the place where Dick and I met you and that blonde you were dating a couple of years ago? I think her name was Terri, Sherri, something like that. She worked in the governor's office."

"I don't know who you're talking about."

"We had a picnic and threw a Frisbee around."

"Oh, yeah," Bill said. "Her name was Randi."

"Whatever. You remember where we went?"

"Yeah."

"Okay, I'll meet you there at nine tomorrow night. I can't make it any earlier."

"Why do you want to meet there?"

"I want to meet there because it's the first place I thought of where I could tell you where I wanted to meet but wouldn't have to say the name out loud."

Bill hesitated as if he was suspicious, then said, "Okay, I'll see you there. But I'm warning you, Marge, if Murdock shows up instead of you—"

"Shut up! Quit flapping your mouth. I'm talking on a fucking radio here. I'll see you at nine and if I'm late, you just wait for me."

After Marjorie disconnected the call, she lit another cigarette and at that moment, wouldn't you know, Bobby opened the door to the garage. She dropped the cigarette on the floor behind her and said, "What are you doing in here?"

"Getting my skateboard."

"You're not going skateboarding. Get back in the house and finish your homework."

"I already finished."

"Then go back in the house and pick up all the crap in the family room."

"It smells like cigarette smoke in here."

"Bobby, if you don't get out of my sight in the next two seconds . . ."

"Jeez, all right. Are you on the rag or something?"

"What did you just say?" She could feel her eyes practically popping out of her head.

Bobby vanished like Houdini.

She found the cigarette she'd dropped. She was lucky it hadn't started a fire since it had landed next to a bunch of dirty rags that Dick hadn't put back in the rag box. She took a couple more puffs on the cigarette, then crushed it out and went back into the house. Dick was making dinner and he glanced over at her as she passed through the kitchen but had the good sense not to say anything. She was going to tell him what Bobby had said about her being on the rag and jump all over his ass—she knew Bobby had heard that expression from him—but not right now. She found her purse sitting on the dining room table, extracted her key ring, and went back to the garage.

There was a metal box on a shelf in the garage that was too high for the boys to reach without a ladder. The box had a padlock on it and she was the only one who had the key. Since she wasn't much taller than her oldest son, she got the stepladder, climbed up, and took the box off the shelf and put it on the workbench that Dick rarely used.

Inside the box were three pistols. The first was a nine millimeter SIG Sauer P226 that Dick had bought before they were married. The second gun was a Smith & Wesson .357 revolver that her father had given her one Christmas when he read about a rapist running around Bismarck. The .357 kicked like a mule and was so damn heavy it was like carrying a brick in her purse. The final gun in the box was a little two-shot Derringer that fired .32 caliber bullets. It weighed less than a pound and was about three and half inches long.

She bought the Derringer when she'd been running all around the Dakotas on Curtis's behalf. She'd been in Beulah, a small North Dakota town in a gas-rich area, having dinner alone one night when some drunken ape started hitting on her—and then followed her back to her motel room. She was able to get into her room and lock the door, but the ape started pounding on it and didn't leave until she called the cops, who took twenty minutes to get there. She purchased the Derringer at an estate sale after her experience in Beulah, so she'd have some protection in the future when she was traveling alone. She thought it was cute and she liked that she could easily hold it in her small right hand.

But when her oldest son started walking and getting into every drawer and cabinet in the house, she decided she didn't want the guns in the house or the cars or anyplace where her boys could even remotely get at them. So she took all the guns they owned, dumped them into the lockbox in the garage, and she kept the only key.

The Derringer was perfect for what she had in mind. It was easy to conceal, it wasn't registered, and, since it was like a revolver, she didn't have to worry about shell casings.

She slipped the Derringer into her back pocket and headed back into the house. When she saw Dick still at the counter making dinner, she took a breath and told herself she needed to quit acting like such a bitch.

"Honey, is there anything I can do to help?" she said.

29

Marjorie Dawkins was a planner.

She was better than anyone she knew in terms of figuring out all the details, scheduling the tasks to be performed, and developing contingency plans in case something went wrong. She never said it out loud to anyone, but she thought she would have made a hell of a general.

At noon, the day she was meeting Bill, she laid out everything she would need: the clothes she'd wear, gloves, a few paper bags. She put the gloves and one of the bags in her car and left the other bags in the garage. Then she drove over to a tavern, and setting the stopwatch feature on her cell phone, she drove from the tavern to the park as fast as she could. She checked the stopwatch: ninety-four seconds. Perfect.

While Marjorie was fine-tuning the details of her plan, DeMarco met with Westerberg only to hear how little progress she'd made. She'd had no luck getting the IRS to audit D&L Consulting, and had been unable to get a warrant to see if Logan or Dawkins had transferred money to an offshore account after Sarah was killed. Nonetheless, he called Doug Thorpe and told him the FBI was still hot on the trail of Sarah's killer, making it sound as if progress was actually being made. He called Mahoney next; he thought about lying to him, too, but told the truth, that he was stuck and couldn't figure out what to do.

He drove to Bill Logan's house a couple of times and knocked on the door, but Logan wasn't home—or was hiding inside his home. DeMarco convinced Westerberg to try to find Logan via his cell phone again, and she appealed to the cooperative judge who'd granted her the previous warrant, but was unsuccessful in locating Logan. It appeared as if he'd disabled or ditched his phone.

At five, after a day filled with frustration, DeMarco decided to go to dinner. But he wanted to go someplace other than the American Grill. He liked the American Grill; he just didn't want to run into the teacher again. He called the front desk and they recommended a place called Jack's Steakhouse.

He decided to have a drink in the bar before he sat down to dinner, and was halfway through his martini when who should walk into the bar but the long-legged, raven-haired beauty he'd seen in the American Grill. It seemed odd he should run into the same woman two nights in a row, but then thought that Bismarck was a pretty small town and there weren't all that many places to go. When the woman saw him she made an oh-my-gosh expression, as if she was equally surprised, and DeMarco waved her over.

He hadn't been in the mood for companionship earlier, but his mood suddenly changed.

———◆———

Marjorie was just leaving the house to drive over to the boys' school when her phone rang. It was Heckler.

"Yeah?" she said.

"He's at Jack's Steakhouse and your pal, Christie, just walked into the place."

"Are you sure DeMarco hasn't seen you following him?"

"I don't think so. My girlfriend's with me and she's driving, so if he looks at the cars behind him, he'll see a couple instead of a single guy. And I switched cars again."

Marjorie was flabbergasted that Heckler would have a girlfriend, but all she said was, "Good," and hung up. By tomorrow, DeMarco— Bismarck's newest rapist—should be in jail.

She drove about a block farther, then something occurred to her: the rape charge would give DeMarco one hell of an alibi—and maybe that wasn't good. She called Heckler back. "I've changed my mind. Call Christie and tell her to get out of that bar right now. Immediately. Tell her I'll pay her half of what I promised her, but I don't want her to do anything with DeMarco. You got it?"

"Yeah, okay," Heckler said.

"And you and your girlfriend can stop following DeMarco, too. Take your girlfriend out for dinner, then go home. I'll pay for the dinner."

When DeMarco told Christie that he lived in Washington, D.C., she asked if he knew the president. He was beginning to think that she wasn't the brightest female on the planet and she was nowhere near as interesting as his little teacher friend—but she was so damn good-looking that he was willing to overlook a few minor flaws.

She was rambling on about some mean thing her boss at Walmart had said to her, when her phone rang. "I'm sorry," she said. "I better take this." She listened to whoever had called for less than a minute and hung up.

"Problem?" DeMarco asked.

"Oh, no. Nothing important. Anyway, I'm just standing there at the checkout counter and Horace says to me . . ."

———◆———

Marjorie arrived at the PTA meeting promptly at seven thirty and shot the breeze with some of the other moms until the meeting started. The topic that night was alerting parents if there was a lockdown. A couple weeks ago, over in Fargo, some schizo nut had been walking around with a shotgun, firing at stop signs and garbage cans and mailboxes. The Fargo cops called the nearest school and told the principal to lock it down until they located the whacko, who had somehow managed to disappear. The cops eventually found the crazy guy talking to a tree but the school never notified the parents that their kids were in danger. The parents learned about the lockdown only if they happened to be listening to the radio or if their kids had cell phones and called home; some moms didn't hear about it until their kids got home that afternoon.

Marjorie had decided that that kind of shit wasn't going to happen at her boys' school, and she wanted the school to develop a system where parents and nannies and whoever else would be notified on their cell phones as soon as a lockdown commenced. Then everybody spent an hour yelling, the moms saying they didn't want to be the last to know that their kids were in danger and the principal and his lackeys saying they didn't have the time, the budget, or the expertise to develop and maintain a system that would send a text message to every mom in the district.

Marjorie finally took charge and said she knew a guy—meaning Gordy—and he would develop the system for the school and set it up so it would be easy for some secretary to add and delete phone numbers from it. And her guy wouldn't charge the school a thing— meaning Marjorie didn't intend to pay Gordy for doing a public service.

Everybody needed to pay back once in a while, including a pot-smoking hacker like Gordy. The meeting ended with the principal saying he'd take Marjorie's suggestion under advisement, and Marjorie said fine, but her tone of voice made it clear that if he didn't do what she wanted she was going to make his life a living hell.

———◆◆◆———

Bill Logan arrived at the park half an hour early. He wanted to scope the place out. What he particularly wanted to do was make sure that Murdock wasn't lurking about. There weren't any cars in the parking lot and there weren't a bunch of places to hide, so it looked okay but it still made him nervous meeting Marjorie here after dark. He thought about what she'd said about why she'd picked the meeting place—because it was the first place she could think of where she wouldn't have to say the name on the phone—and that made sense. Still, he would have felt more comfortable if they'd met in a bar. It wasn't like they were trying to hide that they were partners.

On the other hand, maybe this was a good place to meet her because after he gave her the copy of the document he'd prepared, she was going to go crazy and start screaming at him. But that was all right. After tonight, he might not ever see Marjorie again and she'd have to find somebody else to scream at.

He walked over to a picnic table and took a seat. He started to place the document in the center of the table so it would be the first thing Marjorie would see, then noticed the table was a bit damp and grimy. So he rolled up the document and placed it in the inside pocket of his jacket; he'd hand it to her after he explained what he'd done and why Curtis had better leave him alone.

As he sat there waiting for Marjorie, he thought about all the things he'd have to do before he moved to Fargo. He'd have to put his house on the market, of course, but the market was booming right now so he ought to turn a decent profit. Then he'd have to find a place in Fargo to buy, but he was thinking that maybe for a while he'd just rent. He'd probably have to put some of his furniture in storage and would have to get someone to drive one of his cars to Fargo. Yeah, relocating was going to be a hassle but he was actually starting to look forward to moving out of Bismarck and working for Concordia. He was anxious to see how the big boys played the game.

⚬

After the PTA meeting was over, about ten of the moms went to a tavern, which they always did after the PTA meetings. The mothers pushed tables together, ordered glasses of Merlot and Chardonnay, and started gossiping. At one point, Marjorie tossed into the ring that she'd heard that Amelia Moore, the fifth-grade math teacher, spent damn near every night at the American Grill and would screw anything with a dick between its legs.

At ten after nine, Marjorie said to the woman sitting next to her, "Jean, would you mind watching my purse? I need to go outside for just a second."

"Aw, geez, Marge, are you smoking again?"

Marjorie tried to look sheepish.

Inside Marjorie's purse was her cell phone. She knew cell phones could be used to locate people and trace their movements, and by leaving her cell phone next to Jean no one would be able to use it to prove she'd left the tavern. Marjorie had thought of everything.

She walked to the rear of the tavern, pushed through the back exit, then she really started moving. She hopped into her car, put on the gloves lying on the passenger seat, and drove like a maniac to the park where Logan was waiting—which took exactly ninety seconds, four seconds faster than when she'd timed the trip earlier in the day. And there was Bill, sitting at the picnic table, and no one else was anywhere in sight. It was actually dark enough outside that she couldn't really tell that it was Bill sitting there, but who else could it be?

She fast-walked toward him like she was in a race, and when she was about six feet away, she pulled the Derringer out of her jacket pocket and pointed it at his face.

Bill said, "Whoa, Marjorie. What—"

Marjorie shot him right in the center of his forehead and Bill fell off the bench and onto the grass near the picnic table. "Whoa, Marjorie, my ass," she muttered. She walked around the table, bent over, placed the muzzle of the derringer directly against his left temple, and shot him once more in the head. The .32 caliber bullets didn't make any more noise than a popcorn fart.

She ran back to her car, tossed the Derringer into the glove box, stripped off the gloves and placed them on the passenger seat, and started the engine. Two minutes later she was a little out of breath, but sipping a glass of wine and seated next to her friend, Jean, who'd been watching her purse. It was 9:17 p.m. She'd been gone from the bar exactly seven minutes—about the time it takes to finish a smoke then maybe go to the bathroom.

Marjorie finished her glass of wine, ordered another, gossiped some more, and again excused herself. She went out to her car, put on her gloves, took the Derringer out of the glove box, and placed it in the paper bag she'd staged for that purpose. She then walked up the street a little ways and shoved the bag deep into a trash can. If the Derringer was found—which seemed highly unlikely—Marjorie wasn't worried, as the gun wasn't registered to her. As for fingerprints, she'd wiped hers off the gun and the bullets the day she decided to use the Derringer and had always worn gloves when she touched the gun after that. But most likely the murder weapon wouldn't be found because tomorrow was garbage pickup day, and by tomorrow night her cute little Derringer would be under ten tons of trash in a landfill.

She dropped the gloves she'd been wearing into another trash can, then went back into the tavern and sat down with her friends again. At ten o'clock she told all the moms good-bye, that it was time to head on home to Dick and the boys, and they all praised her again for taking the initiative on the lockdown-notification project.

When she returned home the boys were in bed and Dick was watching TV. "How'd the meeting go?" he asked, like he could give a shit.

"I'll tell you about it in a minute," she said. She walked into her home office and sent out three emails sitting in the draft folder. The times she sent the emails would be recorded in her machine and on the Comcast server. Next she grabbed a robe, went into the bathroom, took off her clothes, and took a quick shower. She shampooed her hair and she really scrubbed her hands and arms even though she'd been wearing a long-sleeved blouse and gloves when she shot Bill. She went back into the bedroom and put on sweatpants and a sweatshirt and slipped into some tennis shoes. She picked up the clothes she'd been wearing when she shot Bill, including her shoes, and placed the clothes and shoes into the paper bags she'd staged for this purpose.

She went back into her office, sent out three more emails, then told Dick she'd forgotten something in her car. He'd figure she was probably sneaking out to the garage for a smoke. She went out the back door with the paper bags that contained her clothes and walked down the alley, placing the bags in her neighbors' trash cans—which would all be picked up first thing in the morning. As she walked back to the house she was humming but didn't realize it. If there had been blood or gunshot residue or little chunks of Bill's DNA on her clothes or skin, she'd just taken care of those problems.

Back in the house she used the landline to call a mom she'd seen at the PTA meeting, made an excuse for calling so late, then jabbered with the woman for a few minutes. Although Dick could testify that she came home right after she left the tavern, the emails and phone call would further establish the fact.

Marjorie figured that when the cops found Bill Logan's body—most likely tomorrow morning when it was light out—they'd think that the person who killed him was the same guy who'd tried to kill him before. This time the guy just succeeded. And although she didn't know anything about forensic science other than what she'd seen on those CSI shows, she guessed that the cops would most likely establish the time of death at sometime the night before. She didn't know if taking liver temperatures and all that stuff could pin the time down to around nine p.m., but she almost hoped so. Marjorie had a solid alibi from seven thirty until almost midnight between the PTA meeting, the gossip session at the tavern, and all the emails and phone calls after she got home.

She was going to miss Bill Logan—she really was—but Bill just had to go.

30

"Where are you, DeMarco?" Westerberg asked.

"In my motel room. Why? What's going on?"

"You need to get down to the Bismarck police station. Right now."

DeMarco drove to the station and asked the cop at the main desk where he could find FBI Agent Westerberg. The cop told him to wait. Five minutes later Westerberg arrived in the station lobby to meet him. "Come with me," she said.

"And good morning to you, too."

Westerberg ignored him. She led him to what looked like an interrogation room: a table, a chair on one side, two chairs on the other, a camera up on the wall. Sitting in one of the chairs was the big detective with the kind eyes who'd interviewed him after Sarah was killed.

"Sit down, DeMarco," Westerberg said—directing DeMarco to what he thought of as the suspect's seat.

"What's this all about?" he asked

"Mr. DeMarco," the Bismarck detective said, "you have the right to remain silent. Anything you say—"

"Hold on. What's going on here?"

The detective—whose name was Fredericks—ignored him and continued with the Miranda warning, concluding with, "Do you understand your rights as I've explained them to you?"

"Yeah, I understand them. Now what's going on?"

"Bill Logan was shot last night. He's dead. Would you mind telling me where you were last night?"

"You gotta be shittin' me," DeMarco said to Westerberg.

"Answer the question, DeMarco," Westerberg said. "Where were you last night?"

"Well, from about five thirty until eight, I was at a restaurant called Jack's Steakhouse. I had dinner with a woman."

"What was her name?"

"Uh, Christie something. A tall brunette. I don't know that I ever got her last name. But I know she works at Walmart and should be at work today."

"And where did you go after dinner?" Detective Fredericks asked.

DeMarco looked away, feeling sheepish, particularly with Westerberg there. "I went back to Christie's apartment and spent the night there. I left about seven this morning."

"Jesus, DeMarco," Westerberg said, like he'd done something wrong.

"What?" DeMarco said.

"Would you object to a gunshot residue test on your hands and arms?" the detective said.

"No. Swab away. Or whatever it is you do."

After the gunshot residue test was complete—the results were negative—the detective said he was going to Walmart to talk to Christie and see if she'd confirm DeMarco's alibi.

"Let's go back into the interrogation room," Westerberg said. "I want to show you something."

Inside the room, DeMarco again back in the suspect's chair, Westerberg placed a multipage, handwritten document on the table in front of him. "Take a look at that. That's was in the inside pocket of the jacket Logan was wearing when he was shot. It's already been dusted for prints, and the only prints on it are Logan's. If that document is authentic, which I think it is, there's enough there to get Marjorie Dawkins, three state legislators, and two judges. I'm not sure we can get Leonard Curtis, however. Logan said Curtis ordered him and Dawkins to bribe the judges and legislators, and he provides enough details that maybe what Logan wrote will convince a jury, but I'm not sure."

DeMarco was scanning the document as Westerberg talked. While still reading, he said, "It doesn't matter. If we can get Dawkins, she'll give us Curtis."

"This will work," DeMarco said, tapping Logan's statement. "What you don't do is give Dawkins immunity for testifying against these politicians. Tell her she only gets immunity if she gives up Curtis and tells us who killed Sarah. Let's go talk to her."

"You are not going near Marjorie Dawkins, DeMarco. As I've told you about sixteen times, you are not law enforcement. I have enough now to make a case against her and five other people, and I am not about to let you screw it up. *I'll* go talk to Dawkins. In fact, I'm going to arrest Dawkins. And Detective Fredericks is going to come with me and ask where she was last night."

"You think she might have killed Logan?"

"I don't know. If she knew he'd prepared that document, she certainly wouldn't have left it on his body."

"If she didn't kill him, then who did?"

"I don't know. Maybe the person who tried to kill Logan the other night at his office. Maybe the person who killed Sarah Johnson. I don't know."

The bell rang and Marjorie answered the door. Dick was grocery shopping and the boys were in school. She opened the door to find a woman and a big guy she didn't know standing on her porch. The big guy identified himself as Detective Harold Fredericks, Bismarck Homicide, and introduced the woman as Agent Westerberg, FBI.

"Mrs. Dawkins," he said, "Bill Logan was shot and killed last night."

"What?" Marjorie said, backing up, holding her hands over her mouth. "What are you talking about? Oh, my God, this can't be true. Are you sure it's Bill? He just can't be dead."

Marjorie thought she did a pretty good job of feigning surprise. She tried to squeeze out a few tears, but couldn't make that happen.

"I need to ask you some questions, Mrs. Dawkins," the big cop said.

"Yeah, sure. Anything," Marjorie said.

"But first I need to tell you your rights."

"What?"

"You have the right to remain silent. You . . ."

After he finished, he said, "Would you like to have a lawyer present, Mrs. Dawkins?"

"A lawyer? Why would I need a lawyer? What's going on here?"

"Can you tell me where you were last night, Mrs. Dawkins?"

Marjorie didn't spit it all out at once. She said she'd had dinner with Dick and the boys about five, went to the PTA meeting, and had drinks afterward with a bunch of moms. When Fredericks asked, she filled in the details regarding the time and where she went for drinks. When he asked what time she got home, she told him. "Dick can tell you I got home about ten, ten thirty, and didn't go out for the rest of the night."

"Can anyone beside your husband verify you didn't leave the house?"

"Beside my husband?" she said, acting confused. Then she pretended to remember the emails she'd sent out and the phone call she'd made.

"I'm guessing you can confirm those emails were sent from the desktop computer here in the house," she added.

"Will you give permission for one of our technicians to examine your computer and gain access to your phone records?" Fredericks asked.

"Sure. I don't have anything to hide. But I can tell you I'm starting to get a little mad here. My partner, who was also my friend, was killed and you people are treating me like a, like a . . . like a suspect or something."

Marjorie noted that the FBI lady hadn't said a word since the detective started questioning her. She just sat there, with this sort of half smile on her face.

"And why is the FBI here?" she asked. "I mean, I don't know anything about legal jurisdictions and all that, but is Bill's murder some sort of federal crime?"

"No," Westerberg said. "Mrs. Dawkins, I'm arresting you on five counts of bribing public officials in two states. You've already been read your Miranda rights and I'd suggest you not say another word until you have an attorney present."

"What!" Marjorie shrieked.

"Turn around, Mrs. Dawkins. I'm going to handcuff you."

And that's when Dick walked through the side door that led to the garage. "Hey, you're not going to believe what I heard down at the store. I ran into—"

Then he saw his wife in handcuffs.

———◆———

In the last five hours, Marjorie had been on an emotional roller coaster.

The roller-coaster ride started when Westerberg and an assistant U.S. attorney gave Marjorie and her lawyer a copy of a document that Bill had prepared and which had been found in the jacket Bill was wearing when she shot him. At first, she was numb with shock as she read what

Bill had written, then she got so mad she was surprised she didn't have a stroke. If Bill Logan had still been alive she would have killed him again. When she read how she'd bribed a federal judge—Bill helpfully providing the day she met the judge, the restaurant where they met, the name of a waitress who could corroborate the meeting, and how she'd obscured the money trail—she began to laugh hysterically, then the laughter turned to tears. She'd probably spent two of the last five hours crying.

It had never occurred to her that Bill would write a document implicating her—and himself—for things they'd done for Leonard Curtis. He must have prepared it to protect himself in case Curtis was thinking about killing him and he'd probably been planning to show it to her, but she'd shot him before he could. It had also never occurred to her to search Bill. Plus, she hadn't had time to search him after she shot him because her whole plan revolved around her being gone from the tavern for the shortest period possible.

Unlike half the women in Bismarck, Marjorie had never slept with Bill Logan—but the man had truly and totally fucked her.

Marjorie never said a word when Westerberg and the U.S. attorney attempted to question her. The U.S. attorney eventually concluded the meeting by saying that the only way she could avoid going to prison for years was to cooperate and testify against Leonard Curtis—and her first thought was: Murdock is going to kill me.

She also realized that she'd made a serious mistake. Her lawyer was from a firm that Curtis used. A firm that made a lot of money off Leonard Curtis. She asked her attorney if he understood that he was representing her and not Curtis, and the weasel said of course, he understood. He was her lawyer, not Curtis's.

Yeah, right. Marjorie was willing to bet everything she owned that as soon as he went back to his office he was going to call Curtis.

Tomorrow morning she'd be arraigned and granted bail—and by tomorrow evening every person she knew would know she'd been arrested. Her sons were going to be humiliated. She needed to figure out what she was going to do, but it seemed pretty clear. She really had only one option. She was going to have to testify against Curtis. She was also going to give up Murdock, although she didn't really know much about Murdock other than his name and that he probably lived in Denver.

She figured if she did both of those things, she might get immunity. But until Curtis's trial—which probably wouldn't take place for a couple of years because his lawyers would delay things as long as possible—they'd have to put her and her family in a witness protection program. She needed to make sure the FBI lady understood that Curtis would kill her to prevent her from testifying. Logan's document alone wouldn't be enough to convict Curtis, but her testimony would be—after which her life would be over.

Her family was going to have to move away from Bismarck—no way would she continue to live in the city and become the butt of jokes. Dick would have to get some kind of job and she would, too. But she knew she'd never get anything in politics after Curtis's trial. She could just see herself working at Walmart, like that bimbo Christie.

<hr />

Leonard Curtis was in Pierre when he got a call from a lawyer named Barrington who practiced in Bismarck. Barrington's message said the subject was urgent, but Curtis didn't get around to calling him until three hours later.

Barrington told him that he'd been retained to represent Marjorie Dawkins. After that, the phone call was like a series of aftershocks following an earthquake: Bill Logan had been killed. Logan had left a document incriminating Dawkins and Curtis. Dawkins had been arrested for bribery. The government was offering Dawkins a deal if she'd testify against Curtis.

The first thing Curtis did was make sure Barrington was going to continue to represent Dawkins while at the same time keeping him informed. "Yes, sir," Barrington said.

Then he texted Murdock: Did you kill Logan?

No. Dawkins did. I saw her do it.

Whoa! He was shocked that Dawkins had killed Logan but then, when he thought about it, maybe that wasn't so shocking. Who else would have killed the man if Murdock didn't? Curtis had told Dawkins that she needed to get Logan under control if she wanted to keep her job and it appeared that she decided the best way to do that was to kill the man. Marjorie Dawkins was one cold-blooded little bitch.

He was less surprised that Murdock had witnessed Logan's murder. He'd told Murdock that he wanted him in Bismarck so he'd be nearby if he had to take care of Logan or Dawkins, and he'd told Murdock to keep tabs on them. But he didn't see how Murdock being a witness to Logan's murder was going to do him any good. Murdock was not the kind of guy who was going to testify against Dawkins in a courtroom.

He texted: Stick with Dawkins. But don't do anything unless I tell you.

Roger that.

Curtis called his pilot and said, "Get the plane ready to go. I want to fly to Bismarck."

He wanted to see this document that Logan had left behind and he wanted to talk to Dawkins's lawyer. He also might talk to Dawkins. He wasn't sure what he was going to say to her, but he wanted to see if it looked like she was going to testify against him. Maybe he could work out some kind of deal with her if she agreed to take the fall without pointing the finger at him. If he offered her a million bucks on top of the annual salary he was paying her, that ought to be sufficient compensation for her to spend a few years in a cell—and he'd probably spend at least a million if he had to defend himself against a bunch of cockamamie charges.

And if that didn't work, there was always Murdock.

31

DeMarco packed his bag and swung by the police station to say good-bye to Westerberg. He found her in a conference room with half a dozen people. He was guessing the other people were more FBI agents and lawyers. With Dawkins's arrest and Logan's confession, the Bureau was in full swing. This was the sort of case they lived for: a witness to testify against a billionaire and five politicians who would soon be doing televised perp walks.

It wasn't clear to DeMarco who had jurisdiction over the whole mess. The FBI was involved because one of the judges bribed had been a federal judge and Curtis's crimes had occurred in multiple states. Regardless of who had jurisdiction, DeMarco was betting that Westerberg was feeling pretty good about things as she'd get the credit for pushing Logan to the point where he virtually wrote a confession and for busting Dawkins. DeMarco certainly didn't care who got the credit. The last thing he wanted was his name in the news.

"I just came to tell you good-bye, Agent," he said.

"You're going back to Washington already?"

"Yeah. My work here is done." He thought *my work here is done* sounded like something the Lone Ranger might say. "Logan's dead and Dawkins will soon be singing like a bright yellow bird against Curtis. But I'm guessing it's going to be months, if not years, before Curtis's trial starts."

"Yeah, we've got a lot of work to do to build a case."

"Do you think Curtis will actually be convicted?"

"I think if Dawkins testifies against him, there's a better than eighty percent chance."

"Eighty percent?"

She shrugged. "He's a rich guy with a lot of lawyers. And even with Logan's written statement and Dawkins's testimony, it's still going to be tough to make a beyond-a-reasonable-doubt case that he ordered Logan and Dawkins to bribe people. Curtis will say that Dawkins acted on her own, *thinking* she was doing what Curtis wanted, and now she's only implicating Curtis to save herself. But I think our chances are pretty good. Dawkins will make a good witness."

"What about Logan's killer? You got any leads on him?"

"No. It was probably the same guy who killed Sarah, although he didn't use the same kind of weapon. And I'm guessing Curtis ordered Logan murdered, but I don't know for sure. What I do know is that it wasn't you or Dawkins since you've both got alibis."

"Did you seriously think that I might have killed Logan?" DeMarco said.

"No," Westerberg admitted.

"That's good. Well, I've got to get going. Best of luck to you, Agent, and thanks for your help. And I'll be sure to tell John Mahoney that you did a good job."

DeMarco turned to leave but Westerberg said, "Hey, hold on a minute, DeMarco. I don't want you to think you're getting away with something here. You may not have killed Logan, but I know you were the guy who fired those shots at him that night at his office. I'm positive it was you. You did it to panic him—and it worked."

"Me?" DeMarco said. "I don't think so, Agent. I don't go around shooting guns at people. I don't even own a gun."

"Bullshit, DeMarco. I know you did it."

DeMarco smiled and walked away.

32

DeMarco called Mahoney and told him where things stood: Logan was dead, five crooked politicians would soon land in the jail, and, unless Marjorie Dawkins wanted to go to jail herself, she was going to have to give up Curtis and whoever had killed Sarah.

"None of that's enough to make up for that girl being killed," Mahoney said.

He could always count on Mahoney to lift his spirits.

"I'm going to fly out of Billings tonight but before I do, I'm going to stop and see Doug Thorpe one last time."

"Yeah, do that. I'll call him later and talk to him."

"Maybe instead of calling, you might want to fly out here and do some fishing. He could use a friend to fish with."

Thorpe was sitting in one of the rocking chairs on his front porch when DeMarco pulled up in front of his cabin. Daisy was sleeping next to him.

"What happened, DeMarco?" Thorpe said. The man sounded tired, like he might never get out of that rocking chair again.

"Bill Logan's dead," DeMarco said.

"Who killed him?"

"I don't know. I think it was probably the same guy who killed Sarah, but I don't know for sure. I thought Dawkins might have killed him but she has an alibi."

Then DeMarco went on to explain how Logan had a document on his body that incriminated Dawkins and Curtis, and how Dawkins had already been arrested.

"The FBI doesn't move at lightning speed on a case like this, Mr. Thorpe," DeMarco said, "but eventually they'll arrest Curtis, Dawkins will testify against him, and Curtis will go to jail. And as old as he is, there's a good chance he'll die in jail."

"What about the person who killed Sarah?" Thorpe said.

"I don't know how to say this and make it come out right, but that guy, whoever he is, was just a tool. The people responsible for Sarah's death were Curtis, Logan, and Dawkins, and Logan was most likely the one who hired the killer. And the FBI still might get the killer if Dawkins knows anything about him, but the main people responsible for Sarah's death are going to pay."

"What do you think the chances are that Curtis will go to jail?" DeMarco really wished he hadn't asked that question. He told Thorpe what Westerberg had told him: eighty percent.

"But Dawkins," Thorpe said, "might get immunity if she testifies against Curtis."

"Yeah, maybe," DeMarco said. "I'm sorry. It's not a perfect world."

"No shit," Thorpe said.

While DeMarco was trying to figure out what to say next, the phone inside the cabin rang. Thorpe said, "I'll be right back."

A few minutes later, Thorpe returned to the porch and said, "That was John. He's flying out here. He'll be here tomorrow morning. Said he wants to do some fishing and drinking. I almost told him to go to hell, but I know it wasn't his fault what happened to Sarah. He was just trying to help." He paused before he said, "It'll be good to see him again."

Doug Thorpe, DeMarco thought, was one of the most decent human beings he'd ever met.

DeMarco told Thorpe that he had to get going as he had a plane to catch, but before he left Thorpe said, "I figured out who to leave all Sarah's money to. There's this group out here who does their best to protect Montana's rivers. A few million bucks ought to make their job easier."

<hr />

Thorpe watched DeMarco drive away, then he sat there in the rocking chair thinking: eighty percent. That's what DeMarco had said, that Curtis had an eighty percent chance of being found guilty. But he wouldn't be found guilty of Sarah's murder; he'd be found guilty of bribing a few slimy politicians.

He'd looked up Curtis on the Internet. He was an old man, like DeMarco had said. Thorpe didn't know how much time a guy could get for bribery, maybe five or ten years, but whatever Curtis got, there was a possibility that he might die in jail. That is, he might die in jail if he actually went to jail. Thorpe knew that the biggest problem the government would have in convicting Curtis was that Curtis was rich.

Thorpe had seen that statue of the justice lady, where she's blindfolded, holding scales in one hand, a sword in the other. Justice was supposed to be blind, but everybody knew she wasn't so blind when it came to the rich and it was amazing how money tipped the scales.

Thorpe reached down and patted Daisy on the head. "Daisy, I can just see that little shit walking. I can see him never spending a day in jail."

Leonard Curtis spent the whole day with lawyers, including Marjorie Dawkins's lawyer. The lawyers told him the chance of him being convicted was less than fifty percent. The good news was that the government's case would be based on Logan—via the document he'd prepared—and Dawkins *saying* that Curtis had ordered them to bribe people. It would be their word against Curtis's. But Curtis hadn't bribed anyone personally. He could show that he didn't control the money he gave Dawkins and Logan to use for legitimate political purposes. Most important, the government had no proof—such as a written order from Curtis to Dawkins or an email or a recording—showing he'd given them an illegal order.

The bad news was that Curtis was a rich guy, and not a particularly likeable one. Juries tended not to side with unlikeable rich guys, and little Marjorie Dawkins, mother of two, was not only likeable but credible. The other bit of bad news was that at least a few members of any jury selected would have an axe to grind with natural gas drillers for environmental reasons. It would be impossible to impanel a jury without at least one tree hugger.

So fifty-fifty, the lawyers said. Fortunately they'd have a lot of time to prepare for a trial. Curtis hadn't been arrested yet and the FBI had a lot of things to do before they arrested him. They had to verify everything Dawkins might say at Curtis's trial to make sure there were no holes in her testimony. Then they had to arrest three legislators and two judges and terrify those people into testifying against Curtis, too. At that point the FBI might arrest Curtis but then the government would subpoena a ton of records from Curtis's companies to see if they could find a money trail supporting bribery, and they'd depose dozens of witnesses to see what else they might find to strengthen their case. Curtis's lawyers were guessing a trial was at least two years away—and a lot could happen in two years.

"What if Dawkins doesn't testify against me?" Curtis asked.

"Oh," one of the lawyers said, as if that hadn't occurred to him. "Then the likelihood of you being convicted would drop to about twenty percent."

Curtis left the lawyers' office about seven p.m. and stopped and had a bowl of chicken soup before returning to the Radisson. When he got back to his room, he took a flask out of his suitcase. The flask contained cognac that sold for more than a hundred bucks a bottle. People thought he didn't drink, and he usually didn't, but every once in a while he'd have one. He poured an inch of cognac into one of the hotel's plastic drinking glasses and stood looking out the window as he drank.

A fifty percent chance he goes to jail if Dawkins testifies.

An eighty percent chance he walks if she doesn't.

Hard to argue with arithmetic.

He still had the option of paying Dawkins a million or so to take the fall for him and refusing to testify against him. But one, he didn't want to shell out that kind of money and two, such a move could backfire on him. He could just see Dawkins coming wired to a meeting where he would agree to pay her.

He tossed back the cognac, liking the way it spread its warmth through his chest. He took out the phone Murdock had given him and texted: Where is she?

In her house.

Stand by. Tonight may be the night.

Curtis didn't normally have a hard time making decisions. He usually made them fast and never second-guessed himself after he made one. But this decision . . . He needed to give it a little more thought—and maybe have one more glass of cognac.

And that's when the fire alarm went off.

33

A couple hours after he met with DeMarco, and after thinking all that time about what DeMarco had told him, Doug Thorpe called Curtis's offices in Houston from a pay phone at a gas station a few miles from his cabin. He said he worked for the IRS and needed to see Curtis immediately. The woman he spoke to told him that Curtis wasn't in Houston, he was in Bismarck, but if there was some sort of tax problem, he needed to talk to Curtis's tax attorney first. She refused to tell him where Curtis was staying in Bismarck or to give him a phone number for Curtis—but that was okay. Thorpe took off for Bismarck and when he arrived there, five hours later, it was almost eight p.m. He went to a 7-Eleven, got ten dollars' worth of quarters, and using a pay phone and the directory in the phone booth, he started calling hotels in Bismarck. It only took him forty minutes to learn that Curtis was a guest at the Radisson.

Thorpe drove over to the Radisson. He knew what Curtis looked like, he'd found his picture on the Internet: a scrawny little guy with sparse, white cotton candy hair. The problem was he didn't know what room Curtis was in. He thought about how to get that information and finally came up with an idea.

Thorpe put on a battered, broad-brimmed Filson bush hat he kept in his truck to wear when it rained, and walked into the Radisson. He need not have bothered with the half-assed disguise as the kid at the front desk was busy with a couple complaining about how they'd been charged for a movie they'd never watched. He walked down the first-floor hallway until he found what he wanted: a fire alarm.

He was standing outside the Radisson as all the guests came pouring outside, most of them acting surprisingly calm and in a pretty good mood. It helped that it was a pretty May night, clear and not too cold, and there were a million stars in the sky. It was almost ten p.m., so although some folks were still dressed, a lot of them were wearing pajamas or robes. Curtis was standing off by himself, apart from the other guests, a sour expression on his face, sipping brown liquid from a plastic cup.

About half an hour after the fire alarm sounded, the kid who'd been at the front desk came out and told everybody that they could go back to their rooms, and Thorpe, still wearing his Filson hat, joined a small crowd of people and followed Curtis back to his room on the second floor. Thorpe walked past Curtis's room but didn't stop. There were still too many people wandering around because of the fire alarm.

At the time the fire alarm went off at the Radisson in Bismarck, it was eleven p.m. in Washington, D.C., and John Mahoney was boarding a private plane at Reagan National. The plane was an executive jet with six first-class-style seats. It was a beauty.

Mahoney had found out earlier that day that Montana congressman Sam Erhart was flying back to his home state that night to attend a prayer breakfast the following morning in Helena. It was a four-and-a-half-hour flight from D.C. to Billings and the jet would drop Mahoney off there, then continue on to Helena. It was almost like taking a taxi. Mahoney had no idea which rich guy had loaned Erhart the sleek jet—and he had no intention of asking.

Erhart was already onboard the plane when Mahoney arrived, talking to someone on the phone. Erhart was a dyed-in-the-wool Republican and impossible to work with, but he really wasn't a bad guy. In fact, when they weren't talking politics, Mahoney actually liked the man.

Erhart hung up on whomever he'd been blabbing with and said, "You want a drink, John? The guy who owns this plane's got a bottle of scotch onboard that's older than you."

———◆◆◆———

At ten p.m. Bismarck time, as Mahoney's jet was taking off from National, Marjorie was sitting in a folding lawn chair near the roll-up garage doors, flicking her cigarette ashes into a Folgers coffee can. Her sons weren't home and at this point, she didn't give a hoot if the neighbors saw her smoking.

Two hours earlier, she'd kicked Dick and the boys out of the house. After she was released from jail, Dick started to drive her nuts. "How could you have done this, Marge? I mean, did you really bribe those guys? How much is the lawyer going to cost? Jesus, what are the boys going to say to their friends at school!" Finally, she just couldn't take it anymore, and she exploded. She told him to take the boys to his mom's place and stay there for a couple of days.

As for the boys, she could see they were scared. Bobby had started crying a couple of times and Tommy . . . He just looked mad, like she'd betrayed him or something. As they were getting into the car to leave, she hugged them both and told them that everything was going to be all right—even though she knew everything wasn't going to be all right.

Sitting there puffing on the cigarette, looking up at the night sky, she knew life would never be the same. She was almost positive that she wouldn't serve time for bribing anyone because she was going to be the star witness against Curtis and everyone she'd bribed. The public—and the FBI—would much rather see a few greasy politicians and a rich guy like Curtis in jail than her.

But what would she and her family do after all the trials were over? They were definitely going to have to sell the house and get something smaller and would have to move away from Bismarck, which would kill the boys, leaving all their friends. And Dick would never find a decent-paying job. It would all be on her—just like it had always been.

———◆◆◆———

Murdock sat in his car, watching Dawkins smoke. She'd been coming out of her house about every twenty minutes to have a cigarette. A couple hours earlier, Murdock had seen a man and two boys throw backpacks and a roll-on suitcase into an SUV and leave the house. Dawkins's husband and children, he assumed. It looked to him like they were going someplace to stay for a few days—which meant that Dawkins would be alone in her house tonight.

Murdock had been surprised when Dawkins killed Logan—and impressed. Curtis had sent him to Bismarck to watch Logan but when he arrived in Bismarck, he couldn't find the man. He had fled the city after somebody took a couple of shots at him. So Murdock decided to start following Marjorie Dawkins, hoping she'd lead him to Logan.

He watched one day when she went to a tavern and made a high-speed trip to a nearby park—and he couldn't figure out what she was doing. Then he figured it out, the night she killed Logan: the high-speed drive to the park had been a dry run for Logan's murder. And that impressed him: the planning that went into Logan's assassination.

He was watching her the night she went to a school for a PTA meeting—there was a reader board outside the school that announced the meeting—and he followed her to a tavern after the PTA meeting ended, thinking he was just wasting his time. But then she came out of the tavern, practically running, and drove to the same park as fast as she could, so fast she almost lost him. He arrived just in time to see the double flashes from her gun as she shot Logan, then she raced back to the tavern. Later, he figured out she was giving herself an alibi because the cops would most likely think—if they suspected her at all—that she'd been in the tavern with all those PTA ladies when Logan was killed.

So he couldn't help but admire Dawkins's ability to plan and professionally execute her partner's murder. He couldn't have done any better himself. But if Curtis gave him the order to kill the woman, his admiration for her wouldn't stop him. He'd just be careful not to underestimate her. And the job itself should be fairly easy since she was alone in her house. It would be as easy as killing Sarah Johnson.

Doug Thorpe stood over by the big ashtray where all the smokers gathered, although right now he was standing by himself. From where he was standing, he could see the kid clerk at the front desk.

Thorpe had noticed that since the fire alarm—and because it was now almost eleven p.m.—the kid was hanging out in a room behind the front desk and he only came out to answer the phone. He was probably back there watching TV.

The kid had just answered the phone again—some guest complaining about something or maybe somebody making a reservation. He hung up the phone and went back to the room behind the desk—and Thorpe decided it was time to move.

Still wearing his floppy-brimmed Filson hat, he walked quickly through the lobby, and took the stairs just off the lobby up to Curtis's room on the second floor.

Okay, Curtis thought. Time to get this done with. And time to get to bed.

He picked up the encrypted burner cell phone—technology these days was goldarn marvelous—but he would get rid of the phone first thing tomorrow.

He typed: Take care of her. But she has to disappear. The body can't be found.

Curtis thought that would be best: Marjorie Dawkins just vanishes, like she'd decided to skip before her trial. He was about to hit the SEND button when there was a knock on the door.

Curtis opened the door holding a cell phone in his hand, the phone down by the side of his leg.

Thorpe said, "This is for Sarah, you little shit"—and he shot Curtis in the face.

He was surprised that the old .38 didn't make as much noise as he'd expected.

He dragged Curtis's body into the room, along with a cell phone that Curtis had dropped. He used a handkerchief to wipe his prints off the cell phone and again when he opened the door, then made sure nobody was out in the hallway to see him coming out of Curtis's room. He didn't really care if he was caught—in fact, he expected he would be caught—but he wasn't going to make it easy for the cops.

He figured the body wouldn't be discovered until tomorrow morning. He glanced at his watch: it was getting close to midnight, but that was okay. He'd be back home in five hours, plenty of time to get there before Mahoney arrived from Washington.

He walked to the stairwell at the end of the hallway—not the stairwell that came out near the lobby, but one of the fire-escape stairways that exited on the side of the building—and left the hotel. He noticed again, as he was walking to his pickup, that it was a beautiful spring night. He didn't notice the tears streaming down his face.

It was funny. In Vietnam, he'd actually felt bad about the men he'd killed, and he'd killed quite a few. He'd always believed that those Viet Cong soldiers were just guys like him: they weren't evil, they were kids that a bunch of politicians sent off to war. But he didn't feel bad at all about killing Leonard Curtis. The tears were for Sarah.

An hour out of Bismarck—and still about four hours from home—he came to a small creek and stopped and threw in the .38. Five minutes later, in case anyone at the Radisson had noticed an old man wearing a Filson hat, he let the hat fly out the window and it blew into an alfalfa field.

Ten minutes later, the right front tire blew out.

It took him over two hours to change the tire. It was pitch black outside, the batteries in the flashlight he had in the glove compartment were old, and the flashlight beam was so weak he could barely see what he was doing. To make matters worse, the spare tire was up under the bed of the truck, and the nut holding it in place was frozen with mud and rust. He had to hunt for almost thirty minutes to find a rock big enough to hammer on the lug wrench so he could break the nut loose holding the spare in place. It didn't help that he was seventy-two years old and not as strong as he used to be.

He remembered teaching Sarah how to change a tire. They'd gone fishing on the Yellowstone that day—Sarah caught a five-pound rainbow—and on the way home, they got a flat. Sarah was sixteen at the time, had just gotten her driver's license, and he made her change the tire by herself so she'd know what to do. And he remembered that thick-headed girl arguing with him that she had a cell phone and she had AAA, and if she ever got a flat she'd make the AAA guy change the tire.

That girl had been so stubborn.

God, he was going to miss her.

34

Leonard Curtis's body was found by a disgruntled lawyer at six thirty a.m. The lawyer—who was a senior partner in his law firm—had been ordered by Curtis to pick him up at six at the Radisson. Curtis wanted to have breakfast with the lawyer, talk some more about the Dawkins case, after which Curtis would get on his plane and fly off to God knows where.

When Curtis hadn't shown up in the lobby by six twenty, the lawyer grew anxious. Curtis was an obnoxious, demanding asshole of a client but he was almost always punctual. He called Curtis's room and didn't receive an answer. He knew that Curtis was an old man. Maybe he'd slipped in the shower. Maybe he'd had a heart attack. He convinced the sleepy kid at the front desk to let him into Curtis's room where they discovered Curtis's body. He'd been shot in the head.

The lawyer told the kid to go call the cops and as he stood there looking down at the dead man, he saw a phone near Curtis's hand. From where he was standing he could see the screen—it was the text message screen of an iPhone—but he couldn't read the words. He knew he shouldn't touch the phone so he knelt down and looked at the message on the screen: `Take care of her. But she has to disappear. The body can't be found.`

Whoa!

The lawyer figured he only had a couple of minutes to make a deci-sion. He had to decide if there was any disadvantage to his law firm if the police should discover a text message that sounded like his client—Leonard Curtis—was ordering a woman's murder. And most likely the intended victim was Marjorie Dawkins, also a client of his firm.

If the police got their hands on Curtis's phone they might be able to identify the person Curtis had been about to send the message to and catch that person. But how did catching a murderer help his law firm? Curtis had children, a son and daughter, and he remembered that Cur-tis's daughter was a businesswoman. She would most likely take over her father's enterprise now that Curtis was dead. If her father was known to be in cahoots with a killer, would that be good for the business—a business that would most likely continue to retain him and his law firm? He suspected not. Furthermore, Curtis hadn't hit the SEND button, so it wasn't like he'd *really* ordered anybody to do anything.

He picked up the phone and put it in his pocket.

Harold Fredericks, Bismarck's most overworked homicide detective, called Westerberg to tell her that Curtis had been killed. "It happened last night, around midnight, but the ME can't pin down the time any better than that."

"You got any leads?" Westerberg asked.

"No, not really. He was shot with a .38, so it wasn't the same gun used to kill Logan or Sarah Johnson."

"I assume you looked at security cameras."

"Yeah, but the hotel doesn't have cameras in the hallways on the guest floors. There is one in the lobby. But last night, somebody set off a fire alarm—maybe the killer did it—and there were a lot of people milling around, coming and going from the hotel after the alarm went off. I saw one guy on the lobby camera who just looked kind of funny, like he was turning his face away so the clerk at the desk wouldn't see him."

"But I take it you couldn't ID him."

"No, he was wearing this floppy hat and, like I said, he had his face turned away from the camera. He was wearing a blue-and-green Pendleton shirt and he was tall, over six feet, but that's about it."

"Huh," Westerberg said. "Well, I know it wasn't DeMarco because he's not over six feet tall and he was supposed to be on a plane back to Washington last night. But you should check with the airlines."

"You seriously think DeMarco could have done this?"

"No, not really. DeMarco's hardly a saint, but he's not a killer. And if you're right about the guy in the floppy hat being the shooter, it couldn't have been Dawkins."

"We don't know that the guy in the hat was the one. Like I said, he just looked funny. And the killer could have entered through one of the side doors instead of going through the lobby, so I can't rule Dawkins out."

———◆———

Marjorie Dawkins had thought that her life couldn't possibly get any worse—then a detective stopped by to tell her that Leonard Curtis had been murdered and he wanted to know where she was last night. She told the dumb cop that she'd been home, all by herself, but the last person on earth she wanted dead was Leonard Curtis.

With Curtis dead, her chance of getting immunity for testifying against him was gone and now she was the only person left to take the fall for bribing the politicians. And she certainly couldn't point the finger at Curtis for the death of Sarah Johnson because, once again, she was now the only one living to blame for that crazy girl's death. Being an accessory to murder was a whole different ball game than buying off a few corrupt lawmakers. Plus, there was always the possibility that Murdock might find out she was talking to the cops about him and he might kill her.

That little son of a bitch, Curtis. Just like with Bill Logan, his death had screwed her. She could see Curtis and Logan in Hell, the flames dancing around them, laughing about what they'd done to her.

When Ian Perry—the man Marjorie Dawkins knew as Murdock—heard on the radio that Leonard Curtis was dead, he was still parked near Dawkins's house waiting for the order from Curtis to kill her. He'd been there all night. He'd seen a cop arrive earlier and speak with Dawkins and, at the time, he had no idea what that was about. Then he heard on the midmorning news that Curtis had been shot and he suspected the cops had come to question Dawkins about Curtis's death.

He wondered who had killed Curtis. Whoever it was had deprived him of a fee that he would have used to demolish the hideous house that spoiled his view when he meditated in his lovely Japanese garden. On the other hand, in a way, he was glad that he hadn't been required to kill Dawkins.

Ian Perry never thought at all about the people he was paid to kill. He didn't sympathize or empathize with them in any way. What would be the point? He didn't even hold himself responsible for their deaths. The people responsible were the ones who paid him. Perry thought of himself—and not facetiously—as being the equivalent of lightning. It was the client who decided a person should die and Ian Perry was simply the instrument that accomplished the physical act—but it was the client who had made the decision. It was the same as when lightning struck some poor bastard walking about in a rainstorm. It wasn't the lightning's fault; it was God who had decided the person's time on this earth was up.

But in the case of Dawkins, and even as much as he wanted the money he needed to purchase and demolish his neighbor's house, he was almost glad that lightning hadn't struck. He would have killed Dawkins had Curtis given the order—he was a professional, after all— but he'd never before killed a mother with two young children. Ian Perry sometimes doubted that God existed—but he did believe in karma.

———◆◆◆———

DeMarco arrived at Dulles at seven thirty a.m. EST—about the time Curtis's body was found in Bismarck.

During the long trip home—made longer because his connecting flight in Salt Lake City was delayed four hours—he had a lot of time to think about Sarah: Sarah laughing over the YouTube video. Sarah's eyes flaring with anger over the way things were—and her refusal to accept that she couldn't change the way things were. She'd been unrelenting, uncompromising, courageous, and naïve. She'd been so very young.

DeMarco wondered what she might have accomplished if she'd lived. She would have matured and perhaps become smarter in her pursuit of the corrupt; perhaps she would have learned how to make alliances and get others to follow her lead. Perhaps—no, certainly—she would have made a difference in this twisted world. The only thing DeMarco could take solace in was that he'd done his best to make Logan, Dawkins, and Curtis pay for their crimes—but like Mahoney had said, nothing he'd done would make up for the loss of Sarah Johnson.

DeMarco caught a taxi home from the airport, and on the way to his house, he stopped thinking about the events that had transpired in

Bismarck. Instead he thought about his rodent problem, praying that, in the two weeks he'd been gone, that Ralph had done his job. According to Ralph, the pests had feasted on the blue-green poison, d-CON, and hopefully DeMarco's backyard would be littered with their decaying corpses. When he got home, he was going to have to put his house in order—put all the stuff back he'd removed from the closets, reinstall new insulation batts down in his basement, and search the house to make sure Ralph had sealed up all the mouse entry holes. But he'd put all that off until tomorrow. After the long flight home, he needed to sleep.

He put the key in the lock and opened the door.

Oh, God! What was that smell!

35

Mahoney got to Doug Thorpe's place at six thirty in the morning—about the time DeMarco landed in Washington and about the time Leonard Curtis's body was found.

His plane had landed in Billings at four a.m. and Mahoney should have been tired after the long flight from Washington, but for some reason he wasn't. He felt great, and was glad he'd decided to come to Montana. Mavis had arranged for a car to be waiting for him in the rental car parking lot, the keys and the rental papers inside it. He hopped into the car and took off, enjoying the solitary drive to Thorpe's place as the sun rose over Montana.

But Thorpe wasn't home when Mahoney got to his cabin, which surprised him. Thorpe knew he was arriving this morning and he was certain the man wasn't inside the cabin sleeping because Doug Thorpe had never slept past five a.m. in his life. He wondered where he could be. Mahoney took a seat in one of the rocking chairs on the front porch and listened to the Yellowstone rolling by. He was looking forward to seeing his old friend in spite of the circumstances.

Half an hour later, Thorpe's pickup swung into the driveway. Thorpe stepped out of the vehicle and waved when he saw Mahoney. He moved stiffly as he walked toward the porch—like his joints were stiff after a long drive. Mahoney hadn't seen Thorpe in quite a few years but he was struck as he always was with how . . . how *noble* Thorpe looked. Some men are blessed with a certain kind of face—men like Jimmy Stewart or Henry Fonda or Gary Cooper—those old movie stars who almost always played the good guy because they just looked like good guys. Mahoney certainly didn't have that kind of face but Doug Thorpe did.

When Thorpe reached the porch, Mahoney stuck out his hand for Thorpe to shake but Thorpe held up his hands and said, "Gotta go wash my hands; had a flat tire."

Mahoney noticed that in addition to his hands being black and grimy, the sleeves of Thorpe's Pendleton shirt were filthy, as might be expected if he'd changed a tire, and again Mahoney wondered where he'd been, but didn't ask. Instead he said, "I'm sorry, Doug. I can't tell you how sorry "

"John, I don't want to talk about sorry." He didn't say anything more for a moment and Mahoney didn't know what to say, then Thorpe said, "I know it's kind of early in the day, but do you feel like sippin' some whiskey?"

"I can't think of a better idea," Mahoney said.

Thorpe went into the cabin and came back a short time later, with clean hands and wearing a fresh blue denim shirt and holding a full bottle of Jack Daniel's and two water glasses. An old black-and-white dog had followed him out of the cabin. The dog plopped down between the two rocking chairs and Thorpe poured the whiskey.

"You remember," Thorpe said, "that time we went into Saigon with that big redheaded kid from Detroit, the one who had lenses in his glasses thicker than the bottom of that whiskey bottle? I can't remember his name."

"Oh, yeah, I remember that goofy bastard. His name was Kellogg, like the corn flakes. I remember once when we were out in a rice paddy and he lost his glasses. I was sure he was going to shoot one of us."

Thorpe laughed. "But that time in Saigon, we were in that club that fat French guy owned, and . . ."

Two hours later, they were both pretty drunk, Thorpe more than Mahoney because Mahoney was no stranger to booze in the morning. A car that said Custer County Sheriff pulled into the driveway and an old cop, a heavyset guy in his sixties, got out of the car. He tugged on the wide belt holding his gun and handcuffs, and Mahoney bet the sheriff spent half the day tugging up that belt.

"Is one of you Douglas Thorpe?" the sheriff asked.

"I am," Thorpe said.

"Mr. Thorpe, can you tell me where you were last night?"

Before Thorpe could answer, Mahoney said, "Why are you asking?"

"And who are you, sir?" the sheriff said.

"United States Congressman John Mahoney."

The sheriff looked at him more closely, then said, "Hell, I recognize you. You used to be the Speaker of the House."

"That's right," Mahoney said. "So why are you asking where my friend was last night?"

"Well, sir, a man named Leonard Curtis was shot and killed last night in his hotel room and the Bismarck cops asked me to come out here and ask where Mr. Thorpe was last night."

"He was right here with me," Mahoney said. "We've been sipping whiskey all night talking about when we were young bulls in Vietnam. Are you by any chance a veteran, Sheriff?"

Epilogue

———◆◆◆———

The guard told Marjorie to take a seat in one of the first ten rows in the plane. The plane was a beat-up old 737 that belonged in a scrap yard and the once-gray seats were almost black with grime. She wouldn't be surprised if she ended up with head lice before the flight was over.

The rear seats of the airplane were occupied by hard-core criminals, all men, being taken to maximum-security federal penitentiaries in Kansas, Colorado, Arizona, and Texas. They were manacled hand and foot and chained to the floor of the plane. In addition, there was a metal gate separating the rear seats from those in the front. If the plane crashed, they were screwed—but who cared?

The front rows of seats were reserved for folks like Marjorie bound for minimum-security prisons and they had on leg manacles that made it hard to walk and impossible to run, but they weren't handcuffed. Marjorie had been told that if she acted up or mouthed off in any way, they'd handcuff her to her seat and gag her.

Marjorie's destination would be the last stop the plane made: Federal Prison Camp, Bryan, a minimum-security facility for females in Bryan, Texas.

Marjorie had been sentenced to eighteen months in prison and would be eligible for parole in twelve. Her sentence would have been longer but she pled guilty, cooperated with state and federal prosecutors, and testified against three state legislators and two judges. The government was more interested in convicting the folks who'd taken the bribes than the person who did the bribing. The feds wanted her to testify that she'd bribed other people than the five named in fuckin' Bill's manifesto, but she lied and said there were no others.

The next eighteen months of her life were going to be bad, but probably no worse than the last eighteen had been. Dick filed for divorce six months after she was arrested and the divorce was finalized four months after that. Naturally, he got custody of the boys since she was a convicted felon. Because of the boys, he also got to keep the house and two-thirds of the money they had in savings. The money she was able to keep was gobbled up by her lawyer. The icing on the cake was she'd heard that Dick was now dating the most successful real estate agent in Bismarck, a woman built like a Sherman tank, but with money coming out of her ears.

Marjorie took a seat next to a skanky-looking white woman whose arms were covered with tattoos and had blond hair that was about a quarter of an inch long. As soon as she sat down, the woman said, "Have you been saved?"

"Saved?" Marjorie said.

"By Our Lord and Savior, Jesus Christ."

Aw, geez. She was going to be seated next to this woman for the next twenty hours.

The first thing she was going to do when she got out of prison was piss on Bill Logan's grave.

———◆◆◆———

Harvey Milton, medical examiner for El Paso County, looked down at the body. The head looked like a chunk of charcoal.

"Well, he's dead," Harvey said to the young Colorado Springs cop who had been dispatched to the house after a neighbor called.

"No shit," the cop said. "The neighbor said he liked to work in his garden and sit on that bench over there and meditate and—"

"It's a beautiful garden," Harvey said. "Looks like one I saw in Tokyo when the wife and I went there last summer."

"Anyway, the neighbor saw it happen. He was up there, looking out that second-story window, the one there on the right, when wham! A great big lightning bolt. Hit the dead guy right on the top of his head. Scared the shit out of the neighbor."

"What's his name?" Harvey asked.

"Ian Perry, according to the neighbor."

Harvey looked up at the sky. "There's hardly a cloud in sight. It's like he just pissed God off or something."

"Karma," the young cop said.

Author's Note and Acknowledgments

Legislation and lawsuits related to natural gas mentioned in this book are, for the most part, real, such as the lawsuits regarding forced pooling, water contamination caused by fracking, and the sales tax case in South Dakota. It's also true that state legislators in the Dakotas and Montana aren't paid particularly well. What is not true—at least as far as I know—is that energy companies are bribing these underpaid lawmakers to do things they want done. I imagine the legislators in these states are decent, honest public servants—but decent and honest doesn't always make for good fiction.

When I was researching this book, I tried to learn how Heckler, the detective, could monitor cell phone calls and was actually amazed to find three companies online that sold software for monitoring calls and tracking people's locations. The companies' websites said everything was aboveboard, completely legal, and that in order to monitor someone's phone you needed physical access to the phone and—wink, wink—the owner's permission. I have no idea if the monitoring software can be downloaded onto a person's phone by embedding it in an email as I do in the book—but I'll betcha it can be.

I want to apologize in advance for poking fun at the name Bertha. My mother had a beautiful name—Antoinette Nicolene—and was usually called Nicky. But for some reason, never explained to me, a number of her childhood friends called her Bertha. My mother hated the name Bertha, but could never shake it. Anyway, the only Bertha I've ever known was a terrific person and I'm sure all the other Berthas out there are wonderful, too.

I want to thank Judge James Donohue for advising me on warrants, although in one case I—or Agent Westerberg—cheated a bit to get around a warrant. I'm grateful to Dale Zimmerman of the Peacock Alley American Bar and Grill in Bismarck for emailing pictures of his restaurant so I could better describe the interior. Also, a couple of folks whose names I won't mention, for advising me on security cameras at the Radisson in Bismarck. As best I was able to determine, there are no security cameras in the guest hallways as it says in the book—and if there are, well, I could see no point in letting the facts screw up a good story.

I want to thank my editor, Jamison Stoltz, for improving this book immeasurably beyond the first draft. Also Allison Malecha, Jamison's assistant, for her help on this book as well as the DeMarco mapping project. (There will be more on the DeMarco mapping project on my website later.) I want to thank my wife, Gail, for reading this book, advising me on titles, and most of all for creating an environment in which I can write. Finally, as always, my agent, David Gernert, for keeping me in the game.